THE
HOME COURT
ADVANTAGE

Lawyers in Love #2

by

N.M. SILBER

Mendelssohn Levy Publishing Philadelphia

Praise for The Law of Attraction

"Between the characters' banter, the preposterous "fixes" that Gabrielle manages to coax her best friend Jess into, and the underlying theme of a blossoming romance that I was completely and utterly pulling for, my verdict is that there is clear and convincing evidence that "The Law of Attraction" is THE stand-out romantic comedy of 2013! I cannot wait for the sequel."

~ Cindy Meyer of The Book Enthusiast

"This book is laugh out loud funny. Fans of Janet Evanovich will get a kick out of this book. There is sweetness and steam and a whole lot of I Love Lucy moments. I cannot wait for the conclusion in The Home Court Advantage."

~Donna Antonio of In My Humble Opinion

"The banter in and out of the court room was hilarious and the sexual tension was just there. The only part that I didn't like was "it ended". I wanted MORE."

~Mayas of Reading by the Book

"The Law of Attraction' has it all — romance, hot sexxx, humor, a sex ring scandal, and great friends! A great read and a must add to your to read list. We can't wait to read Part II. N.M. Silber has definitely been added to our Must Read Authors List! Absolutely loved the book!"

~556 Book Chicks

"The characters were loveable and you just want to see them get what they want. Once I started reading I could not stop and ended up reading it in one sitting."

~Joy Whiteside of Book 2 Book

"If you like to read a book that has a fun love story with lots of humor (who doesn't?) then you NEED to read this book!"

"The Law of Attraction has more to it than just humor and sex, it also has some mystery to it as well. Even now thinking back while typing this has me snorting at parts of the book."

"I am pretty impressed by what I have seen so far and I can't wait until the second book is available. The Law of Attraction has some great lol moments and stars a very sweet and fun couple."

"I LOVED this book. Hardcore, super duper, would recommend it to anyone, marking it as a favorite kind of love. It's cute, adorable, lovely, sexy, panty-melting, heart-warming, laugh-out-loud goodness."

"Gabrielle is the type of heroine I like to read; she's funny, sweet, devoted to her friends and her crazy family. Braden is charming, hot and boy when they tear up the sheets I needed a fan to cool me off. They were H-O-T!!"

"This book was laugh-out-loud funny, sexy, and there was even some mystery and suspense. With a book with all of these qualities, you know it's going to be good!"

"This book seriously made me OMG and LOL from page 1. I could not stop laughing. I love it."

Mendelssohn Levy Publishing Philadelphia
http://mendlevypub.com/

First Mendelssohn Levy eBook Edition November 2013
First Mendelssohn Levy trade paperback edition, November 2013
Edited by:
Julie Roberts
isillote1@gmail.com

NOTICE: This is an adult contemporary romance novel and contains explicit descriptions of sexual acts and mature language. It is intended for readers over the age of eighteen.

This is a work of fiction. Names, characters, places and incidents either are products of the author's imagination or are used fictitiously. Any resemblance to actual events or locales or persons, living or dead, is entirely coincidental.

Silber, N.M.

The Home Court Advantage / N.M. Silber – 1st edition

ISBN 978-0-9895984-2-2 eBook edition

ISBN 978-0-9895984-3-9 Print edition

Cover Design by Carrie Spencer

Formatting, back cover and interior design by Donnie Light

This book is dedicated to the fans who loved *The Law of Attraction*, and made me believe that I could really be an author, and to all the reviewers who helped me to connect with them. Thank you for that.

∿ CHAPTER ONE ∾

JULY

After leaving the police station we headed back to Braden's place. As he turned the key in the door to his apartment, I heard rapid click click click sounds followed by a whoosh and then a thud and a scrambling scratching, sounding not unlike a small dog trying to peel himself off a wall. Bruno still hadn't mastered those hardwood floors. When Braden swung the door open, Bruno was waiting there to greet us as if nothing had happened. He gave us a happy yip and wagged his tail so hard that it almost shook his little Chihuahua butt off.

I reached down to pick him up and give him some attention, walking over to the large windows overlooking Rittenhouse Square. I loved the way that those windows made the place feel warm and open during the day and at night provided a breathtaking view of the twinkling city lights. It was a hot, clear sunny day in Philadelphia and the Square was filled with people walking, playing, reading … and what was that guy doing? Okay, I *didn't* see that and it was *not* going to be stuck in my head all night. I moved away from the windows. Braden had tossed his keys on the kitchen counter and gone into the bedroom to change into more comfortable clothes.

"So, Bruno, did you guard the place for Mommy and Daddy?" He looked up at me and panted with his tongue hanging out of his mouth. I took that as a "yes." Actually, I took it more as a "do you *really* need to ask?" I knew that while the world may have seen him as an itty bitty ankle biter dog, Bruno saw himself as a ferocious killer.

I wandered around the apartment that would eventually become my place too, stopping to look again at the pictures hanging on Braden's wall, the Harvard Crew he rowed with, Braden with Adam and Mark at Georgetown Law, Braden with his family in Martha's Vineyard, and finally, the most recent addition, Braden looking debonair in his tux and me not looking too shabby in my gown at his family's fundraiser last month. I smiled and felt all warm and fuzzy. I had made "the wall."

I went over and sat down on the soft leather couch and settled Bruno on my lap, where he promptly flipped over with a not terribly subtle hint that he wanted a belly rub. I obliged. What could I say? The dog had grown on me.

Braden came out of the bedroom looking as good as always. Just to let you know, that was pretty damned good. You know how Phoenix was hot but the tropics were hotter? Well, Braden was like the planet Mercury. Not everybody could rock khaki shorts and an old Phillies T-shirt like he could. He was like a big, blonde, blue-eyed, Norse god. Notice I didn't say Greek God by the way. Have you ever seen a statue of a Greek God? Well, trust me, there was nothing on Braden that a fig leaf could cover.

He sat down next to Bruno and me and took out his cell. First he called Adam, who as it turned out, was with Mark, who as it turned out, was with Cameron. They were watching baseball and drinking beer together at a local sports bar. I guess they were warming up. We had decided that despite some pretty wacky events the night before, Sunday Game Night was officially on.

We still didn't know who had sent me a couple of anonymous notes that seemed aimed at getting me to leave Braden, but we had decided that even though we would be cautious, we were going to go on with our lives as usual anyway. Of course that meant I was probably going to have to talk my father out of borrowing some Navy SEALS to guard me and hiring someone from the Louvre to install a burglar alarm in my apartment. Dad could be a little protective. After hanging up with Adam, Braden checked his voicemail and found a message from his own parents.

"My mom said that she and my dad are going to be in D.C. this weekend. They'll be home Sunday at noon. And Beth is visiting friends until Sunday morning. Drew will be here all weekend though. She suggested that we spend time at their place with him. We can hang out by the pool and there's a music festival in town on Saturday."

"That sounds fun. Are we going to tell them about our plans when they get home?"

"Probably not yet," he said, getting up and heading toward the kitchen.

I started to get a little nervous. I hadn't even completely gotten used to the idea of dating Braden, let alone marrying him. Not only was he gorgeous, he was *so* sexy. He had this way of looking at me that always gave me the proverbial butterflies in my tummy. His eyes would get darker and he would get this cocky grin on his face like he knew a hundred and one ways to make me see God. I called it his "hot Braden sex look" and it made my panties melt because I knew what he was thinking about when he looked at me like that. Actually being in bed with him was almost like an out-of-body experience except, believe me, you didn't want to leave your body if you were in bed with Braden.

Even more important than all that gorgeous sexy, though, he was also strong, well-grounded, confident, compassionate and intelligent. Best of all we were amazingly compatible. From the very beginning we just clicked and it was like we belonged together. We spent our evenings talking about books, history, politics, law, and a million other things. Then we would cuddle up and watch shows on PBS that would make us popular with the geriatric crowd down at the senior center. Even though we argued passionately in court sometimes, we rarely argued privately. We discussed things and we usually saw eye to eye. The only tense point between us was the potential risk that was inherent in our respective jobs. We loved each other so much that the thought of anyone threatening the other was devastating.

As I was saying, though, his answer made me a little nervous because it still kind of blew my mind that this man who I had fantasized about for months, and never expected to even date, actually wanted to marry me. I had pretty good self-esteem and I was decently self-confident, but facts were facts. I could be pretty eccentric and rather awkward at times. I made corny jokes and odd observations. I was the queen of too much information. I was uncoordinated and could manage to trip while standing in place. I had some unconventional ideas and my life often resembled an episode of I Love Lucy. Let's just say that I was an acquired taste. Luckily, it seemed that Braden had acquired me, so I wasn't sure why he didn't want to let his parents know that he had proposed the night before.

"Why don't you want to tell them?" I asked hesitantly, putting Bruno down and then getting up and following along after him.

"I didn't say I didn't want to tell them," he answered over his shoulder. "But I'd like to ask you properly and give you a ring first. I'm not sure I'll have time to do that before they get home." He opened the refrigerator and took out a bottle of water, offering it to me. I shook my head and he opened it and took a big swig himself.

Bruno came sliding into home, crashed into the breakfast bar and scrambled to his feet. I winced and went to the cupboard to get him a treat. I wished that he would stop doing that, but if he insisted on traveling everywhere at light speed, then I should tie a buffer cloth to his butt. At least I could get the floors cleaned.

"Those things don't matter so much."

"They matter to me." He leaned up against the counter and watched Bruno run off somewhere with his tiny Milk Bone. "I don't want you to think back to the moment I proposed to you and remember being dressed in leather and latex. Besides, I'm a guy, and I don't want to introduce you as my fiancée to anyone, even my parents, unless you have a ring on your finger."

"Okay, but you don't have to make big plans. You've already swept me off my feet. Trust me."

He turned his full attention to me and my tummy actually fluttered. "I just want to make it special. Then we'll tell our parents and I'm sure they'll want to make a formal announcement and throw a big engagement party."

"Oh, a *big* party! See this? This is my excited look."

"What's wrong with having a big party to celebrate?"

"I just don't do parties very well, Braden. Gatherings are fine. Get-togethers I can handle. Parties, not so much. My chit chat leaves a lot to be desired. I usually wind up standing in a corner petting a cat or sitting on a flight of stairs talking to somebody's kid. Once I did someone's laundry."

"Don't worry about anything, baby." He laughed. I amused Braden a lot. "We'll have a very nice engagement party with no pressure. Pet as many cats, talk to as many kids and do as much laundry as you want. Just let me keep you company." He finished the water and tossed the bottle in the recycling, then came over to put his arms around me. I leaned up against him and enjoyed the feeling of his warmth and his hard muscles. Then I breathed in deeply to enjoy his familiar spicy scent.

"I don't mean to sound so anxious. It's just hard to wrap my head around the idea of getting married, let alone marrying you. Sometimes I still can't even believe that I get to see you naked."

"You can see me naked whenever you want," he said, putting a finger under my chin and tipping my head back so he could look at me. He smiled and leaned down to kiss me lightly on the lips. "In fact, I highly encourage you to ask whenever and wherever possible."

"There are moments in court ..." I smiled back lasciviously. The adrenaline we built up arguing with each other in court seemed to stoke both of our libidos more and more.

"That might have to be the one exception, or we could wind up in jail, at least if you're talking about open court. Ever since our rendezvous in the interview rooms, I've been fantasizing about getting it on with you in all kinds of places around the criminal courts building."

"We should make a map of doors that lock," I joked and rubbed his back, enjoying the feeling of his taut muscles under my fingertips.

"Personally, I think that with what we do every day, we deserve to relieve our tension whenever and however we can." He lowered his hands to my bottom and pulled my hips up against him. The bulge pressing against my abdomen told me that this discussion was starting to give him some interesting ideas.

"Relaxing by the pool will be fun," I said, pressing against him even closer and enjoying all of that warm, hard, Braden-ness.

"I was thinking that we could invite Adam and Mark. Are you okay with that?"

"That's okay with me. It would be nice if you invited Cameron too though. After last night he's probably worried."

"He should be worried, but fine, we'll invite Cameron. I still want to make sure that we have alone time while we're there though. Maybe we can skinny dip in the Jacuzzi when everyone's gone to bed." He looked down and gave me a sexy smile that made me feel all tingly. I noted that he was starting to look quite aroused.

"Can we invite Jess too?" An idea was forming in my head.

"That could be fun, although it might be better for our relationship if I just watched." He backed up and retreated beyond my reach just in time. "So violent!" He laughed.

"You had *better* watch or you'll be sleeping alone tonight, mister."

"You would deny me? I'll bet I could get you to change your mind if I tried hard enough." He came back over to me and reached under my shirt to stroke my ribs with his thumbs. He knew how much I loved that. In fact, he was an expert when it came to my body. He knew just how and where to touch me to drive me out of my mind. I had to stay focused though, because I needed something to distract me from my nerves. Matchmaking was always a good project, and besides, I was Jewish. It was in my blood – like the instinct to tell corny jokes, go to law school, and migrate to Florida at age sixty.

"Can we invite her or not?" I asked throatily, starting to fidget.

"If you want." One hand traveled up and started to trace the lower curve of my breast and my heart started hammering to a salsa beat. I'm sure that he knew how aroused I was becoming myself. The fact that I was panting more than an obscene phone caller was probably a dead giveaway. I was becoming lightheaded, but I was on a mission, so I toughed it out and backed out of his reach as I started thinking about how I could manage to get Cam and Jess together.

I knew they were both attracted to each other and both of them were intelligent, successful and good-looking. Even more than that, though, they had fun together. They always seemed to be laughing about something but I knew that Cameron tended to hesitate and that Jess wouldn't push the issue. I, on the other hand, could be very pushy.

"Good. Then I won't be the only girl." I looked up and gave him an innocent-looking smile, or so I thought.

"Why do you have that look on your face?" he asked suspiciously. I obviously would have to work on my innocent smile. This would have to be my own private project as I was smart enough to realize that Braden probably had the typical male aversion to the idea that somebody might be maneuvering a guy into a relationship.

"What look?"

"The 'I'm planning something' look."

"I don't know what you mean." I even managed to sound vaguely offended.

"Even though I'm sure I should explore that subject further, I'm feeling pretty amorous at the moment," he said, pulling me to him again. "Maybe you should…" My cell started to ring then, "…answer your phone," he finished with a sigh, releasing me.

Speak of the devil, it was Jess herself, wanting to know what had happened at the police station. I filled her in quickly and then let her know I would be over shortly to grab some more clothes. We had been spending more and more time at Braden's place and slowly but surely my possessions were making their way there. I also wanted to have a chance to talk to Jess alone about Cam, but as soon as I hung up with her, Braden was offering to escort me. He could be pretty protective too. Actually, he and my dad were a lot alike in general.

"Braden, it's only two blocks." Silence. "In daylight." He continued to stare. "In a major city." No response. "The guys are going to be here soon?" We had a winner, folks!

"Fine. Take Bruno then and invite Jessica to come back with you."

"Yes, dear." I smiled sweetly and leaned up to kiss him goodbye. Bruno and I headed out, hopped into the elevator and descended to the opulent Art Deco style lobby of the luxury high-rise where Braden lived. I waved to the concierge, and let the doorman know we would be right back. Braden had made it clear to everyone in his building that I was a permanently welcome guest and future resident. I was barely outside when I started to get a funny feeling. The back of my neck felt prickly and I got goosebumps, even though it was very warm outside. I paused to try to process it and realized that it felt like somebody was watching me. I looked around me in every direction, and while there were plenty of people out and about, everyone seemed to be going about their own business. I told myself that it was just my imagination and Bruno and I headed off down the sidewalk. As we walked, the little hamster on the wheel inside my head starting running faster. What if it wasn't my imagination? What if whoever wrote the notes was following me? That would explain how they knew I was in New York. Great, just what I needed; more weird things going on. Then that thought sunk in and I stopped in my tracks, nearly causing Bruno to do a back flip as his leash became taut. It must be difficult to be that small. He turned around to give me an inquisitive look.

"That *is* what we need Bruno, more weird stuff! Jess and Cameron got to know each other and spend time together when they were helping Mommy. If they help her more, they'll spend more time together." Hey, maybe there was an upside to being stalked by some wacko. Who knew?

∽ CHAPTER TWO ᝈ

The apartment that Jess and I shared was also in a very nice building, although not nearly as luxurious as Braden's. I greeted our own front desk guy, Carl, who I thought was a little afraid of me. I really couldn't blame him. This was a building filled with nice upper middle class people and I had shown up in our lobby covered in garbage and dressed like a dominatrix.

I took the elevator to our floor and dug my keys out of my purse. Opening the door, I called out to Jess, who called back from her bedroom to let me know that she would be right out. Then I took Bruno off his leash, and as per his custom, he took off to go check the place out. Bruno was always the point man. Mommy wasn't allowed past the front room until he gave the all clear. I took out my cell and quickly alerted Braden to our safe arrival before he had the National Guard out looking for us, and then I went into the living room and plopped down in my favorite comfy chair. We had spent many an evening in this living room drinking wine and sharing gossip. I was going to miss it. Jess came out a minute later, escorted by Bruno.

"Braden let you out on your own?" she asked, taking a seat across from me and putting her feet up on an ottoman.

"I have my attack dog." I looked down at my teeny tiny Chihuahua who I was sure would yip his ass off for me if I were in danger. The fact that nobody might care was another issue. Bruno placed two tiny front paws on my leg and gave me an imploring look not unlike the one I frequently gave Judge Channing. Bruno and Mommy both knew how to beg. I picked him up and settled him into my lap, rubbing him behind his ginormous ears. He made the doggie equivalent of a sigh. Bruno loved to be rubbed. He and Mommy had that in common too. "He asked if you would come back with me though," I added.

"For Game Night?" She didn't look thrilled.

"Yeah, I know, pizza, beer, and sports we don't fully comprehend may not *sound* like a magical evening, but Cameron will be there," I said with a big suggestive smile.

"And?" she asked, brushing some imaginary lint off of her sleeve. Ah - the imaginary lint brush - a classic evasive maneuver. I had used it myself on many an occasion. Lawyers knew all about this stuff because juries watched our body language very carefully. Two could play at that game though. I went to law school too.

"And so, you guys are getting along really well. Maybe it's time to explore something more than friendship." I gave her the earnest sincere look. She countered with the dismissive eye roll but I didn't buy it. I knew what *she* was thinking about exploring.

"He was here alone with me for hours last night. He could have explored a whole continent if he had wanted to. We talked; we laughed. There was some sexual tension but he didn't do anything." She shot me a raised eyebrow – a direct challenge. I sidestepped it with the thoughtful look, complete with the lean forward, to demonstrate my sincerity.

"I suspect he overthinks it with women he's interested in for more than a night."

"Great. Just what I need." She sighed. "An over-thinker. That's usually the same thing as an under-committer." I needed to make her understand that this was well within her power.

"I know that he *wants* to explore more but he may need a little nudge."

"What kind of nudge?" she asked suspiciously. Why did everyone seem to distrust me?

"I don't know. Maybe you should just kiss him. He wouldn't refuse *that* and then you could talk about the details before doing anything else." I paused as the irony sunk in. "That last step was the one that I forgot myself before our wonderful college encounter, incidentally."

"Kiss him! That's your plan, General MacArthur? Okay, Should I do that in the office with our two hundred colleagues or in open court? Maybe I'll just do it at Game Night so that Adam and Mark can cheer me on. I can't count on even being alone with him unless we go on a date, let alone kissing him out of the blue."

"So maybe you should ask him out, then."

"No. I'm not making the first move and I'm not asking him out. I want him to do it because I need to know that he's worked through whatever he feels about you and Braden being together. Besides, I may be a shameless hussy but I'm kind of an old-fashioned shameless hussy in some ways. Braden asked *you* out."

"He asked me to hook up with him and when I demanded dinner first, he challenged me to a round of Beer Sex Trivia and then we negotiated a settlement that included pre-sex dating."

"So it wasn't the Notebook ..."

"Look, I know that Cam's interested in you. He said so. And I know that he's *happy* for me and Braden too, even if it was weird at first. You just need to spend more time together. Braden's parents are out of town this weekend and it's just his younger brother at their place. His mom invited us to stay over. They have a pool and there's a music festival going on near there on Saturday. Mark, Adam, and Cam are invited. You should come too."

"I told Lily that I would hang around with her this weekend and I don't want to ditch her. Now that her parents are living in Florida she doesn't have anywhere to go on weekends and I think she needs more socialization. She works in a law library and she spends every night in her apartment writing her books. She's going to start hoarding stuff and having deep conversations with the neighbor's cat if she doesn't get out more."

Bruno yipped. He didn't like cats. Whenever he saw one he would follow it around and give it what I'm sure he imagined were very intimidating looks. Wait - he followed it around. Okay, time to test out my new idea.

"The thing is, Jess, I may need some help anyway. I think somebody may be following me. It could be the person who left the notes."

"Following you?" She sat up straighter and looked concerned and I hoped that I wasn't getting her all worked up for nothing.

"Yeah, it could be nothing but I just got this weird feeling. Anyway, I was thinking that I shouldn't keep this stuff to myself anymore after what happened last night and so maybe we could all discuss it or something over the weekend. In fact, why don't we invite Lily along too?"

"You know that she and Adam don't get along?"

"Oh that's right." I paused. "Definitely invite her then."

"You don't think anyone would mind that you're inviting all these people to Senator Pierce's house while he's away?" she asked with a laugh.

"Of course not," I replied. *Probably not.* I stood up and tucked Bruno under my arm. "Now, I've got to grab some more clothes." I headed down a short hallway to my room and Jess followed me in and sat down on my bed. I put Bruno down and grabbed my suit bag, tossing it on a chair. I would kind of miss this room too when I moved. It was small and cozy and crammed with books just like my room in my parents' brownstone in New York.

"So, what was Cam like in college anyway?" Jess asked as I moved around my room figuring out what I needed. I paused and thought about her question for a minute, remembering our days together at Yale. What was Cam like then?

"He had lots of friends and he got involved in all kinds of activities. He was very intelligent, but not intellectual, more the cute, fun, easy-going kind of guy. He was in a fraternity and he was very popular."

"You were close?" she asked and I hesitated. We hadn't really gotten into a lot of detail about Cameron's and my former relationship.

"We hung out together a lot," I replied, hoping that maybe we were done talking about it.

"What did you do when you hung out?" Okay, we weren't done talking about it. What, was she cross-examining me? I quickly started grabbing toiletries and tossing them into an overnight bag like I had sixty seconds to evacuate the building.

"Um, sometimes we went out to eat or to the movies. Sometimes we just talked," I said while digging around frantically in my closet. Obviously, I still felt a little uncomfortable talking about this, for some reason.

"But you weren't dating? I only ask because you did the same stuff with the gay guy you supposedly *were* dating. The only difference was that you actually had sex with *Cam*."

"We were friends," I answered as I shredded a few garments in my haste. "And I told you, we only had sex that one night." I rifled through my blouses, grabbed one and tossed it in the general direction of my suit bag. If one considered five feet away the general direction.

"But never anything other than that? Not even a little fooling around?"

"No. Just that one night." I came barreling out of the closet and started frantically digging through my underwear drawer. For something. Not really sure what.

"Gabrielle, stop! Step *away* from the dresser! You do *not* need your bathing suit to spend the night at Braden's apartment! And for the record, you probably don't need the shoe polish that you packed either." I stopped digging, put the bathing suit down, turned and slowly walked over to sit next to her on my bed in defeat. The Grand freaking Inquisitor over here wasn't giving up. What in the hell difference did it make now anyway?

"There was sexual tension between us but nothing happened other than that one night."

"So, what happened *that* night?"

"There was one of those moments, the kind where you look at somebody and think, 'wow I really want to kiss him.' So I kissed him. And he kissed me back and he just kind of took it from there. I was planning to tell him that I was a virgin, but I really liked what we were doing, and I seemed to be holding my own pretty well," I said defensively.

"I think you should have mentioned it, honey."

"Ug! I know," I admitted, banging my head a few times against the bedpost. "Anyway, hc freaked out when he realized the next day that he had deflowered one of his closest friends. I said that I wanted to date him and then he freaked out more. In retrospect, I probably should have mentioned that *before* I kissed him."

"And he should have handled it better, even at nineteen. There were more sensitive ways to tell a good friend that you didn't want a romantic relationship."

"He said that he was confused, and that he *did want* to be involved with me romantically but he couldn't deal with those feelings at that moment, because he was really down on himself at the time. Afterward, when I wouldn't talk to him, he figured he had damaged our relationship beyond repair, so he just decided to leave me alone."

"This is like a bad movie," she said, shaking her head.

"Everything seems more dramatic when you're a teenager. It's hormones and chemicals from all the Clearasil and Axe body spray. At least that's my hypothesis."

"You really should tell Braden, you know."

"What? That I made him negotiate an international treaty to take me out to dinner, but I let his cousin take my virginity on a whim? He already knows."

"I mean that you should tell him that Cam said that he cared about you but that he just couldn't deal with it. At least Braden will know that he wasn't just using you as a convenient place to come."

"You've got such a way with words."

"I know, honey. Now, getting back to the point …"

"He's already guessed that it was more than just a casual hook up for both of us. He's still a little jealous about Cam having gone where no man had gone before, so I don't want to rock the boat when they just made up." We both sat there quietly for a minute, lost in our own thoughts, while Bruno chewed on a pair of my stockings.

"He really said he was interested in me?" she asked finally.

"Yeah! Last night when we were waiting, and he said he found you really attractive too." She nodded her head silently. I knew she was thinking about it!

"Does he have nice boy parts?" she asked after another minute of silent contemplation.

"*That's* what you want to know?! Does that matter so much?"

"I already know that he's cute and funny and smart! I even know what kind of food and books and music he likes," she said defensively. "We had a lot of time to talk while we were staking out Braden's crazy call girl ex-girlfriend for you." Okay, she had a point there. He had nothing to be ashamed of anyway in that department.

"He's a healthy boy," I replied. "Not quite as healthy as Braden, but Mother Nature was generous to the men of their line. Stamina and the ability to recover quickly also seem to run in their family. Both he and Braden are like Energizer Bunnies."

"Did you do it more than once?" she asked, sounding surprised.

"Five times," I answered, blushing a little with the memory of our one wild night together. In some ways I had actually lucked out as far as first-time experiences went. Even at nineteen Cam was good in bed. Must have been something in the genes.

"*Five* times! Mary, Joseph and a fucking donkey! This was the first time you had sex? Did they carry you out of there on a stretcher?"

"I was a bit sore the next day. I was too busy having an emotional breakdown to really notice much, though."

"You've had very interesting experiences," she said, shaking her head again. "Come on Mrs. Pierce. We had better get going before your very healthy husband comes looking for you."

"That sounds so weird! I'll have to get used to that."

"Is Braden acting any differently now that you're engaged?"

"Well, first of all, we're not officially engaged. He wants to propose to me in a more romantic way."

"I can't imagine why," she said dryly.

"Secondly, it's been less than twenty-four hours, so it's kind of early to tell."

I called Bruno who came scurrying over with a yip, and when I had him leashed again, we headed out. It happened again as soon as we cleared the front door! I looked around in confusion.

"What's the matter, honey?" she asked.

"I have that weird feeling again, like somebody is watching me."

"Right now?" she asked, suddenly stopping and looking around frantically in every direction. She gave some folks some suspicious looks that probably made them think that *we* were stalking *them*. A little kid ran away from us. We weren't really good at the whole spy game thing. We would probably have to work on subtlety a bit.

"I don't see anybody, Gabrielle. It's probably just nerves because of everything that's happened. Don't worry about it."

"Yeah, I'm sure you're right, but we should still mention and talk about it as a group this weekend," I said as we headed back toward Rittenhouse Square.

∽ CHAPTER THREE ∾

I had my own key now and I let us in to Braden's apartment. Bruno went off to check things out as usual and I heard male voices from inside acknowledge our presence. The gang was all there. I hung up Bruno's leash and headed toward the TV area behind Jess, who greeted everyone and sat down next to Cam with a smile. She was much cooler around guys she was attracted to than I had ever been.

"Hi, Gabrielle! I understand that I dressed up like an ass for no reason last night!" Mark said in a falsely cheerful voice.

"You looked very cute," I replied sincerely. It was the truth. Mark always looked cute, in a carefully disheveled way. He knew how to pull it off so that he looked like a sexy hipster rather than a messy derelict. That took skill.

"You're lucky that you're sleeping with one of my best friends," he said, not looking terribly overwhelmed by the compliment.

"I'm sorry," I replied, and he raised his eyebrows at me. "That I made you dress up like a naughty schoolboy and go to an underground sex party." He cleared his throat.

"For no reason," I finished.

"Yeah, whatever. You owe me. I think I see some really annoying trials in your future."

"Are you mad at me too, Cam?" I turned toward him, with what I hoped was a contrite expression. He gave me his charming Cameron grin. Have I mentioned the charming Cameron grin? Well, if not, trust me, it was very charming. It had charmed the panties off of me once.

"Me? Nah. I'm not mad that I dressed up like a gay biker for nothing. Now, when my multi-millionaire client caught me digging through garbage cans for you …"

"I already apologized for that!"

"I'll get over it eventually. I'm getting to be pretty good at criminal defense anyway. Maybe I can do that when my father and the other partners at my firm find out."

"I'm not mad at you at all." Adam smiled brightly. "In fact, I think you're fucking hilarious. If you weren't dating Braden, I'd go out with you myself just for the entertainment."

"Well, she is dating Braden, so find your entertainment elsewhere," Braden said and moved over, patting the loveseat beside him. I went over and sat down and it was as if Bruno just magically knew somehow that Mommy and Daddy were sitting together. (Which meant double team petting.) He came flying around a corner, hurtled himself back into the room like a missile, stopped short, and slid ten yards on his ass to arrive at our feet and beg us to pick him up, which Braden promptly did. Bruno was a very enthusiastic animal and Braden was a doting doggie daddy.

While Braden petted Bruno, I petted Braden, running my fingers up and down the hard muscles of his inner thigh. Bruno was blocking what I was doing from sight, and I could sense that Braden was enjoying it, so I teased him a little by moving a bit higher periodically as we watched the game. At the time I didn't realize *how much* he was enjoying it.

"So how was Pittsburgh?" Jessica asked during a commercial break. Braden and Adam had just returned from a conference there the night before.

"First night was just introductory stuff and a cocktail party," Adam said. "The keynote speech was okay. The party was pretty good although Braden wanted to leave early because he missed Gabrielle."

"Oh, poor Braden," Mark teased. "What had it been? A whole ten hours?" Adam and Cameron laughed. Braden just glared.

"The next day," Adam continued, "we did our presentation, went to a couple other presentations, and then Braden wanted to leave early because, you guessed it, he missed Gabrielle. Apparently he can't survive outside of her for more than a day."

"We had done all the important stuff!" Braden argued. "The third day was just more bullshit. I didn't want to go to any more lunches or dinners. I can eat here."

"One *month*!" Mark laughed. "Jesus, Braden, you went down like the fucking Titanic, man! Dating for four weeks and you can't make it two whole days without her."

"Six weeks," Braden corrected. "I don't dick around when I know what I want, and I want to be with her." Braden and I smiled at each other stupidly for a minute.

"I guess you *don't*!" Cam muttered with a laugh. "I have to admit I kind of admire that."

The game came back on and we watched another inning. My fingers brushed up against Braden's boy parts a little more and I realized that it wasn't just his muscles that were hard. I had gotten him excited right here in the middle of Game Night! Something about that felt very sexy and I liked having the power to do that to him. At the next commercial break Adam picked up the conversation again.

"Do you think your parents are going to be okay with you getting engaged so quickly?" he asked Braden.

"My dad proposed to my mom after six weeks and they've been happily married for thirty years. He said that he just knew and he didn't want to waste his time."

"What about your parents, Gab?" Jess chimed in. "Your dad's pretty protective; do you think he'll be okay with it?"

"You're kidding me, right? My father's biggest fear is that I'll die alone with a bunch of cats." Bruno yipped. "He'll probably ask Braden what took him so long. Incidentally, *he's* definitely a guy who doesn't dick around when he knows what he wants. That's why he's a CEO." My fingers traveled up again and rubbed a little harder.

"Gabrielle, can you help me in the kitchen? Excuse us for a minute," Braden said, sounding a little hoarse. He got up, put our yippy dog down, and took my hand, gently pushing me in front of him off into the other room. Bruno trotted along after us. The layout of Braden's apartment was very open but there was a wall that obscured part of the kitchen from those in the TV area.

"What's up?" I teased. He backed me up against a black granite counter, out of view.

"I think you know the answer to that. You're driving me crazy. I can't wait until tonight," he said in a low voice. "I need it now." Uh oh. I had gotten him a bit more excited than I realized. As much as that turned me on, he couldn't be serious, could he? I looked at him carefully. He looked flushed, he was breathing quickly and his eyes were dilated. He could be serious.

"What do mean you need it now?"

"Sex. I need sex. I've moved beyond amorous and now I'm into really horny. Stage three is physical discomfort and mental anguish. Just letting you know." His eyes dropped to my lips.

"I knew *what* you meant but we have company!" I whispered back. He was stunningly sexy-looking when he was aroused like this, and I headed for stage two with a bullet myself, but come on, during Game Night? I just thought I was building anticipation for tonight when they all went home and we were alone.

"Just a quickie to tide me over until later." He ran his hands over my hips. Oh, that felt nice. While my brain was still saying, "sex isn't a spectator sport," my cha-cha was starting to come around to his point of view. My brain was still ahead though. At least for the moment.

"Braden, you don't do quickies." My eyes went to his lips and I started to feel flushed.

"We got off together in ten minutes in an interview room at the courthouse once."

"That was different. There was a whole other level of pressure involved there. And there are logistical problems. We would have to walk past them to get to the bedroom." I knew that if Braden and I just strolled off toward the bedroom together it wouldn't be really difficult to figure out where we going. That could be kind of awkward when one had guests.

"We'll say we're going to the bathroom."

"Together?"

"So we'll say we're going to have sex and we'll be right back. Honesty is the best policy anyway." He obviously knew he was going to have to work harder to convince me, so he upped his game and leaned in to start kissing his way up my neck. His lips felt so good against my skin. He gently nipped me with his teeth and a bolt of heat shot straight to my lady bits, which were now firmly on his side.

"It's rude to have sex while you're entertaining," I said throatily. I was sinking fast and we both knew it. He was going to have me down on the kitchen floor in another minute.

"Mm hm?" I guess that was the best he could do with his tongue in my ear.

"Oh God. Okay, but give Bruno a treat first because he's making me nervous." We both looked over at our Chihuahua who was sitting happily watching us, panting and wagging his tail. Braden quickly grabbed a doggie bacon strip out of a cupboard above my head and leaned down to give it to Bruno, who ran off with his prize, as was another one of his habits.

"Now where was I?" Braden muttered, going back to business. "Business" being introducing my earlobe to oral play that was usually reserved for my lower regions.

"Ahh!" I whimpered quietly. "I hope you have a permit for that tongue." I wrapped my arms around his neck and pulled his mouth to mine. The tongue in question began tracing delicious little circles on the roof of my mouth and I made a contented sound and arched my back to press my chest tightly against him. I wanted to haul him to the floor with me and have my wicked way with him. So much for good manners. Emily Post would be so disappointed.

He groaned and grabbed my bottom to pull my hips tightly against him too. The now very *big* bulge pressing into my belly told me that my baby was rock hard and ready to rumble. I started rubbing against him shamelessly and I was about to suggest we head to the bedroom while we still had some good judgment left, when I heard a phone ring and Adam call out.

"Pizza's here, Braden. You going to get it or should I?" It sounded like Adam was getting up. Braden broke the kiss and leaned his forehead against mine in breathless defeat.

"I'll get it!" he called out, sounding a bit tense.

"Poor baby," I said with a giggle. "I hope this doesn't lead to stage three."

"Laugh it up. You're not going to be able to walk tomorrow. The quickie option is off the table. I'm going to bang you so long tonight they'll send out a search party for you," he said, pulling his shirt down over the evidence of his healthy maleness and heading off to get the food. I didn't know what in the hell I was laughing at. I felt more than just "warm" myself at that point and I probably looked like I had just jogged a few dozen miles. I splashed a little water on my face before grabbing some plates out of the cupboard and napkins out of a drawer. I had a feeling that we were going to have a night of volcanic sex later and I wondered if I should try to get cardiac clearance.

Braden brought the pizza back and we all grabbed a piece and sat down to eat and watch the game again. The teams were evenly matched and there was plenty of excitement, shouting, and cheering. I wasn't a really big baseball fan, but now that I knew most of the rules, it was much more entertaining. Did you know that those guys weren't actually translating things into sign language, by the way? Those were secret signals they were using. Tricky, huh?

"Any interesting cases this week?" Mark asked during another commercial.

"A few," Braden answered, pulling me closer to him and nestling me in his arm. I loved it when he nestled me. It made me feel wonderfully small and girlie. I had learned my lesson earlier, and

Bruno, who was eyeing up my pizza suspiciously, was the only one who I was petting during the later innings.

"I've got a really fun one with Gabrielle coming up," Adam said with a smirk. "It involves a young man who, shockingly, may not be terribly bright. I'm afraid that I'm going to have to make her life a bit difficult, but I'll try to be gentle. "

"Don't worry, Captain Ego. I can take it."

"Well, alright then! Bring it, baby!" he taunted.

"Don't call her baby," Braden warned. "Only I get to call her baby." He reached up and stroked my hair possessively. It didn't bother me when Braden got possessive. In fact I was perfectly happy to let him claim his territory on a nightly basis.

"Uh oh. Are other guys *allowed* to argue with Gabrielle?" Mark teased. "What's going to happen when it's Adam getting her all fired up instead of you?" He could be such a pot stirrer. He really was like a naughty schoolboy sometimes.

"He can get her all fired up as long as she works off her adrenaline with me," Braden said. "And as long as I can watch her get all fired up." He gave me a slightly lecherous look.

"I think I saw that movie on cable last night," Cam joked.

"Yeah, that sounds pretty voyeuristic," Adam noted with a laugh.

"And your point is?" Braden asked, dropping his hand back around my waist and stroking my ribs. The looks he was giving me clued me in to the fact that he was still somewhere in the vicinity of the really horny stage. He very subtly moved his hand a little higher and brushed the underside of my breast, giving me a wicked smile. Oh boy.

The game was tied and the Phillies were up to bat with the bases loaded and two men out. Suddenly the batter hit it straight into left field and the runner on third headed home. Everyone's attention was riveted to the game and they all started yelling and cheering. Braden decided to take that opportunity to get to first base himself, squeezing my breast and pinching my nipple in just the way that he knew drove me wild. I almost moaned but I caught myself. The Phillies scored and Braden gave me a cocky grin, content in the knowledge that he had scored too. He dropped his hand back down and began stroking my ribs again. I guess that he had proven to me that two could play at that game.

"Oh by the way, Gab, do you want me to take that client in that gang case you got hauled into?" Mark asked me, turning away from the TV again for a moment.

"Why? There's no reason I can't handle it just because it's a gang case. My client's not a shooter. I think he's just charged with theft."

"Let him take it anyway, Gabrielle," Braden said, sounding unhappy. Anyone in a street gang was potentially a violent criminal, no matter what he was charged with. He hated it when I had to represent the violent ones, mostly because I had to be locked in with them alone to interview them. His fears weren't completely unrealistic, even though incidents were rare.

"Why, Braden? I can handle it."

"Because I care about your safety."

"Gee thanks," Mark said with a laugh.

"Not that ..." Braden said hurriedly, glancing up at him.

"It's alright dude. I'm not your fiancée."

"Braden. I have to do my job just like you do," I said gently.

Just then the game came back on and everyone turned their attention back to the TV, but I could sense that we weren't done discussing this subject. It was the one real source of potential conflict that we had. If I was going to do this job, though, I was going to do it like everyone else did. I didn't want any special treatment because I was the daughter of a very rich man or the fiancée of one either, for that matter. The Phillies eventually won six to four and our friends got up, stretched, and got ready to go. Cam offered to take Jess home and before they left I pulled her aside for a little strategy session and pep talk.

"Remember what you told me," I whispered.

"Never try to wax your own hoohah?"

"Not that!" I rolled my eyes. "Just flirt with him and see what happens."

"Okay, but I have a feeling that what will happen is nothing."

"Just try it," I said with a sigh. We said goodnight to all of them and as the door closed, I grabbed the stack of dirty dishes and darted into the kitchen to start filling the sink. I had been enjoying our little back and forth teasing game and it was my turn again now.

"We need to clean up," I said, smiling brightly and filling the water with bubbles. All I needed was some pearls and I could have been June Cleaver. I was looking like such a wholesome little housewife.

"We'll clean up later," Braden said, coming up behind me as stealthily as a panther and putting his arms around my waist. "I've been really horny for over three hours. It's unhealthy."

"According to you I'm going to be too tired later," I reminded him.

"The cleaning lady's coming tomorrow." He ran his hands over my hips.

"You can't leave a bunch of crusty dishes out all night. You'll get bugs." I didn't feel guilty about building up a little more anticipation, because I knew that I was going to rock his world that night anyway.

"Fine. You do the dishes. I'll just occupy myself while I wait," he said as he leaned down and nuzzled the base of my neck. I could feel his warm breath and then his soft lips and then finally his hot tongue as he trailed open-mouthed kisses all the way up to my ear.

"Braden." A warm tingling sensation flowed through my body and I started breathing faster. My panties were probably wetter than the dishes already.

"Don't mind me," he said huskily, and began sucking on my earlobe and once again moving his tongue the way that he moved it when he went down on me. It was a not-so-subtle reminder of what else we could be doing besides housework. My clit screamed at my brain in protest. Then he started lightly brushing his fingers across my breasts and I moved from tingly girl parts to achy girl parts. I pushed my bottom back against him and I could feel how hard he was again. I rubbed up against him like a cat. Mother Nature was good – so very *good*. Even though I wanted him desperately at that moment, I also liked how much he was trying to convince me. Let him work for it a little. I was worth the effort.

"If you would stop distracting me…" I swallowed hard and let out a ragged breath.

"Don't let me stop you. I know how important the dishes are," he said as he reached back and unhooked my bra. His hands traveled up under my shirt to cup my breasts and pinch my nipples the way I liked it again, and it felt infinitely better against my bare skin. When he began gently squeezing them between his fingers, chills ran through my body and goosebumps formed on my arms.

Have I mentioned that I *love* doing dishes? The smell of Palmolive would probably make me come like a Pavlov dog after this. Okay, so technically Pavlov's dogs didn't come, they salivated, but you get the point. I could feel his breathing getting heavy and his heart racing. I knew how much he wanted me too and that his self-control was stretched thin. That, in and of itself, would have been enough to drive me crazy, but then one hand left my breast and slid into my panties and all bets were off. My brain had left the building and my cha-cha had stayed behind to party down and get funky.

"You must find doing dishes very stimulating, because you're really wet, baby," he teased.

"I didn't say I didn't want you," I said breathlessly. "I just said I wanted to tidy up a little first so your cleaning lady wouldn't think your fiancée was a slob." My voice sounded as rough as sandpaper and I was starting to tremble.

"I'll tell her that you make up for it in bed," he whispered in my ear seductively and I almost hit the floor. Jesus Tap Dancing Christ! This man was off the charts sexy! I started pushing my hips forward and I leaned back against him, panting. "What's the matter? Don't you want to finish the dishes?" he teased.

"You're so naughty, Braden," said the woman grinding her cha-cha against his hand.

"You're so ready, Gabrielle," he practically purred. Oh that was just too much!

"Oh God! Braden, I need you!" I gasped and reached down to put my hand over his and press his fingers against me harder.

"You need me to what?" he asked in a low sultry voice. "Dry?"

"I need you inside me," I panted, feeling myself about to lose control.

"Now?"

Oh shit! I give up! You win! You win! You win the freaking teasing game! AARGH! I heard the click click of nails on the floor. Oh no. No! No! No!

"*Yes* now, Braden! Bruno, honey, go play with your toys for a while," I said desperately.

"That's right, Bruno, Daddy's playing with *his* toys," Braden said, sounding amused. He was keeping pressure on my clit with his thumb and teasing me by skimming his other fingers over my entrance but not giving me the penetration I was aching for. My entire body felt like it was on fire. How did he *learn* this stuff? Okay, don't think about that, Gabrielle. Bruno looked up at us curiously, checked out the scene from a few different angles, and then thankfully, got bored and moved on.

"Oh God, Braden, I need it so badly right now, baby," I moaned. "And just to be clear I mean sex! Stage three! Stage three!"

"But what if we get bugs?" I could hear the laughter in his voice.

"Braden, fuck me right now! Please?!" After all, my parents raised me to be polite. Apparently "please" *was* a magic word! Although I think that the "fuck me" was pretty effective too. He spun me around and yanked my shorts and panties down over my hips. Then he lifted me up to seat me on the counter, and while I slid them the rest of the way off, he opened up his jeans and freed Mother

Nature's generous gift to both of us. Sweet baby Jesus and two hump camel, it never ceased to amaze me that I managed to accommodate him so well. I must have a vagina like a Tardis – a Dr. Who-hah. And, *Oh my God*, I'm a geek! He pulled his T-shirt over his head and stood there looking more appetizing than anything in any other kitchen anywhere. I wanted to count his muscles with my tongue. He smiled with naughty anticipation, pushed my legs apart, positioned himself at my entrance, grabbed my hips… and froze when he heard the really loud scream-like noise that wasn't coming from me for a change. Bruno started barking immediately.

"Oh no! No! Not *now*!" he shouted.

∽ CHAPTER FOUR ∾

"Is that a fire alarm?" Maybe my body wasn't all that was on fire. Or maybe I was already in stage three and it involved a bunch of Dementors shrieking in my head.

He groaned, swore and managed somehow to close his pants over one raging example of healthy maleness. Oh man. No fair. I was just going to get to play with *my* toys.

"They do drills periodically for insurance purposes," he said, in a very angry voice, pulling on his T-shirt again and yanking it down to cover the evidence of said healthy maleness for the second time that evening. I wouldn't want to be a Prudential agent right now. "Baby, get dressed while I get Bruno's leash."

When I came back out to the entry, he was at the closet by the front door. "Here, put this on so you don't get chilly." He handed me a sweat jacket and grabbed another one for himself.

He picked up a frantically yipping Bruno and tucked him under one arm, grabbing my hand and leading me toward the stairs. Other residents were already on their way out and we joined the crowd.

When we got to the sidewalk, we crossed the street where emergency personnel were directing people. We waited on the sidewalk as Bruno paced around at the end of his leash, probably on the verge of passing out with excitement. Braden put his arm around me and held me close to him. We mostly just watched what was going on around us as the minutes started to tick by. I eventually began to get the weird feeling again, like someone was watching, and my eyes started to wander over the immediate vicinity.

"You know, we've never had alley sex," I said, staring at a fairly dark side street.

"That's because alley sex is also known as disorderly conduct and public indecency. Talk to me again in ten minutes." More time went by.

"Braden, why don't we just go to my place?" I asked after we had been out there for what felt like quite a while. I looked around us at the crowd of tired-looking people and saw something odd. There was a guy in a baseball cap standing alone some distance away and it almost looked like he was staring directly at us.

"It doesn't usually take this long. Normally we're back in in less than ten minutes." I turned toward Braden when he spoke, and when I turned back, the figure was gone. I assumed that I must have been mistaken. My imagination was working overtime these days. Still, it didn't hurt to mention it. I had learned my lesson not telling Braden about the notes.

"Braden, I need to tell you something. I had a weird feeling like somebody might be following me earlier and just now I felt like someone was watching us. When I looked around, I saw a guy over there who seemed to be staring in our direction."

"Where?" he asked, suddenly sounding very alert.

"He was standing over in that direction. When I looked back a couple of seconds later though, he was gone. Like I said, I just had a weird feeling and I also had one earlier, although I didn't see anybody at all then."

"I don't see anybody there now. Are you sure he was looking at us? It's pretty dark out here and there's a lot going on."

"No, I'm not sure. He was wearing a baseball cap and it hid part of his face. It was probably just my imagination or nerves or something." The crowd started to move then and people began re-entering the building. Braden stopped to talk to the concierge on the way in.

"So, what's going on, Anthony? They don't announce nighttime fire drills anymore and it takes twice as long to do them?" Braden wasn't in a good mood and Anthony was in the line of fire. It's a good thing we weren't in court or a whole lot of people would be doing hard time. No pun intended.

"It wasn't a fire drill, Mr. Pierce. Somebody pulled a false fire alarm."

"Do you know who it was?" For their sake I hoped that if they ever got caught they wound up in someone else's courtroom. Braden might go after the death penalty.

"No sir. We think that the person might have snuck in through Roxie's," he said, referring to a restaurant and lounge located in Braden's building. "Either that or it might have been a kid who lives here." That kid might not be living here for long. Or living for long in general. We thanked him for the information and headed back up to Braden's apartment. The elevator doors slid open disgorging us and half a dozen other disgruntled-looking residents, and just as we began to head down the hall, I saw it. There was a small, white object sitting in front of Braden's door. I felt adrenaline rush through my body and I got goosebumps.

"Braden! Look!" I pointed. "You don't think that's another note, do you?" We quickly went over and I retrieved the object. It wasn't an envelope, though, it was just a cocktail napkin that said 'Club 51' on it.

"I didn't see that here when we left," he said, looking confused.

"Somebody must have dropped it on the way out," I suggested.

"Right in front of my door?" he asked dubiously.

"Maybe they were checking to make sure everybody was out. Why a firefighter had a cocktail napkin on him is probably something we shouldn't contemplate too deeply." I turned it over and saw that there were numbers written on the back. "It says seven one six ..."

"Maybe this litter was intended for a different apartment. If you want, we can give Mr. Lewis in seven sixteen his trash."

"Seven one six, one zero three zero," I continued. I thought about it for a minute and then a light went on in my head. "Seven sixteen, ten-thirty! It sounds like a date and time!"

"So, maybe somebody's got a date at this Club 51 on Friday," he said, as he unlocked the door and stood aside to let Bruno and me go in. Bruno took off to check the place out as usual and made his way back speedily with a twelve foot butt slide that made the base runners in the game earlier look bad. Luckily, he didn't hit the wall this time. His aim was improving. We gave him a treat for being such a good boy and he ran off somewhere with his treasure. Then Braden turned and gave me his hot sex look and my cha-cha cheered for joy. We were finally going to get grand slammed. Thank you, Lord!

"So, Gabrielle, are you going to be a good girl for me now?" he asked in a low husky voice as he started walking toward me slowly.

"Define 'good'." I started feeling shaky again. I could feel my face heating up and my pulse started to race like a stock car engine. Not that I knew what a stock car engine actually sounded like.

"What are you thinking?" he asked, looking at me like he knew exactly what I was thinking. Braden could read me far too well. I think he could probably detect my sexual arousal from the next room. Or the next county. Or the next planet. He was getting closer by the second and I was starting to pant.

"That sometimes I like it when you get all 'take charge' like that. You going to show me who's boss, bad boy?" I taunted seductively, standing my ground firmly even though my legs felt very wobbly at that moment. I knew that within half an hour I would be having a screaming orgasm and the fact that I was still vertical, let alone still teasing him, was a minor miracle.

He gave me a sexy smile and then he was only a couple of feet away. "I'll be happy to take charge anytime you want." He reached out and pulled me into his arms a little roughly, kissing me hard, possessing my mouth, and rubbing his tongue up against mine forcefully. He was claiming me and consuming me and I wanted him to do it. I started kissing him back with just as much heat, pulling his hair and pressing my body up against him brazenly. In seconds he had me pinned up against the wall. We were frantically trying to undress each other while grinding our hips together and never breaking our burning kiss. I wrapped my leg around him and felt his erection pressing into my belly as I grabbed onto that tight gorgeous ass. "Bedroom," he said, breaking away and breathing hard, "or I'm going to take you right here, right now."

"And that's bad why?" I panted.

"The lights are on and we're standing in front of really big windows."

"Bedroom!" I grabbed his hand and ran like a track star. I probably could have handled high hurdles too at that moment. Fuck! I probably could have handled the high *jump*!

Bruno followed along eagerly. This was a new version of the humping game and he obviously didn't want to miss anything. Usually Bruno was banned when Mommy and Daddy were playing full-force in the bedroom but at the moment Mommy and Daddy had more pressing matters on their minds. We set a world speed record for cross-apartment sex-sprint, made it to the bedroom in seconds flat and continued desperately undressing each other. Okay, let's be honest, Braden ripped my panties off. This wasn't one of his more tender, gentle moments. It's a good thing he did, though, or I would have ripped them off myself and I'm not very coordinated. There could have been bloodshed.

"Lay down and spread your legs for me, baby," he said without preamble.

"That's so romantic, Braden. Maybe you can have that engraved on my wedding ring."

"Gabrielle, you're beautiful; you know that I love you and that I want to spend the rest of my life with you. Now spread those legs for me and show me that sweet pussy, baby," he said, peeling off his boxers. He stood there in all of his naked glory, looking all naked and glorious. Lord have mercy. I didn't care how many times I saw it, the sight of Braden Pierce without clothing took my breath away and sent my hoo-hah into a state of emergency. He was quite obviously ready. I was quite obviously willing. I hit the bed flying, and God help me, I showed him that sweet pussy. I would have shown him anything at that moment.

He came over, crawled onto the bed with me, knelt between my legs, and surprised me by grabbing my wrists and pinning them above my head. As he smiled down at me with a truly wicked look, it suddenly dawned on me that he hadn't forgotten about the petting or the dishes.

"Well, hello, Gabrielle."

"Hi?" He wasn't moving.

"Didn't your mother ever tell you it's not nice to tease?" he asked seductively.

"Didn't your mother ever tell you that patience is a virtue?" I shot back.

"I'm not very virtuous," he purred and I swallowed hard but I held his gaze. "I believe that when we were so rudely interrupted you were ordering me to fuck you."

"I said please," I reminded him.

"You did," he acknowledged. "So polite. My mother was right. You are a good influence on me." He lowered his hips and rubbed his readiness up against my willingness. I started breathing hard but I swallowed my moan and I still didn't look away. "You like that, baby? Well maybe you should beg me for some more." He started to pull back and I quickly wrapped my legs around his hips and held on tight, rubbing up against him deliciously even though he had me pinned down. His smile got bigger. "Naughty girl. Maybe I'll tie you to the bed and go finish the dishes myself."

"You're the one who said, 'I need it now' first. Maybe I should make *you* beg *me*."

"And maybe I should spank you too while I'm at it." The way that he was looking at me at that point was so hot that I thought I might combust.

"Yeah. Good luck with that," I taunted. I was pretty cocky for a girl my size pinned under a guy his size. Have I mentioned the muscles? Like lightning he sat back, yanked me across his lap and then that bastard really did spank me! I was shocked! And angry! And incredibly turned on! Oh my God! That was *so* hot!

"Such a saucy mouth," he said as he slapped my ass kind of hard. Okay, not super hard. But hard *enough*!

"I thought you liked my saucy mouth," I bit out.

"Oh, believe me. I do," he said in a low silken voice and slapped the other cheek. "And I think *you* like *this* too." He slapped me again. "Don't you, baby?" he said and his palm connected with my ass three more times. Then he caressed my bottom and slipped two fingers between my legs and up inside me. I couldn't help it, I squirmed and moaned with pleasure. "Oh, you *do* like it, my bad girl. You're soaking wet and really ready."

"You just wait, Braden," I groaned. "I'm going to make you my fuck toy." He gave a startled laugh and loosened his hold. That was the opportunity I had been waiting for. I pushed myself off his lap and threw my weight against him, pushing him down on his back. In retrospect, I'm pretty sure he let me. He looked incredibly turned on and *amused*. Bastard! I climbed on top of him and straddled him. Then I grabbed his cock, positioned it at my entrance and without any further discussion slid down on it. That was quite a journey with Braden. I felt him fill me up completely and I whimpered with pleasure and threw my head back for a second. Then I looked down at him again and saw that he was flushed and breathing rapidly, gazing back at me with a combination of adoration and naked lust.

"God, I love you," he said thickly.

"Who's on top *now*, Braden?" I gasped. Some of those words were probably even understandable. And then I started moving up and down, sliding him in and out of me, getting faster and faster until I was riding him like I was going for the Triple Crown. Soon, I was slamming down against him so hard I could feel his balls hitting up against my bottom; my boobs were bouncing like crazy and I was crying out with pleasure, all of which I'm sure made Braden quite happy. He definitely looked happy. In fact, he looked positively euphoric.

"That's it, baby. Teach me a lesson," he ground out. "Oh yeah! Like that! *Fuck* me! Fuck me *hard*, Gabrielle!" His voice was strangled and he was groaning loudly as I bounced up and down, frantically grinding my clit up against him. In between my cries and moans and screams I tried to speak coherently. Unfortunately, it came out kind of like "waaannnacummm" (I just said that I *tried*.) I think he actually understood me, though. He sat up and pulled us toward the headboard where he braced his back and bent his knees. Then he grabbed my hips tightly, tilted them forward and began thrusting up beneath me, helping me slide up and slam down on his cock. There were no more clear thoughts then, just an incredibly pleasurable sensation between my legs, and building pressure and tension throughout my lower body. I reached higher and higher trying to get to where I needed to be. Finally when my body couldn't take any more, I felt myself explode into blissful relief as my inner muscles contracted sharply and I trembled and shook.

"Braden!" I screamed, looking at him helplessly as I came.

"So beautiful," he gasped. Through the haze something surprising registered. Braden was still moving. He had never finished with me on top before but I could see that's where he was headed very quickly. He kept thrusting hard for another minute or so and I could see in his eyes he was right on the edge.

"Gabrielle! Oh yeah! I'm going to come! Oh fuck! Baby, I'm going to come so hard!" He thrust up deeply into me one last time, shuddered, groaned and went still, his muscles tensing and then immediately releasing as he spilled himself into me.

"I guess I showed you who was boss," I said, staring into his gorgeous blue eyes.

"Kiss me," he said, still sounding out of breath. I leaned in and gave him a very warm tender kiss and then I gently eased off of him and he laid back down and cuddled me into his arms. I loved cuddling as much as nestling. I looked over to Bruno's doggie bed and saw that he had fallen asleep despite all the noise. We had trained our dog to sleep through rowdy sex.

"You're not mad at me for teasing you?" I asked, rubbing my hand over the sprinkling of hair on his chest and trailing gentle kisses there.

"No. You drive me crazy but in a good way. Are you mad at me for spanking you? Do you need me to get you any aspirin or ice or anything?" he asked in a concerned voice as he gently caressed my bottom.

"No, baby." I laughed softly. "You didn't spank me that hard and you were right. I liked it and I thought it was really hot. Don't think I'm going to let you get all Marquis de Sade on me though."

"Don't worry. I won't flog you," he said moving his hand back up and stroking my hair as we caught our breath. "I think I really would like to tie you to the bed though. Just playfully."

"With something soft?"

"No. With cable ties. I *said* just playfully!" He laughed.

"Well, it depends on how rough you play. I think that I would let you as long as you promised to let me go if I wanted and to not go hang out with the guys and leave me there."

"Of course I would let you go if you wanted! I'm not talking serious BDSM stuff. Just fooling around. And for the record, Adam and Mark are great guys but I'm pretty sure I would choose you naked and tied to a bed over hanging out with them. I would choose being with you even if you weren't naked and tied to a bed."

"Now that's *really* romantic! Let's put that one in our vows. Would you Braden, choose Gabrielle, even if she were not naked and tied to a bed?" I teased, leaning up to kiss him softly on the lips. He hugged me close and gently rubbed my back. He made me feel so loved and cared for. No other guy had ever made me feel like that.

"So, when do you want to get married?" he asked softly.

"You haven't even officially proposed yet," I replied, running a finger over his biceps.

"I will soon and I'll make it special. I promise."

"It would be special no matter what."

"Do you mind if I borrow one of your rings? I need to know your size and what you like. I want it to be perfect for you."

"Of course you can. And you can look at all my jewelry if you want. Most of it came from my parents but they know my taste."

"I think I'm starting to get to know it pretty well myself already," he replied.

"How long have we known each other altogether?"

"Seven and a half months. It feels like longer though."

"What did you think the first time you met me?" I asked curiously.

"I thought 'I'd like to hit that'." I jabbed him in the ribs. "Hey! I'm a guy." He laughed. "But right after that I thought 'wow, she's really intelligent too and she's a damned good lawyer.' What did you think when you first met me?"

"I thought 'wow, he's so confident and in control. I'm going to have to be on my game if I want to hold my own with him'."

"Really?"

"That and 'I totally want to have hot sweaty monkey sex with him'."

"I love that!" He laughed. "In fact, I think you had me at the hot sweaty monkey sex comment on our first date."

"I think you had me way before that. I had such a huge crush on you and all kinds of naughty fantasies about you. I named my vibrator Mr. Pierce Junior."

"Well, I'm flattered!" He laughed. "I had a big crush on you for a long time too, and trust me, you were the regular star of my dreams and sexual fantasies," he admitted. "I think I engaged in more self-love in the months just before we started dating than I had since I was thirteen."

"I didn't know you had a crush on me."

"Couldn't you tell?"

"Jess thought so. It seemed too good to be true, though, and besides I had heard that you were a player."

"I was," he said, sounding amused, "before I met you, but I had definitely slowed down a lot by the time we started dating. I really didn't have much interest in that anymore."

"If I hadn't flirted with you, would you have ever asked me out?"

"I wanted to. I had finally figured out that you were interested in me too, when you told me I could comfort you after that shoplifting trial you did." He laughed. "I was trying to figure out how to go about it, though. Your flirting that night was very helpful! Negotiating with you was a lot of fun too, not to mention a really huge turn-on."

"I love you Braden. I was going to tell you that when you got back from Pittsburgh but you told me first."

"I was going to wait until we were together again too but at that moment I missed you so much, and I just felt like I had to let you know. Now let's go to sleep and dream about each other some more." He kissed the top of my head and cuddled me closer.

∽ CHAPTER FIVE ∾

Monday

The Defender Association of Philadelphia

When I got into the office the next morning, Cameron was there working, but Jess was out. I glided in, tossed my bag onto the floor and plopped down into my desk chair, which promptly tilted backwards, nearly causing me to splatter my extra grande cup of doubly caffeinated coffee all over me. I put it down before I injured myself.

"Where's our office mate?" I asked, settling in at my desk. As usual there was a pile of files waiting that could probably kill me if it fell on me. No matter how many times I worked my way through the pile it would always be rebuilt when I came in each morning. Like magic.

"She and Mark got called out to do preliminary hearings in the districts," he replied, writing something in a file. I fired up my computer and did a little quick research to satisfy my curiosity about Club 51. It was a fairly new place and it sounded kind of interesting. I personally thought that finding that napkin was a little too convenient and that it would definitely be worth checking it out on Friday at ten-thirty. Besides, if we went as a group, that would give Jess a reason to get all dressed up and gorgeous-looking and it would give Cam a chance to see her looking that way. I was such a brilliant strategist. Napoleon could have taken lessons from me.

Unable to put it off any longer, I dug into my pile of case files for the next day. Luckily, with one exception, most of the cases seemed pretty straightforward. Unfortunately, the exception was a real winner. I sighed. Cameron and I worked quietly until eleven-thirty and then I took a break and stretched a little, turning toward him and starting a conversation.

"So how long are you going to be here with us, Cam?"

"Why? Trying to get rid of me?" he asked with a laugh.

"Are you kidding? I like having you here. It's nice to have help and I've always enjoyed your company. Besides, you and Jess are just getting to know each other well. Didn't you tell me just the other night that you found her really attractive and you might want to explore that more?" Okay, I was nudging. Cam stopped what he was doing and turned to face me.

"I did tell you that and I have been thinking about it," he confirmed.

"So, why don't you ask her out on a date or something?" I had moved on to pushing.

"Because I like her a lot. I would want it to be a success, so I'm waiting for the timing to be right. I still need to work through some things before starting a new relationship."

"What ..."

Then it dawned on me, Jess might have been right; the "some things" he had to work through might be his feelings about having me pop up out of the blue dating his cousin. Oh God, was I standing in the way of their happiness and ruining it for both of them? Some small part of my brain registered what was about to happen just in the nick of time. I flew out of my seat and bolted toward the door. "I'm having an allergy thing," I said, my voice catching.

I made it to the ladies room and hurtled myself into a stall just as the first heavy hot tears started to fall. Oh fuck! This wasn't happening. I could just *tell* that this was PMS! Even on the pill I always became an emotional basket case a week before my period. God, I hated freaking hormones! I assured myself that even if he needed some time to wrap his head around it, that didn't mean he was broken-hearted or anything. He would work through it and they would get together and be happy. I needed to get a grip. Get the estrogen under control, Gabrielle! It's all good. I took a few gulps of air and dried my eyes with toilet paper. I stepped out of the stall and looked in the mirror … at my red eyes and tear-streaked makeup. Shit. Okay, I needed to wash my face. I turned the water on full blast and started frantically pumping icky, thin pink soap into my hand. I heard someone coming through the door and I looked up into the mirror to see Kim, a friend and fellow PD, whose office was at the other end of the hall from ours. Kim was a gorgeous Halle Berry look-alike with short dark hair, beautiful mocha-colored skin, and amazing style and taste and here I stood looking like someone had just dragged me out of the river.

"Hey, Gab. You okay?"

"Allergy attack."

"Oh, sorry, girl. Want some Claritin?"

"No, thanks. I took something already." She went into a stall and at that moment my arm started to feel cold and wet. I looked down and saw that while I had been looking up at her, pink soap was running all over one sleeve of my suit jacket, and the other sleeve was sitting in the sink basin, which was rapidly filling with water. I yanked my arms away, managing to splatter pink goo all over my white blouse in the process. I grabbed some brown paper towel and wet it, attempting to scrub it off. Unfortunately, all that did was smear brown all over the pink. Needed more water! I started splashing water across the stain and immediately realized my mistake. Oh fuck! I looked like a contestant in a wet T-shirt contest and I had to interview clients in an hour! *In jail!* It would probably dry but what if it didn't?!

Okay, think, Gabrielle! The air blow hand dryer! I went over and tried to turn the air blower upward but it wouldn't move. Shit! I hit the button, bent my knees and squatted below the pipe. And that's how Ellen Anderson, *the* Philadelphia Public Defender, one of the most highly respected attorneys on the East Coast, and my boss, found me as she walked in the door. Then I heard the stall door open and saw Kim's startled expression in the mirror.

"Ms. Ginsberg? Are you all right?" Ellen sounded like she wasn't quite sure if she should help me or get the hell out of there.

"Uh, I'm good! Thanks. I had an accident with the soap. And the paper towel. And the water."

"Hygiene can be a complex thing," she said, looking at me strangely and heading for a stall.

"Do you need another blouse, Gab?" Kim asked, looking like she was trying not to laugh. "I have an extra in case of emergency. I can bring it to you."

I glanced up nervously at the stall where my boss was peeing and suddenly all I wanted to do was to get the hell out of there myself. "I'll come with you to your office. Thanks." I started following Kim and I was about to pass my office when I saw that Cameron had gone. Not wanting to go down the rest of the hall looking like that, I ducked in. "Can you bring it here?"

"Sure, I'll be right back."

I peeled off my sopping jacket and waited. Kim came back in a couple of minutes with another white blouse.

"Thank you so much!"

"No problem. I'll close the door on the way out," she said and left.

As soon as she was gone, I ripped off my wet blouse and quickly realized that my bra was wet too. I turned my back to the door and started fanning my chest in an effort to dry it a little. Movement caught my eye and I looked up and out the window to the building across from me, where a group of rather startled-looking businessmen stood gaping at me. I spun around in a panic just as the door opened and Cameron came back in looking down at a file. He looked up at me and then he looked down at my wet see-through bra. Oh, and by the way? I was cold. He dropped the file he was holding and his jaw nearly hit the floor with it.

"Oh," he said, sounding stunned. "I had forgotten how nice those were." He started slowly backing up toward the open door.

"Cameron!" I charged at him to push him out faster. "Close the fucking door, for Christ's sake!" I hissed loudly. Just as Braden walked in. I stood there. In my bra. With my arms around Cameron. After telling him to close the door. Frozen in shock.

Braden looked at me with confusion. Then Braden looked at Cameron with fury. Cameron looked at Braden with horror.

"Not what it looks like!" Cameron sputtered backing up away from me frantically. Then Adam walked in and stopped short. His eyes immediately dropped and he openly admired my boobs for a long moment and said, "Hi, Gabrielle. Nice tits. I'm going to find Mark to help me save Cameron's life." Then he ducked out quickly.

"What. The *fuck*! Are you doing? With my girlfriend *now* Cameron?!" Braden's voice was deadly.

Mark and Jess came through the door next.

"Holy shit!" Mark exclaimed, looking at me in shock. Then, seeing the look that Braden was giving Cameron, he flew into action. "Braden! It's Gabrielle! I'm sure there's some wacky explanation for this!" Jessica literally threw herself in front of Cameron as Adam came back in and quickly assessed the situation.

"Whoa! Braden! Down boy! You've found her dressed in garbage and BDSM gear. This is just par for the course, man!" He and Mark put themselves physically between Braden and Cameron then too. Finally, I snapped out of it and I grabbed Kim's blouse and threw it on, buttoning up as well as I could with shaking hands.

"Braden! My blouse got wet and another PD lent me an extra one. I was changing when Cameron walked in. He was only in here for a few seconds and he was trying to leave but he was shocked and he was moving too slowly and so I was pushing him faster. I wanted him to close the door on the way *out*!"

I watched Braden take deep breaths and force himself to calm down. Cameron visibly relaxed then and let out a deep breath of his own. I hurried over to Braden and put my arms around him, hugging him tightly and rubbing his back. His muscles felt like piano wires and I could feel his heart beating fast.

"Braden, baby. Listen to me. You need to stop worrying. I love you and Cameron knows and respects that! He's not going to try anything with me."

"I do know and respect that! I really do! I would never touch her as long as you were together! I've only ever touched her once before! Well, a few times, but only one night, and it was eight years ago when I was nineteen years old!" Cameron said emphatically.

"You've slept with Gabrielle?" Adam asked. "You haven't slept with her too, have you, Mark?"

"No!" Mark answered.

"Good, or I would have felt *really* left out," Adam, who was apparently suicidal, added.

"It was when we were in college!" I seethed. "Before I even *knew* Braden."

"Thanks for trying to protect me, by the way," Cam said, looking at Jess. "Didn't *you* wonder why Gabrielle was half naked with me?"

"It's Gabrielle and so I just assumed that there was some nutty reason for it. I've learned not to question why she does anything. It's better that way," she answered with a smile, collapsing into her desk chair.

"Okay, I'm sorry!" Braden said finally. "You have to admit it was kind of weird!"

"Well, that was fun," Adam quipped.

"Braden, man," Mark said, "you're planning to marry this woman." He looked at me and his eyes dropped to my chest for one second before he shook his head and looked away. "You really need to get used to walking in on weird shit, dude!"

"Did you say 'nice tits, Gabrielle'?" Braden asked Adam with a hint of menace.

"So, we came by to see if you wanted to have lunch together!" Adam said cheerfully while slowly backing away from Braden.

"That's a great idea! I need to talk to everyone about something anyway," I said grabbing my purse and bolting out the door. Luckily, they did follow me.

We all sat around a table at Reading Terminal Market eating our lunch and chatting much more calmly. Probably because we were all fully dressed and nobody was in mortal danger.

"Should I be brave and ask Gabrielle what she wanted to talk to us about?" Mark asked, taking a bite of his sushi.

"I wanted to tell you about a napkin that we found on the floor," I explained.

"You wanted to talk to us about litter, honey?" Jess asked. She didn't really sound surprised, for some reason.

"We found it right in front of Braden's door after someone had pulled a false alarm and we had to leave the building. It wasn't there when we left."

"Somebody must have just dropped it when people were evacuating," Adam said, eyeing up his corn dog a little suspiciously. A corn dog? Really, Adam?

"It was a cocktail napkin," I explained. "How many firemen do you know who go out for cocktails before going on duty?"

"Maybe another resident dropped it," Mark suggested.

"It was right in front of my door," Braden admitted a little reluctantly.

"It was from a place called Club 51 and on the back someone had written 7161030.

"What's that supposed to mean?" Cam asked.

"I think it's a date and time. This Friday at ten-thirty and I think we should go check it out!" I said excitedly.

"What do you mean 'we'? Who do we look like? The Scooby Doo gang?" Adam asked, biting into his dubious looking food-like product.

"Oh trust me, man!" Mark broke in, "you haven't lived until you've gone with Gabrielle on one of her little adventures. What should we dress up as *this time?*"

"Aliens," I answered dryly. "The club has a conspiracy theme. The 51 refers to Area 51." I took a bite of my veggie lasagna. All the adrenaline had given me a big appetite. I could probably eat a whole pan of this stuff.

"Uh oh! Conspiracies!" Adam said. "Maybe your litterbug read the article in the New York Times and is worried about the senator's son dating the kingmaker's daughter."

"You know, even though you're just being a wiseass, you may not be wrong," I said thoughtfully. "Maybe it's a message, and in more ways than one."

"I think it's a message that Braden should take you out on a date," Jess said, playing around with her salad. "You two haven't really gone out anywhere since the first time. Although, I'll admit that it's hard to top a kabob joint and a train station."

"You want me to take you out?" Braden asked me. "Why didn't you say so?"

"I hadn't really given it much thought, but sure. That would be fun," I said just before bending down to pick up my napkin and smacking my head on the table. Braden checked to make sure that I wasn't bleeding. He was so sweet. He was always checking to make sure that I wasn't injured too badly. That was true love.

"Personally, I think that if you want to marry her, you should at least court her *a little*," Jess went on. She gave Braden a stern look before finally locating the elusive crouton she had obviously been searching for and popping it into her mouth.

"*Court* her? What is this, 1800?" Adam asked. "He banged her at a fundraiser. I think they're a little beyond the 'courting' stage, Jane Austen."

"I'm just saying that maybe it would be a good idea if they went out on a few dates before they got married," Jess responded. "He should romance her. What kind of memories will she have otherwise?"

"Well, let's see," Cam said. "She can remember being covered in garbage, dressing up like a dominatrix and running around South Philly at night …"

"I would be happy to take you out," Braden interrupted. "I don't know about a club though. I would rather we didn't go somewhere filled with players and women who are looking to hook up with them."

"Uh, Braden? Wouldn't that include the criminal courts building?" Mark asked.

"We work there," Braden said testily. "There's nothing I can do about that."

"Oh come on, Braden," I broke in. "We'll go as a group. We can invite our friend Lily along. I meant to ask if she could come to your parents' place for the weekend too."

"Oh no!" Adam said in a tone of voice most people reserved for discussing IRS audits, septic tank overflow or hemorrhoids. He tossed down his corn dog stick in disgust.

"What is your problem with her?" I asked.

"We don't get along," he said, sounding almost petulant.

"How can you not get along with her? She's so nice," Jess chimed in.

"She's a bi … a bit overbearing," he said catching himself just in time. He would be lucky if he lived through this day.

"When's the last time you even saw her?" Jess asked, sounding annoyed.

"I don't know. A year ago? It doesn't matter! We *don't get along*!"

"Oh come on!" I said, again. "Adam, you can be civil for a little while and Braden, you and I will be together so there's nothing to worry about. We should check it out. We might find out something important and it would be fun!"

"Fine." Braden sighed. "If that's where you really want to go, that's where we'll go, but you stay near me the whole time."

"Okay, although the other women in the ladies room may not like it much. Let's go on Friday at ten-thirty. Then we can see for ourselves if there's anything to it or if it was just somebody's trash."

"I'll take trash for twenty," Adam said to Mark. "Tell me, Gabrielle, what does that cigarette butt on the floor say to you?"

"Do you really want to know?" I asked with a smile.

"Okay, I'll take that action," Mark told Adam. "Enough weird shit happens to Gabrielle that there's always a possibility. Besides, she's been wrong so far; she's got to guess something right eventually."

"Come on, Braden!" Cameron coaxed. "Take your girlfriend out on a date to the conspiracy joint with all of us. You can't beat that for romance." Braden shot him an amused, if exasperated, look.

"Okay! We'll go check out that club Friday at ten-thirty. Saturday we can all meet at my parents' place," Braden said resignedly. "We'll hang out by the pool, go to the festival that evening and then spend the night there."

"And can we invite Lily?" I asked.

"Sure!" he said, smiling at Adam.

"This is because I said 'nice tits, Gabrielle.' Isn't it?" Adam muttered, rolling his eyes.

After lunch Mark and I walked to his car together. He had to go out to the prison too so I was grabbing a ride with him. We were talking about some of the cases we had coming up, when I accidentally tripped over a crack in the sidewalk and fell on my ass. As Mark helped me back up, I turned around to pick up the pad I had dropped and noticed a figure that looked familiar some distance behind us. I couldn't place him, though. There was just something about him that made me think I knew him. We were in a hurry and the guy turned a corner anyway so I just forgot about it. The whole thing probably only took about ten seconds. It was a few hours later when it came to me. I thought that it might have been the same guy I had seen in the alley the night before and it made me feel pretty uncomfortable. Even if it was mostly a convenient way for me to get Jess and Cam together, I did want to get to the bottom of this.

∽ CHAPTER SIX ∽

Tuesday

IN THE COURT OF COMMON PLEAS OF PHILADELPHIA COUNTY, PENNSYLVANIA

Commonwealth v. Luchinsky

"Ms. Luchinsky," Judge Channing began, "you understand that you are pleading guilty to criminal trespass and disorderly conduct?"

"Yes, judge." My client, Tammy Sue Luchinsky, six feet and two inches of badass mama, with tattoos covering her arms, wild long dark hair and a gold tooth, did her best to sound contrite and ladylike. Good luck with that last one. That fact that she sounded like she smoked about three packs a day didn't help. I shuffled around a little nervously. I couldn't *wait* until the judge heard the facts of this case.

"And you understand that you have a right to a trial and you are waiving that right?" Judge Channing was eyeing her up suspiciously. He probably couldn't wait to hear what Tammy Sue had done either.

"Yes sir." She smiled and the light glinted off of her tooth. Lovely.

"Mr. Pierce, please summarize the facts of the case." Here we go, folks!

"Your Honor, just after midnight on June first in the County of Philadelphia, alarms were triggered at the Curren Fromhold

Correctional facility and the defendant Tammy Sue Luchinsky, was found by guards climbing a wall."

"She was breaking out?!" Judge Channing cut in. Suddenly he looked very serious, but then it dawned on him. "Wait a minute! Curren Fromhold is a men's prison!"

"That's correct, Your Honor. She was breaking *in,*" Braden answered, *trying* to look very serious. The key word being "trying". He set his lips in a firm line and looked like maybe he was reciting baseball statistics in his head in an effort not to think too much about this one.

"Breaking *in* to prison?!" the judge asked incredulously. I wondered how many times a day he wished that he could say, "What the fuck?!" Okay, time to tell Tammy Sue's side of it ...

"Your Honor." I sighed. "My client was a bit intoxicated and she missed her boyfriend. A lot. The alcohol and the, uh, missing, clouded her judgment. I think that we've *all* had nights like that." I nodded my head and tried to look sympathetic.

"Most of us don't try to break into prison, though, Ms. Ginsberg. She was scaling a wall not drunk dialing," he responded irritably.

"She's voluntarily sought counseling for alcohol abuse, Your Honor, and she's seeing a therapist about possibly going on anti-depressants. She just has to make sure that she can operate heavy machinery on them. She works on a loading dock. She also understands that she's only allowed in to see Hank at visiting hours. It was a momentary lapse."

"Ms. Luchinsky, why would you do something like this?" Judge Channing asked, shaking his head in wonderment.

"Well, judge, my man's been locked up for six months now and that night, 'I Changed Her Oil and She Changed My Life' came on the radio. That's our song, sir, and I guess that I had just drunk a few too many cans of Pabst. You know how it is when a gal's been drinkin' especially when she's been alone for a while. I'm a hot-blooded woman and I got hot-blooded womanly desires! I've been alone too long! I need some lovin' and I need it bad!" I saw Braden put his fist to his mouth and squeeze his eyes shut. Judge Channing looked slightly alarmed like he thought that Tammy Sue might be trying to tell him something. Hell, maybe she was.

"Maybe Ms. Ginsberg could try to get you some conjugal visits," Judge Channing muttered, looking like he found the thought rather distasteful. I can't imagine why. Tammy Sue coughed up a lung into her hand. "Is there an agreement in place?" the judge asked, appearing a bit ill.

"Um," Braden cleared his throat. "The Commonwealth has agreed to the defendant completing her alcohol counseling program and serving two years' probation with random urinalysis." He didn't sound like he was going to make it much longer without losing it. I figured we had better wrap this up.

"That's your understanding of the agreement, Ms. Ginsberg?"

"It is, Your Honor," I answered quickly.

"Tammy Sue Luchinsky I accept your plea of guilty to criminal trespass and disorderly conduct and I hereby sentence you to complete your alcohol counseling program and serve two years' probation subject to random urinalysis, and to pay fines and costs." He banged his gavel "Court is in recess for five minutes! Wayne get me some Pepto!" With that he left the bench.

A female probation officer escorted Tammy Sue off to pee into a cup. I knew what was coming. I turned toward the prosecution table and prepared myself.

"Gabrielle, would you scale a prison wall for Braden's lovin'?" Adam asked with a smile. I knew he had been waiting so patiently to ask me that.

"She might knock it down," Braden teased, his voice cracking with suppressed laughter. "She can be very demanding."

"You'd probably tunnel in one spoonful at a time to get to her junk, honey," Jess answered tartly from the defense table. Jess always had my back.

"You know, I think I would!" Braden agreed and finally let go and cracked up.

"I'd like to talk to that guy," Adam said. "I want to find out what he's giving Tammy Sue there that would make her willing to break into a prison to get some."

"The poor woman probably doesn't have many opportunities," Jess chided. "She looks like she could kill a man."

"You should set her up with that old guy who was willing to risk his life to make a booty call." Braden joked. "He'd give her some lovin'." He pulled himself together and looked at me in such a boyishly cute way that I wanted to scale *him.*

"So, Gabrielle's demanding, huh?" Adam asked suggestively. "All the time or just when she's been drinkin'?"

"I think I've only ever seen her drunk once, that night at O'Malley's," Braden replied, calming down and wiping tears of laughter from his eyes.

"I wasn't drunk!" I protested, sorting through my files for my next wonderful case.

"You walked face first into a door," Adam pointed out.

"I've done that before. I've been known to enter a party with a screen door stuck to my face before I've had a single drink."

Having finished teasing me, Adam let Jess know that he had an offer on a case and she got up and went over to the prosecution table to discuss it. Braden, in turn, came over to the defense table to talk to me. When they were out of earshot, I turned to him.

"Do you really think I'm demanding?" I asked, sorting out some files.

"Hmm, let's see, fuck me right now, Braden, I'm going to make you my fuck toy, Braden..." I felt my face get hot.

"Am I *too* demanding?" I put the files down and looked at him almost shyly.

"Are you serious? Just thinking about it makes me want to go negotiate a deal in one of the interview rooms with you," he said, giving me a flirtatious look.

"We can't keep doing that. We're going to get caught if we continue using the interview rooms to satisfy our lustful urges." I sighed and looked at my sexy boyfriend, indulging myself for a moment in some hot fantasies. "I think on Friday night I'll dress up for you and we can do some of those naughty things we talked about. Maybe we can find some nice silk scarves and you can tie me to the bed and have your way with me."

"You had to put that image in my head, didn't you?" He groaned quietly and raked his fingers through his hair, giving me a seductive look.

"I have a feeling Harvard will bring Yale to her knees that night and you'll get to handle my saucy mouth and my sharp tongue up close."

"Stop! Please! I'm begging you. I can't picture *that* now too." His eyes went to my lips. "Oh shit. I'm picturing it. You're such a tease sometimes." He laughed.

"Am I *teasing* you too much?"

"No! I love it. You're so fucking hot, Gabrielle. I'd love to bend you over that table right now and make you scream my name."

"Are you two finished whispering sweet nothings to each other?" Adam called out. "I want to get out of here."

"Leave them alone. They're in love," Jess answered him.

"They're in court!" Adam shot back. "Let them be in love after work."

Wednesday

IN THE COURT OF COMMON PLEAS OF PHILADELPHIA COUNTY, PENNSYLVANIA

Commonwealth v. Stemple

"Ms. Stemple," Judge Channing began, looking like he would have rather been anywhere else at the moment. "You wish to enter a guilty plea to driving under the influence of alcohol, fleeing and eluding police, and reckless endangerment?"

"Yes sir," she answered. I strongly suspected that she would have rather been back at the bar that she was probably at until last call the night before. Either that or her perfume was called Eau d' beer.

"You understand that you have a right to a trial and you're waiving that right?" Judge Channing was looking at her suspiciously. He probably smelled the barroom too.

"Yes judge."

"Mr. Pierce, please recite the facts of the case."

"Your Honor, in the afternoon hours of May twenty-fifth in the County of Philadelphia, police responded to reports of a vehicle being operated in an erratic matter. Officer Luke McClusky got behind the vehicle, a white Hyundai Accent operated by the Defendant, Lucy Stemple, in his patrol unit, activated his lights and siren and motioned for the driver to pull over. In response, Ms. Stemple instead increased her speed and began veering in and out of traffic. Officer McClusky called for assistance and two other patrol units responded. After a chase lasting approximately ten minutes Ms. Stemple pulled into the parking lot of a liquor store and exited the vehicle as if she intended to enter the establishment. When officers ordered her to freeze and put her hands on her vehicle, she responded, and I quote, 'just give me a second to grab some Jack Daniels, baby.' At the time she was wearing cowboy boots."

"What's wrong with that?" Judge Channing broke in irritably.

"That's all she was wearing, Your Honor," Braden replied and the judge rolled his eyes.

"Ms. Ginsberg?" He glared at me and he sounded like he thought that I'd put her up to it! Jesus. I was doing my job here, you know? So much hostility.

"Your Honor, my client has been going through a difficult divorce. On the day in question she had just received word that her estranged husband would be getting remarried. She was feeling very emotional and not thinking clearly. She's employed as a waitress at Denny's and this is her first offense. She's willing to seek drug and alcohol counseling."

"Do you have anything to say, Ms. Stemple?" the judge asked.

"That asshole took the best years of my life!" she slurred. "And now he's marrying some little slut he met at his gym! You know, I may be thirty-eight but I still look good! I'm the same size I was in high school and my tits hardly sag! Ask that cop!" Well, at least she was dressed. I hoped she hadn't driven there.

"About the case, Ms. Stemple," I prodded, glancing at the judge nervously.

"Oh, sorry. It probably won't ever happen again."

"Well, I certainly *hope* not!" Judge Channing retorted, looking at her dubiously. "Is there an agreement?"

"Defendant served twenty-four hours, Your Honor. The Commonwealth will agree to a sentence of time served plus six months probation, mandatory drug and alcohol counseling and random urinalysis."

"That's your understanding Ms. Ginsberg?"

"Yes, Your Honor."

"Ms. Stemple, I accept your plea of guilty and I hereby sentence you to serve twenty-four hours with credit for time served, six months probation, and you'll need to complete drug and alcohol counseling with random urinalysis. Fines and costs. Off the record." The stenographer stopped typing. "No more driving drunk. That's not safe. Or naked. That's not hygienic."

"Yes judge," she answered with a big smile.

"Court's in recess. Ten minutes." He banged his gavel and left without a backward glance. I grabbed the court order and went over to the defense table to wait for the comments. Braden decided to go first this time. At least he didn't let our relationship stand in the way of teasing me.

"Yee haw!" he said with a laugh, leaning up against the prosecution table and looking far sexier than anyone had a right to.

"And I thought you dressed funny," Adam added with a smile, leaning back in his chair and looking highly amused. Despite the seriousness and stress of the criminal justice system, there were plenty of moments for levity and this was clearly one. I wasn't going to deny it.

"Just ignore them, honey," Jess said patting me on the back as I sat down next to her at the defense table. Jess never let it get to her. I admired her for that.

"I loved how she wanted to go buy her Jack first before they arrested her," Braden continued, obviously on a roll.

"It *probably* won't happen again!" Adam laughed. "She's not quite sure, but probably."

"Hey, that asshole took the best years of her life. *Obviously* the answer was to drive to the liquor store naked," I noted dryly.

"She's right, though," Jess noted. "Her tits really don't sag. She must not have any kids, thank God. What did he mean, that's not *hygienic*?" She laughed.

"Who knows? I wish he wouldn't look at me like I helped her plan it. It's not like I was riding shotgun with her," I added.

"He's just ready to retire, Gab," she consoled. "Ignore him, too."

"So, Gabrielle, when you were in law school dreaming about providing the poor with access to justice, is this what you had in mind?" Adam asked. "Representing naked drunk drivers, eighty-five-year-old potheads, people who use their underwear as a shopping cart…"

"Yeah, okay. Maybe I should go back to the office and tell them that I'd like to represent a better class of criminals. It's not like Cam's private clients are wandering into the public defender's office for financial planning advice."

"Where's he been anyway?" Adam asked.

"With Mark," Jess answered. "His courtroom partner took a spot in child advocacy and so Cam's been filling in this week."

"No kidding!" Braden said. "He's turning into a regular little public defender!"

"He'll *need* to go out by the end of week," Jess said.

"You know, if we're all going out together Friday night and we're spending Saturday night at your parents' place, Mark and I aren't going to *unwind* this weekend," Adam said significantly to Braden. It wasn't too hard to figure out what he meant by "unwind."

"So, go out beforehand to *unwind*," Braden answered. "You're not looking for a long-term relationship." Jess got up and ran out to the ladies room then and a deputy called Adam over so Braden and I were left alone.

"What a great lifestyle, working in a quick blowjob before going out with friends," I joked, rolling my eyes. "Didn't Norman Rockwell paint that once?"

"Personally, I would much rather *unwind* with you. Speaking of, I think I would like to see you in an outfit like that," he said. He was giving me the hot Braden sex look right here in the courtroom which made me feel rather flirty.

"Cowboy boots? Wouldn't you prefer my high heels?" By the way his eyes got even darker and his smile even cockier I could see that he most certainly would. Hmm. I think Braden had a thing for high heels. He wasn't just a boob man after all.

"How high?" His voice sounded a little husky.

"I have a couple of pairs that are six inches. I'm not a material person but I do have a weakness for pretty shoes and clothes." His eyes dropped to my body and traveled down. I saw him swallow and start to breathe a little faster. He tore his gaze away and raked his fingers through his hair. He did that when he was stressed, especially when he was stressed because he wanted me but couldn't have me at the moment.

"I'm not thinking about it. I'm *not* thinking about it. I am absolutely not thinking about what you would look like in just a pair of six inch heels." His eyes returned to my body. "Okay, I'm thinking about it. Oh shit, Gabrielle. They don't have cold showers here, baby."

"You started it," I reminded him. "Picture the cute little black dress I'm going to wear for you on Friday instead. That will take your mind off of it."

"What does it look like?" He looked back to me and I could see he was torn between wanting me to describe something really sexy and something that looked like a nun's habit.

"Well, it's got like a halter top and it comes down in a V. It wraps around me so if you just untied it, it would come off. It comes to about two inches above my knees. It's padded and more structured on top, so I don't have to wear a bra under it. The material is jersey knit, which is smooth and stretchy so I was thinking about maybe not wearing anything under it on the bottom either. I hate panty lines. Did I mention that the heels are Louboutins by the way? They buckle at the ankle and I'm so tall when I wear them. We could probably have sex against the wall without you even picking me up or bending your knees!"

"You're being very naughty, Gabrielle," he said in a quiet seductive voice. "Remember what happened last time you were naughty." He took a step forward toward me and I swore that I could feel the heat coming from him. "Do I have to put you over my knee, my bad girl?"

"Now you're being a tease." I was breathing quickly and I could feel that I was flushed. The judge came back out of his chambers and ascended the bench. Jesus! We still had legal argument to do!

Commonwealth v. Chapman

Braden and I were engaged in another fierce battle over a Motion to Suppress Evidence and the judge was giving us both a lot of leeway so we were really going at it.

"Your Honor, the case law provides that flight, in and of itself, does not provide probable cause to search!" I argued. Braden and I were circling each other again as we argued. We always looked like prize fighters in the ring.

"But it wasn't just the flight in this case, Your Honor! There was a totality of the circumstances," Braden shot back. He was coming at me full force on this one but I wasn't going down. There was a bigger issue here. There were times that I did get to fight the good fight and today I felt like I really was defending the Constitution so I wasn't giving in.

"What circumstances? That it was night in a poor neighborhood?"

"That it was dark in a high crime neighborhood!" Braden believed in his position too, though, and I respected him for it. Things were rarely simple in law. There were always two sides.

"If you allow that argument, it will mean that anyone who can't afford to live in a good neighborhood could be searched at night!" I argued passionately.

"If they run from the police!" he countered fiercely. "And then not because they're poor but because there is greater likelihood that a crime has taken place! Should we assign just as many patrol officers to low crime neighborhoods as high crime neighborhoods so that we equalize everything?" He was a smart and strong opponent and when he brought it he brought it hard.

"Okay!" Judge Channing finally stopped us. "I have your briefs and I've heard your arguments. I'll let you know when I've made my ruling. That's all that we have on the docket today. We're adjourned." He banged his gavel and left the bench. Braden and I looked at each other and it was clear that we were both very worked up. The combination of flirting and arguing had excited both of us. A lot.

"I have an office meeting that I have to be at in thirty minutes," he said, looking at his watch and sounding kind of edgy.

"I'm supposed to interview a witness in half an hour," I said, looking at him a little desperately. I was mentally calculating how long it would take me to get back to my office if we visited the negotiation room first.

"What is it with us, Gabrielle? This can't be normal," he said, looking flushed. "If it were, they would put beds in those interview rooms. Oh fuck. I just pictured you in bed."

"I think we just have an exceptional amount of sexual attraction and chemistry between us. It's got to be biological, like pheromones or something," I answered, feeling pretty warm myself. "I've met a lot of attractive lawyers before but I've never pictured them naked while they were cross-examining a witness."

"Yeah, well, you're the only lawyer who's ever made me fantasize about demanding sexual favors in exchange for a plea bargain. Do you know how many erotic dreams I've had about nailing you in the jury room while court was in session?" he asked with a tense laugh.

"Yeah, I'm not really sure how I made all those months without breaking any laws. I remember I had this dream once that you were sitting up on the bench presiding as judge over a case and I was down on my knees …"

"Stop! Please! Baby, I'm begging you. I can't take anymore. I'm approaching stage three here!" He plowed his fingers through his hair and started striding back and forth at an almost frantic pace. I had a feeling he was trying to redistribute the blood flow in his lower regions.

"We'll be home in four hours," I said. I tried not to think about what kind of condition I would be in by then, though. I had a feeling that I might be knocking him down again.

"Four hours. That's what? Two hundred and forty minutes. Just to let you know, at two hundred and forty-one I'm going to need those panties off, baby."

"I'll take them off before I leave. It'll save us a few seconds. I don't think we have to go all the way to the bedroom either."

"Hell, no. I'm going to nail you right there inside the front door."

"I'm good with that," I said with a nod.

"Sounds like we have a plan. Good working with you, counselor," he said decisively. We packed up our briefcases and off to respective offices.

Thursday

IN THE COURT OF COMMON PLEAS OF PHILADELPHIA COUNTY, PENNSYLVANIA

Commonwealth v. Blakey

"Officer Standish," Braden began, striding up to the witness stand with his usual confident demeanor, "would you please describe the events that brought you here today?"

"On June third of this year I was traveling westbound on the Schuylkill Expressway when I noticed a gray Toyota Corolla following closely behind me. The driver seemed to be trying to catch my attention." Officer Standish was a young guy and I noted that he looked very earnest.

"How so?" Braden asked. He had such a powerful voice. I loved his voice. Especially when he was talking dirty to me ... okay, pay attention, Gabrielle! I shook my head to snap myself out of it.

"He was leaning out the driver side window shouting, 'hey cop'." Yep, seemed like he was trying to catch his attention all right. Brilliant deduction on Officer Standish's part. He was going to make detective! Braden quickly glanced at me with amusement.

"What happened then?" he asked. Braden walked over to the prosecution table and put his hands down, leaning over, looking for some report, and the image of him leaning over me like that in bed flashed through my head. Concentrate, Gabrielle! Concentrate. He found his report and strode back to the witness.

"The Corolla pulled up alongside my patrol vehicle and the driver, defendant Wayne Blakey, called out 'catch me if you can, copper'." Copper? Oh great. A gangster wannabe - as in the 1920's kind – driving a freaking Toyota.

"What happened next?" Braden asked.

"He pulled into the passing lane, cutting off another driver, and accelerated, weaving in and out of traffic in a dangerous fashion. I activated my lights and siren and began to pursue him."

"He was trying to outrun a Philadelphia police cruiser on the Schuylkill Expressway?" Judge Channing cut in. "In a Corolla?!"

"Yes, sir. He began the pursuit himself. For no reason," Officer Standish said very sincerely. He seemed genuinely baffled as to why someone would do something so incredibly stupid. He was obviously new to the force. Give him a few years.

"And then what happened?" Braden asked, tilting his head to the side in a really sexy way. In case you haven't figured this out, I pretty much thought that everything Braden did was sexy. I was also, obviously, still feeling the effects of hormones in my system, because even though I usually wanted him, at that moment I wanted to rip his clothes off. I crossed my legs and pressed my thighs together.

"He committed approximately forty-two moving violations, which I could see, and refused to pull over so I called for back-up and continued my pursuit." I looked over at Mr. Blakey who turned to me with a proud smile. Wow, bad boy here actually outran a cruiser in a Toyota. That was weirdly impressive.

"What was the outcome of this chase?" Braden asked. He glanced over at me and my tummy flipped. God, he was hot. I needed to see him naked very soon. Like right after this case.

"We managed to cut him off in several directions, essentially herding him toward a parking lot where fellow officers had set up spike strips. His tires were punctured and he came to a stop. We ordered him out of the vehicle with our weapons drawn and we cuffed him."

"Did Mr. Blakey offer any explanation for his actions?"

"Yes, sir, he told us that he had always wanted to try that."

"Were there any witnesses who gave statements describing the events that you just related?"

"Yes sir, uh, I believe one hundred and twenty-three? The parking lot in question was at police headquarters." I looked over at Mr. Blakey and raised my eyebrows. He just shrugged and smiled.

Thankfully, Mr. Blakey's case was the last of the afternoon. After holding all of the charges for trial and having his clerk schedule it, Judge Channing left the bench in his usual good mood. Jess and Adam had already left and the courtroom was emptying. I came over to the prosecution table where Braden was grabbing his files.

"So, you know, maybe we should discuss a deal," I said.

"On that case? Don't expect much," he answered. "Hey copper? Who is he, Al Capone?"

"Give the man some credit. Anybody could outrun a cop in a Lamborghini. We could at least discuss it," I said, hoping he would get the hint. He got the hint. Braden's a bright boy.

"Did you want to discuss it right now?" he asked with a smile, packing his files into his briefcase and turning to face me, looking rather interested.

"Are you too busy?" I felt myself blushing and I realized that I was being coquettish, running my finger along the edge of the table and looking up at him through my lashes.

"Not too busy for *your* negotiation style." He laughed. "Although I will point out that you were right when you said that we can't keep doing this and we may want to save it until after a more intense case than that one."

"Yeah, you're right about that. Mr. Blakey may be one badass Toyota owner but his case is pretty lame as far as adrenaline goes." It was more like excess estrogen that was my issue but it would be selfish not to wait until he was revved up too.

"How about if we just get really seriously freaky when we get home tonight," he suggested. "The entry hall was a lot of fun last night. Maybe I'll take you up to the roof garden again this time."

"Okay, it's a deal," I said with a smile. He hesitated for a moment and then looked around the now nearly empty courtroom. Wayne, the judge's bailiff, was near the door talking to Jerry, the sheriff's deputy, and their attention was diverted at the moment.

"Come here for a second though," he said and grabbed his briefcase. He walked over to the deliberation room behind the jury box. I grabbed mine and followed him, wondering what exactly he had in mind. Well, I had an idea that he wasn't interested in deliberating, but the details were kind of fuzzy. When we got inside, he shut the door and backed me up against it.

"Was there something you needed, counselor?"

"I want to at least kiss you goodbye," he said, his eyes dropping to my lips before he leaned down and gently pressed his to mine. He started to pull back, but he must have changed his mind, because he leaned in and deepened it instead.

Oh Lord! He was such a good kisser and he tasted all minty and delicious. I slid my tongue up against his and rubbed it back and forth, burying my fingers in his hair. He groaned a little and slid his hands up to cup my breasts. I pressed against him and reached down between his legs to see how interested he was. There was emerging interest when I got there but my little exploratory mission quickly changed that to great interest. In fact, enormous interest wouldn't be an exaggeration.

"Mm, you're a very good negotiator," I said breathily, moving to kiss his neck.

"Baby, we're in the deliberation room. There's a deputy right outside."

"I guess that means we would have to be really quiet," I whispered as I started trailing kisses along his jaw and stroking him on the outside of his pants.

"Oh Jesus, Gabrielle." I took his earlobe between my teeth and unzipped his pants. "I'm not kidding around. I sense my good judgment leaving," He was protesting, but I noticed that he wasn't stopping me, and so I reached into his boxers and gripped him gently. Then I sunk to my knees and looked up at him with my bad girl smile.

"Braden, baby, I'm going to serve your subpoena," I said and dragged my tongue along the length of his cock. He groaned and started breathing hard. I started sliding him in and out of my mouth as far as I could take him, and stroking him with my hand, sucking on the tip and running my tongue back and forth on the sensitive underside. All the things he loved best.

"Ah! Fuck! Oh, that feels so good! I'm serious Gabrielle, if you don't stop, I'm going to nail you right on the jury table, and that may not be a great career move for either one of us." I could tell that he was barely holding back. I popped him out of my mouth and looked up at him.

"Do it," I said and cupped his balls, squeezing gently. That was it. His hand flew to the door knob. Luckily, it locked. I was sure that the deputy had the key but at least it would buy us a couple of seconds. Unfortunately, I could hear people starting to come back into the courtroom outside. There must have been a special hearing scheduled. It didn't matter at this point, though, because he had warned me and I had insisted. I was about to get nailed on the deliberation table with court in session on the other side of the door. I really hoped that there wasn't a jury empaneled! I was glad that we were independently wealthy because if we got caught, we would be screwed in more ways than one.

He pulled me up to my feet and over to the table and pushed my skirt up over my hips. I wondered vaguely if they could disbar us for this. That would sound great in the papers. Noted CEO's daughter loses law license getting laid in court by senator's son.

He pulled my panties down and sat me up on the table. On the other hand, law was a stressful career, maybe it was time for a change. I heard the bailiff call court to session. Jesus! The judge was taking the bench! *All rise!* Braden was way ahead of him! I now had his full attention. Holy moly! He pulled my panties the rest of the way off. *The Court of Common Pleas of Philadelphia County is now in session! The Honorable Louis Channing presiding!* Braden leaned in and started kissing me hungrily and I responded like a starving animal with a steak. He unbuttoned my blouse quickly and I opened his belt and undid his trousers.

Eric Jeffries for the Commonwealth. The lawyers were entering their appearances. *Mark Patterson for the defendant.* Oh great! Mark was out there! Braden unhooked my bra and leaned down first to lick and then to start vigorously suckling one hard nipple and then the other as I grabbed his head and arched my back, biting my lip to keep myself quiet. *Your Honor, we have to resolve the matter of the introduction of the telephone call into evidence before the jury is brought in.* Shit! The jury! It was a pre-trial motion but obviously the jury was waiting somewhere else. Braden moved up to kiss my neck as he reached between my legs and started teasing my throbbing clit.

"Mmm, my baby's ready for me," he whispered.

"Braden, there's a jury," I whispered back.

"He said that they had a matter to resolve. They'll probably have a hearing."

He slid two fingers up inside me and starting circling my clit with his thumb. I buried my mouth against his neck and started kissing him frantically. I was breathing hard and occasionally whimpering quietly but I was managing to stifle my usual moans.

"Oh God," I panted. "This is really scary but really hot."

"This is like a sexual fantasy come true, Gabrielle," he said thickly.

Your Honor, allowing that phone call in would be highly prejudicial. I wrapped my hand around the base of Braden's stiff cock and began stroking him slowly just how I knew he liked it. Then he was pressing his mouth against my neck too. Braden was actually rather vocal in his lovemaking. He began moving his hips in rhythm with my hand. *Call your witness Mr. Jeffries!* His fingers slid in and out of me and I rode his hand feeling the sweet ache of wanting more, wanting to be totally filled up. It was a good thing we were getting married because Braden's generous proportions had ruined me for the average man. *Do you solemnly swear or affirm to tell the truth, whole truth, and nothing but the truth?* I couldn't take it anymore. I needed him inside me.

"Fuck me." I whispered it in his ear and then I nipped it kind of hard. I didn't have to say it twice. He pushed me down so that I was lying on my back and then he grabbed one of my legs and pushed it open to the side and took the other and placed my ankle on his shoulder. I was spread open wide before him on the jury table with my skirt bunched up around my hips and my breasts displayed for his viewing pleasure. I said a silent prayer that the bailiff didn't decide to check out the jury room or put a water pitcher in here or something.

"Do you know how many times I've thought about doing this to you here?" he asked, looking like he was about to lose control.

"So do it to me. Hard," I panted and he officially lost it. Positioning himself quickly he thrust into me and we both paused for a second, stunned. We were actually having sex in the jury room with court in session. Clearly, we were nuts.

"Oh yeah!" he ground out under his breath. And then he started doing it to me. Hard. And I loved it. *Officer Michaels, would you please tell the court how you obtained the transcript of the phone call in question?*

Soon he was slamming into me and I was trying desperately to keep myself quiet. Our skin was slapping together and my boobs were jiggling up and down. We really should write to Penthouse about this one.

"Oh God! Don't stop!" I moaned as quietly as I could.

"Is this what you want, baby?" he said through gritted teeth as his hips crashed against me, driving him even deeper.

"Yes!" I panted. "I'm close."

Officer Michaels, the informant hadn't mentioned my client by name. Isn't that true? I was holding onto him and moving my hips to meet his thrusts, loving the feeling of him banging up against the end of me inside. The combination of intense pleasure with just a little pain drove me closer and closer to a powerful orgasm. Then he reached down and began fingering my clit again and I quickly started to climb.

The Commonwealth rests, Your Honor. Defense rests. Oh shit, we needed to get out of there soon. They were done arguing and if the judge ruled from the bench, the jury would be on its way. I relaxed and cleared my mind and just let it happen. The tension built second by second, my inner muscles getting more and more taut, the pressure in my lower regions growing. I was right on the edge, and as usual Braden sensed it.

"Come on, baby," he hissed thrusting into me so hard I could feel his balls slapping against my bottom. I went over the edge and I felt the first wave hit as I clamped down on him. Intensely pleasurable relief flooded through me as a tremor shook my body and my muscles continued to contract around him. *I have my ruling. I'm going to allow in portions of the call but not all of it.*

He thrust into me several more times and then held himself tightly against me and went still. With a groan and a shudder he came, staring at me intently with a euphoric smile. *Okay, Wayne, go get the jury.* I sat up immediately and Braden kissed me sweetly as we quickly fixed our clothes and gave each other a once over to make sure everything was in place.

"How do we get out of here?" I asked, feeling flustered.

"Through the door." He smiled. He strode over confidently and swung it open, allowing me to walk out. Heads popped up as we exited.

"Mr. Pierce? Ms. Ginsberg?" Judge Channing said, raising his eyebrows inquisitively.

"Sorry to interrupt, Your Honor," Braden said casually. "Defense counsel and I went in to quickly discuss a deal and we were in there when your hearing started."

"We didn't want to disturb the court," I added.

"Did you reach a satisfactory result?" the judge asked.

"Oh yes, Your Honor," Braden answered. "We were both quite satisfied in the end."

"Good! That's what I like to hear! Keep it up!" He turned his attention to something on the bench. I glanced over at Mark, who looked highly amused. Somehow, I don't think that he bought the negotiation story. When we cleared the courtroom doors, Braden turned to me.

"That was crazy, you know," he said, looking flushed and happy.

"I know but it was crazy hot," I said. "I agree that it was like a sexual fantasy come true."

"We can't ever do that again." He shook his head in wonderment.

"Definitely not. I think next time you should sit on the judge's bench and let me go down on you," I joked.

"What?!" He looked panicked as he reached out and pushed the down button for the elevator.

"I'm kidding!" I smiled at him as the doors slid open and we stepped inside.

"I'm never sure with you! You're going to give me a heart attack one of these days but at least I'll die happy." He pushed the button for the lobby.

"I have a feeling that Mark didn't believe our story."

"Oh, ya think?" He laughed.

"Judge Channing believed it, though. In fact he wants us to keep it up!" I teased.

"Keeping it up is not a problem with you. Keeping my job might be, though."

Friday

IN THE COURT OF COMMON PLEAS OF PHILADELPHIA COUNTY, PENNSYLVANIA

Commonwealth v. Sanders

Adam was enjoying himself immensely as he questioned the convenience store clerk who my client had allegedly robbed. I knew there had to be one hell of a bomb he was going to drop for him to be this giddy, and I braced myself.

"So, Mr. Oberman, you testified that the defendant, Joseph Sanders, came into your store wearing a mask and holding a gun and told you to empty your register. What happened next?

"I gave him the money and he was going to leave but he stopped and ordered me to give him a carton of cigarettes too."

"What did you do?" Adam stole a glance at me and I knew it had to be coming. I searched the police report again to try to figure out what it didn't say.

"I said, no way, man. You sound like you're about sixteen. You gotta be eighteen to get cigarettes in PA."

"And what did Mr. Sanders say?"

"He told me he was eighteen but I said, man, but I need some proof."

"What happened then?" Adam asked and turned to look at me, obviously wanting to see my reaction. This had to be the bomb he was going to drop and I had a feeling that I knew what it was. Please don't tell me that this schmuck ....

"He took out his driver's license and he showed it to me." Kaboom.

"Wait a minute!" Judge Channing broke in incredulously. "He's wearing a mask but he shows you his driver's license?" You would think that nothing would shock this man by now.

"Yes sir." Mr. Oberman and Judge Channing shared a moment. Adam could barely contain his mirth. I hoped that he peed himself.

"What happened then?" Adam asked, looking immensely pleased. Oh great! There was more! Why did I always get the scholars?

"I said, hey buddy I can't tell if this is you or not with that mask on."

"What did he do?"

"Well, he ripped off the mask he was wearing and held the driver's license up to his face so I could compare." What a freaking rocket scientist this kid was.

"And then?"

"I said, okay I guess that's you and you're eighteen. I asked what kind of cigarettes he wanted and he told me. It so happens that the cigarette company is doing a contest for a thousand bucks and I told him about it and gave him an entry form to fill out. He wrote down his e-mail address and cell phone number." I sighed deeply. I wanted to leave.

"I said, okay and then I gave him the smokes. When he left I called the cops and gave them his name and address."

"No more questions." Adam sat down looking very smug indeed.

"Ms. Ginsberg, any questions?" Judge Channing looked like he expected me to say 'no' so when I got up to question the witness, he shot me an annoyed look. Jeez! So sorry to be a pain by, you know, trying to defend my client.

"He was holding a gun to you and you refused to give him the cigarettes? Pretty dangerous decision, wasn't it?"

"Probably, when I look back on it, but something about him just didn't seem like he knew what he was doing. For example, he was holding the gun wrong. If he would have shot it like that, he would have blown his fingers off." I heard Adam cough behind me to cover a laugh. I was so glad that he was entertained.

"No further questions," I said and sat down.

"Prosecution rests," Adam said merrily.

"Defense rests," I said irritably.

"Are you actually going to bother to argue, Ms. Ginsberg?" the judge asked. Somehow I didn't think that question boded well for my client.

"I'll reserve argument, Your Honor."

"Uh huh," he said dubiously. "I find that the Commonwealth has made out all of the charges listed in the complaint. Schedule it, Wayne. Mr. Pierce, call the next case." Braden stood up and got the case he and Jessica had together started.

I went over and picked up a copy of the court order. Adam wasn't as thoughtful as Braden was about walking the order over to me.

While Braden and Jessica started in on their own preliminary hearing, I went over to talk to Adam.

"Make me an offer."

"Are you kidding? He did everything but fingerprint himself and give a blood sample to the clerk. How the hell could I lose that case at trial?"

"Oh come on, Adam. The kid is harmless."

"Harmless?! He held up a convenience store. With a *gun*."

"He couldn't even hold the gun right."

"That's right! He could have shot somebody by accident. I should have added reckless endangerment on there. He showed the clerk his driver's license, Gabrielle. This guy is too stupid to be on the streets. He should be kept out of the breeding pool."

"Do you hear yourself?"

"Do you hear *yourself*? I should give your client a break because he's an idiot? What is that, 'the dumbass defense'?"

"Fine, at least consider the fact that if you make a fair offer *you* won't have to try this case and a jury won't have to be empaneled."

"I think I would enjoy trying it and you can always elect to go non-jury."

"Adam, you *need* to work with me and we both know it, so stop screwing around!"

"I'm not screwing around with you. You want a deal, you should only try cases against the guy who is screwing around with you."

"Are you saying you think Braden goes easy on me?"

"No. I think he's a pro, but I think you're used to trying cases with him and you forget that other prosecutors do things their own way. I also think, though, that the two of you are going to have to stop facing each other in court soon or some people *may* say that." God, he pissed me off, even though I knew he was probably right.

That was my last hearing of the morning and I went over to get my files together. When his case was done, Braden came over and leaned against the defense table. I looked up at him and sighed. I was still totally in lust with him. I just happened to be in love with him now, too. Before I could say anything, though, I saw Jack Davis, one of the senior defenders from my office, approaching me.

"Gabrielle, I've got some news on that West Six Ten thing," Jack began. "Turns out your guy's a shooter." This was the case that Mark had offered to take for me. The West Six Ten was a West Philly street gang and it sounded like the young guy I had been assigned wasn't as uninvolved as they originally thought.

"They're charging him with homicide? So, are you here to tell me that the office is taking the case away from me and transferring it upstairs?"

"That's just it. No word yet on if or when they're going to add the homicide charges. It's your case until they do, unless you want somebody else to take him."

"I'll only have him for the preliminary hearing. If he's really a shooter they'll charge him and then our office will transfer it up to you homicide guys anyway."

"Okay, I just wanted you to be aware."

"Thanks, Jack. I appreciate it." Jack patted me on the arm and left. I knew immediately that Braden was upset. Very upset.

"Gabrielle, let someone else take it," he said immediately and he sounded deadly serious and very tense. He started pacing and raking his fingers through his hair and this time I knew it didn't have anything to do with sexual tension.

"Braden, I'll only have him for the preliminary. I've represented lots of shooters in prelims before. I'm a criminal defense attorney. That's what I do – defend criminals."

"Not gang members charged with homicide." He paused in his effort to wear a hole in the carpet long enough to give me a look announcing that he was very serious about this.

"He's not charged with homicide," I reminded him carefully. I knew that I had to tread lightly here because we were close to having this escalate.

"Not yet!" Now, Braden sounded angry. This was it. The moment of truth. Did I dig in and tell him that I would make my own decisions when it came to my career choices, or did I try to understand where he was coming from and figure out if I could honor his request? Suddenly, it was like time slowed down and I saw the two paths ahead that I could take. I had a decision to make and after a few moments of thoughtful analysis and searching my feelings, I made it.

This was how the thoughtful analysis part went. If I gave up the gang case, Braden would be relieved and if he were less stressed out, he would be more reasonable about the other cases I handled. It wouldn't have any impact on my career to give it up and the case didn't have any special significance to me. Braden wasn't doing this to try to control me or because he didn't respect me. His fears weren't totally unrealistic, even if amazingly few public defenders were actually lost, or even injured, in the line of duty. Mark had offered to take it and I would take whatever case he wanted to give me in return, so it wasn't like I was unloading it on someone.

And this was how the searching my feelings part went. I don't *want* to fight! Especially not over something stupid!

"Okay," I said, committing to my choice. "If it means that much to you, I'll trade cases with someone else. I can see if Mark will still take it and I'll take one of his really lousy, but nevertheless, nonviolent cases."

Braden looked stunned. I think he had been prepared for this to turn into a battle. I saw all kinds of emotions cross his face but the strongest ones appeared to be relief and love. I knew immediately that I had made the right decision.

"You would do that for me?" He had stopped pacing.

"Yes, if it means that much to you. It's just one case. We are going to have to come up with some plan, though, because there will be others, and for the record, I would rather you didn't handle them either; so we had better think of something fast."

"Okay," he agreed. "And thank you. I promise that I'll try to come up with a plan." Phew. Crisis avoided. Amazing what a little discussion and compromise could accomplish.

"What's the plan for *tonigh*t?" I leaned against the defense table and looked up at my beautiful, and very happy looking fiancé.

"Some guys from my office invited me out to O'Malley's with them for beers after work. I haven't hung with them in a while and I think that I'd like to go." He walked over to me and pushed a strand of hair behind my ear.

"They're not going out to pick up women, are they?" I teased, giving him a raised eyebrow.

"No," he assured me with a smile. "That's Adam and Mark and they usually go out later and somewhere besides O'Malley's. Most of these guys are happily married."

"Well, okay then." I smiled. "As long as you promise to say nice things about me. I'll pick up Bruno and go back to my place and then Lily and Jess and I can get ready and have some fun of our own together. Remind Adam to be nice to Lily, by the way."

"I'll do my best but I can't make any promises."

"Don't forget that we're also there tonight to see if someone was trying to send us a message with that napkin."

"Yeah okay, Nancy Drew. I'm just happy that I get to be included in The Mystery of Club 51. I would hate to think of what I might walk in on this time." He leaned down to kiss me goodbye and promised to call me later.

As I walked back to my office, I told myself that this would be exciting. Not that I was a big fan of clubs but it really had been a while since I had gone out with a bunch of friends. Speaking of friends, Jess would get to put on a sexy dress and some high heels with Cam there to check her out. That should give him a nice little nudge. And there was always the possibility that someone had left the napkin on purpose, and they would try to contact us there. Maybe we could figure out who had sent me those notes, and whether or not someone was really following me.

Best of all, though, I was going on a date with Braden! Thinking about how good he looked on the last date almost made my mouth water. All that sexy in one package. It almost wasn't fair. It didn't matter that he had ridden me like Secretariat in the jury room the day before, I was going to put on my sexy clothes and get my boyfriend's engine revved. He had seen me in an elegant gown but he had never seen me in a little black dress and six inch heels.

∽ CHAPTER SEVEN ↻

Lily Adler and I had been friends since we attended Penn Law together. She had gone to law school mostly to please her family. It was her dream to be an author, and presently she worked as a law librarian rather than as an attorney because it gave her more time and freedom to write. She and Jess had hit it off immediately when I introduced them. The three of us were close, although lately Lily had been distracted by her career as an author and I had been distracted by Braden.

She came over to our place at eight and she looked great in a red dress that flattered her curvy figure and her dark brown hair and eyes. The three of us chatted and managed to polish off a bottle of wine while Jess and I got dressed. I really was starting to get excited! We danced around Jess's room to 80s music which we all liked, and in between choruses of *Don't You Want Me Baby*, I filled Lily in on the details of everything that had happened to me in the past month. Bruno, not being one to discriminate when it came to petting, made his rounds between the three of us, busting all of his most adorable Chihuahua moves.

"So Braden's cousin was *that* guy from college?" Lily asked. She had heard the most basic details one drunken night back in law school. "But you're friends again now. So, I guess you forgave him?" She took another sip of wine. We had just opened bottle number two.

"He says that he really did have feelings for me, but he was going through a hard time and he was feeling really down on himself," I said, standing with my back to Jess's mirror and nearly dislocating a few vertebra attempting to examine how my ass looked in the dress. "I took him by surprise when I told him that it had been my first time and it made him feel even worse. Like he had taken advantage of me or something."

"So I guess he didn't realize that he was entering uncharted territory at the moment of truth, huh?" she asked, raising her eyebrows and scratching Bruno's belly. He had rolled over on his back and turned his head to plead with her silently with those big brown eyes. He was a little doggie flirt.

"I guess not. It wasn't a big deal for me though," I said fluffing up the waves in my hair. "When it wasn't going in very easily, he just had to push a little harder and that worked! He was in! It hardly hurt at all even though Yale was almost as well endowed as Harvard and Harvard is *really* well endowed, let me tell you! I swear that thing's got to be almost ten inches."

"Oh my God, honey!" Jess laughed, rolling her eyes at me.

"I guess that it's safe to assume that Braden went to Harvard?" Lily asked Jess with a surprised sounding laugh. I had a feeling that I might have been a bit overly candid again.

"Uh oh. Was that too much information? I'm sorry. I guess I shouldn't be talking about the size of my boyfriend's endowment, or Cameron's endowment for that matter either, since he's probably Jess's future boyfriend."

"It's okay, honey. I asked you about that myself," Jess reminded me. "I was more amused by how you put things." She was just finishing up her makeup and she looked amazing. Her long auburn hair was gleaming and her skin looked like ivory. She was also wearing a killer dress in a deep green that was perfect for her. Cam would pass out when he saw her. Bruno was duly impressed. He decided that it was her turn to love him and so hopped down and went over to sit at her feet adoringly. He was more than a flirt. He was a little doggie player. She bent down and picked him up to pet him and he looked at her with pure bliss.

"Why is he probably Jess's future boyfriend?" Lily asked, sounding very curious as she paged through a copy of Vogue.

"Because they make a great couple," I explained. "You should see them together. They're always laughing. And he said he thought she was very attractive and that he was thinking about exploring it more." Jess blushed but she looked very happy.

"And do you want to be explored?" Lily asked Jess with a suggestive smile.

"Well, he's really cute and smart, and sexy," she said, blushing even more. "And I do have fun with him. So yeah, I would like to be explored, but there's no rush. I want him to work through anything he has to work through with Braden being Gab's boyfriend and me being her friend first. Then I'll know that he's ready to be involved, because I'm not interested in a one-nighter with a meal plan either." She threw me a smile.

"I want to be as well-grounded as Jess when I grow up," I said and poured myself another glass of wine.

"Slow down there, you lush," Jess chided. "You're not drinkin' for the gold."

"I hardly ever drink!" I pointed out and for some reason at the moment that argument seemed to make sense to me. Probably because I was drinking. I took another sip of wine.

"Uh oh, I see some drunk dancing on the horizon!" Lily teased.

"For an uncoordinated person I'm a *very good* drunk dancer. In fact, I think I dance better drunk," I answered thoughtfully, wondering why that was.

"I hope so, if you're planning to try to dance in those Loubies, honey. Maybe we had better bring a first-aid kit along with us," Jess said, looking worried.

"Very funny. So, tell us about your latest novel!" I said to Lily, changing the subject.

"I assume you mean my latest thriller," she teased. Lily wrote legal thrillers but she also wrote erotic romance under a pen name.

Jess and I had definitely become addicted to her naughty books and we weren't the only ones. She was developing quite a little following.

"You know what *we* want, honey!" Jess piped up. "Spill it! What kind of smut are you writing now and how soon can we buy it?" Lily sketched out the details for us and we made a show of fanning ourselves and giggling with wine-fueled, dirty-minded delight. Speaking of dirty-minded delight, Braden called just before nine. I grabbed my phone and headed into my own room to talk to him.

"Hey there, sexy guy," I answered. Just hearing his voice made me all fluttery and I couldn't help the big goofy grin that I saw gazing back at me from my vanity mirror.

"Uh oh, I think someone's been drinkin'." He laughed.

"You could tell from one sentence?" I asked, sort of surprised.

"Well, call me conceited, but I'm assuming that you meant to call me a 'sexy' guy not 'sudsy' guy, although I did just take a shower and I have had a few beers myself, I must confess."

"Uh oh, you've been hanging around with me too long. You're starting to tell corny jokes. So how was hanging out with the prosecutor types?"

"It was fun. I was catching up with everybody and letting them know where I've been. They were joking around saying they were going to put my picture on a milk carton and file a missing person's report on me. Don't worry though. I said lots of nice things about you."

"Did you tell them that I'm a brilliant and incredibly gifted attorney and that you worship the ground that I walk on?" I plopped down on my bed and let his deep rich voice wash over me.

"Even better. I told them that you fondled me while I watched the baseball game and then knocked me over in bed and showed me who was boss."

"Braden." I laughed, hoping he was kidding. I heard him laugh too. Phew!

"Actually, I told them that I've never been happier and that I'm very content to spend my nights with you."

"Oh. That's sweet. Did Adam vomit?"

"Actually, I think he's jealous."

"Adam's in love with you?" I teased.

"No! I think he's jealous of the fact that I found somebody who I can go home with at night and who makes me so happy."

"You must be drunk," I teased. "He wouldn't want to limit himself to having sex with only one woman."

"He would if it were great sex. I *know* he's jealous of our sex life. Just to let you know, not all casual hook-ups are great. Novelty just goes so far."

"You tell him stuff about our sex life?"

"Not details. Just general stuff."

"What kind of general stuff?"

"I don't know. Like for example, if he said, 'Hey, Braden you're looking really cheerful, you must have gotten laid last night, I might point out that I get laid most nights, but I wouldn't mention that I spanked you and you liked it." He laughed.

"Well, that's okay, I guess."

"And I've told him that you blow my mind in bed but I haven't mentioned that you've also blown it in the jury room. Although I suspect that Mark will so I'll probably be hearing about that soon."

"I've told Jess some general stuff about you, too."

"Like what?"

"Like you have the stamina of an Energizer Bunny."

"An *Energizer Bunny*? Oh shit! You did not."

"You're going to complain that other women know that you keep on going?"

"Okay, fine, just don't share anything more intimate than that."

"Define more intimate."

"Oh, fuck!"

"Would that include the information that the Harvard endowment is very large?"

"The Har ... Oh Jesus! Gabrielle!"

"I didn't think guys would really mind women knowing that. I mean isn't that, like, a source of pride?"

"Yeah, when you're twelve! Honey, the size of my dick is nobody's business but yours. How about from now on we both try to be a little more discreet, okay? If you do let anything else slip, though, don't tell me about it. There's some shit that I just don't want to know."

"Okay, it's a deal. So what's the plan, Harvard?"

"Well, this is supposed to be a date, but Adam, Mark, Cameron and Drew are on their way here now and we were just talking about cabbing it because we've all been drinking. Drew's crashing with Cameron, so he's at his place."

"Why is he crashing with Cameron instead of with you?"

"Cameron has an extra bedroom so he wouldn't have to sleep on the couch. Besides, I want to get really freaky and mildly kinky with you tonight and I have a feeling you may have a hard time being quiet."

"Oh! I see." That tickly feeling? Yeah, it was way beyond tickly now.

"Anyway, I got us on the list. How about if you three share a cab and we'll meet you there in the VIP lounge lobby at about ten?"

"Sounds like a good plan. See you later sudsy guy."

"Bye. Too much information, girl." He laughed and hung up.

I went over to the mirror to check myself out one last time. I looked sexy without looking sleazy. Exactly what I had been going for. My long brown hair looked a little tousled and Jess and Lily had done a fabulous job helping me do my makeup. They had used smoky colors to compliment my hazel eyes and a deep rich color on my lips. I had decided to go without stockings and I rubbed lotion onto my legs and slipped on my black heels.

"Who else is going again?" Lily asked suspiciously as soon as I came back into Jess's room. She must have overheard me mentioning Adam to Braden. The walls in that place were so thin. I went over to sit down on the bed and take my turn at adoring Bruno.

"Braden's younger brother Drew, Cameron, Mark from our office, and Adam."

"Oh Christ!" Lily said, making a face. "Why didn't you warn me?" She came over and sat down beside me with a thud, looking like I had just told her she would have to take the bar exam again.

"He'll also be there this weekend too," I admitted and she took on a pained expression and stared at the ceiling. "But I warned him to behave! What is the problem between you two anyway?" I put Bruno on her lap. Nobody could stay upset when faced with that much cuteness.

"He thinks I'm an uptight bitch," she answered with a distinctly unhappy look on her face. Could it really be *that* bad? Bruno nuzzled her hand and she petted him ... and smiled. See, I told you.

"Uptight?" Jess asked, turning around to look at us. "You write raunchy books."

"He doesn't know about those. He sees me as a mousy librarian who writes thrillers to make her boring life seem more exciting." Lily looked very annoyed by that. I wondered why his opinion mattered so much to her.

"Well, you look like one of your sexy book heroines tonight," I said with a smile.

Actually, in the past year, Lily had really blossomed. She had always been attractive, but now she just exuded a new sense of confidence that made her seem very sexy. I wondered if it had anything to do with her parents moving away, and I was also curious to see if Adam would notice the difference in her.

The cab pulled up to a big, plain, industrial-looking building. There was no outside line like at other clubs but there was a sign pointing toward the back. We went through a pair of heavy steel doors and immediately saw that everything was hidden behind the facade of what looked like an old abandoned factory.

We followed along a winding hallway with bare brick walls. Videos were being projected in various places — newsreels with reports about Elvis sightings, Lone Gunmen, and aliens. There were framed editions of papers like *News of the World* and the *National Enquirer* hung on the walls and various Masonic symbols and hieroglyphics painted or scrawled here and there as well. This joint was really well done. We approached two large men dressed all in black of course. (Men in Black? Get it?) They had ear pieces in and held clipboards. I gave them our names and they directed us to what looked like an elevator from a sci-fi movie to our left. Apparently the VIP area was on the second floor.

When the doors slid open again with a whoosh, I saw people mingling about, a bank of TVs on a wall, all showing UFO footage, and another set of doors straight ahead just beyond a sign for restrooms. Jess said that she had to make a pit stop and Lily decided to go with her. I told them that I would go in and let the guys know we were here. I let another set of men in black have my name and they directed me through the doors. I walked down a hallway that turned around a bend. Up ahead I could see a large room with several sofas and low tables scattered around. The bare brick walls were lit only by the ominous glow of recessed green neon lights but I could still make out the details of the room and what was going on inside. I figured that this must be the VIP lounge lobby.

There were arches on the left and on the right that looked like they led into the actual VIP lounge and club area. Like everywhere else in the building so far, the décor was industrial with a sort of *Metropolis* feel. There were people sitting on the sofas and others standing in groups chatting, including our gang of guys.

I paused to take it all in. Leaning against a wall, tall, blonde and beautiful, Braden stood in the middle, wearing a white linen shirt rolled up at the sleeves, and a pair of tan pants. Adam, with his dark hair and eyes looked sexy dressed all in black. As usual Mark looked funky, dressed in a black jacket over a white T-shirt. And then there was Cam, stylish as always, in what looked to me like Armani. Drew looked just like a younger version of Braden, but I saw that he had his own style – a horizontally striped baby blue and white shirt that showed off his blonde good looks in a summer beach boy way. There was something for everyone.

I watched them as they talked and laughed looking all masculine and confident. Occasionally a club chick would pass by wearing a dress that was too short, too tight and too revealing, and one or more of them would check her out. Braden didn't look interested, though, which made me very happy. It was only a couple of minutes but it was enough time to see what kind of impact they made on their surroundings. Suffice it to say, by the looks they were getting from the other women who saw them, I didn't think any of them would want for partners to help them *unwind*.

I started walking in their direction. Just then Drew looked up and I saw him mouth the words, "holy shit." I almost stopped in my tracks. I looked quickly behind me in case I was about to be mugged or something. There was nobody there, though. Was one of my boobs hanging out? They all looked up then and by the looks on their faces I realized that it was probably just that the sexy designer dress and shoes had been a good choice. I did glance down to make sure it wasn't the boob, though.

A few things happened in the next couple of seconds. Braden's eyes glazed over; Adam's eyes fixed on my six inch heels, and Mark's eyes just got wider. Cam and Drew immediately started a conversation between the two of them that included a lot of eye contact. I figured it was because they were Braden's relatives and likely assumed that they were in the most possible danger if caught ogling, so they were taking precautionary measures.

"Hey guys," I said with a smile. Braden continued to stare openly but the other guys quickly snapped out of it and looked curiously at him. Were they waiting for him to do something? What did they expect, that he would throw me down on the carpet and share our love with the crowd? When he didn't appear to be doing much of *anything*, they just looked anywhere but at me.

"Hi, Gabrielle," Cam said, talking to the ceiling. There was a chorus of 'Hi, Gabrielle's' addressed to various locations around the room. Braden seemed a little stunned.

"I don't think we should stay much longer," he said, sounding very distracted. His eyes dropped to my body and his gaze slowly traveled back and forth from my boobs to my six inch heels. Several hundred times. He looked like he had just seen a miracle performed. What, did I normally look like a bag lady or something?

"We just got here," I reminded him. "Jess and Lily aren't even out of the bathroom yet."

"Right," he mumbled. Just then I heard someone call out to him.

"Braden! Where the hell have you been?" Two tall, well-dressed, exceptionally good-looking guys who were leaving the lounge came sauntering over. They had an air of wealth and good breeding about them, just like he did. When they noticed me, they stopped in their tracks. They both checked me out, but a bit more subtly than Braden, who was *still* checking me out.

"Well, hello," said the blonde guy who had called out. The look he was giving me practically screamed 'player'. I figured there would be a line coming momentarily.

"Girlfriend!" Cam suddenly exclaimed, sounding like he was shouting, 'abandon ship!'

"This is your girlfriend, Cam?" the other guy, who had dark hair, asked.

"Mine? No! She's just my friend! I swear!" The two newcomers looked understandably confused. Cam collected himself and went on. "She's Braden's girlfriend!"

"Ah!" blonde guy said, and they both nodded politely as if that explained Cam's little outburst. "Wait, his *girlfriend*?" he asked dubiously looking at Braden for confirmation. Normally, this would have been the point where Braden would have come over to drape a possessive arm around me but he was still busy making the visual journey up and down my body. I think that he might have been experiencing some kind of fugue state.

"Gabrielle, this is Kurt van Ryland and Kevin Bryce. We grew up together," Braden said still sounding very distracted.

"Evan. Evan Bryce," said dark haired guy who Braden had grown up with, but whose name he apparently didn't know, while reaching out to shake my hand. "We also went to college together."

"Yeah, they went to Howard," Braden mumbled.

"Harvard," Kurt corrected with a smile as he shook my hand.

"Gabrielle went to Yale," Cam put in. "That's where we became friends. *Just* friends!"

Kurt and Evan were looking at Braden and Cam like they thought that maybe they were high or something. Drew decided to help out at this point. So, of course, things just went downhill from there.

"Kurt, Ev, this is Gabrielle Ginsberg, who's Braden's actual girlfriend. She's like the *only* woman he's sleeping with now. And Cameron's not sleeping with her at all anymore." Well, I was glad he had cleared *that* up. I saw Cameron look up at the ceiling. He may have been praying. Luckily, Braden still wasn't really completely with us.

"Any relation to Ruth Bader Ginsburg?" Evan asked, tactfully avoiding Drew's little revelation. Kurt was looking back and forth between Braden and Cam with what looked like confused amusement.

"Uh, no, sorry. Just Ben and Judy Ginsberg," I said with a smile.

"Not Ben Ginsberg, the CEO of Marlton Radcliff?" Kurt asked, suddenly turning his attention back to me and looking very intrigued.

"Yeah, he's my dad," I answered and I saw Kurt and Evan share a surprised look. Then they looked at Braden like he had just become their new hero.

"Uh, wow. It's nice to meet you!" Evan said with what sounded like suppressed excitement. "We read about that PoliCon case in the *Wall Street Journal*. Your dad's really a brilliant man."

"Yeah, we're both admirers!" Kurt explained. "I work in finance myself and Evan is a legislative aid. That case is going to lead to some interesting business reform in New York."

"What case was that?" Mark asked.

"PoliCon," Kurt explained. "Marlton Radcliff was considering a buyout and when the CEO, Ben Ginsberg, took a good look at everything he figured out that the company had been involved in an incredibly complex money laundering scheme. The whole business was a front for illegal activity and nobody knew."

"He tipped off the authorities and now he's helping them to create some new regulations and legislation to make sure nobody else can ever do something like that again," Evan added. "It's really groundbreaking stuff."

"Uh oh, we were supposed to meet friends of ours ten minutes ago," Kurt said, looking at his watch. "I guess we had better run. It was a pleasure meeting you, Gabrielle, everyone. Nice seeing you guys, especially out together."

"Yeah, it's about time you two buried the hatchet," Evan added with a smile and a glance at Braden and Cam. They waved and then turned and left.

Just then Jess and Lily came walking in and Kurt and Evan gave them an admiring look as they passed. Adam had been looking off in the direction of the lounge and when he turned and caught sight of Lily, he immediately did a double take. Even though he quickly hid it, the look he gave her appeared to be filled with more attraction than dislike. So, of course, he had to compensate.

"Why Lilith," he said. "Do they let you out at night?" His body language reeked of cockiness and disdain. What a charmer he could be! I could see why the ladies flocked to him.

"Gentlemen," Lily said. "Adam." She looked at him dismissively. Lily knew how to give as good as she got and she wasn't anybody's little groupie. No wonder they didn't get along. Although I wasn't his groupie either, and I gave it back to him too. Same thing with Jess and we seemed to get along with him okay. Interesting.

"Your full name is Lilith?" Jess asked, looking at Lily curiously. "I didn't know that."

"No. Lily is my full name, but Adam finds it amusing to call me by the name of a female demon." She threw him a sarcastic smile.

"If the shoe fits..." he said, returning the smile. As she turned away, though, he gave her a thoughtful look like he wasn't sure that it was really her. She didn't look like a mousy librarian tonight, did she, Adam?

Braden *finally* seemed to be getting over being in alcohol/lust induced shock and he moved over to stand by me and pull me to his side. He looked down into my eyes, gave me a sexy smile, and ran his fingers lightly up and down my bare back, making me all shivery.

"Lily," Jess said, "that's Cameron Clay and that's Drew Pierce. Guys, this is Lily Adler." Cam and Drew greeted Lily and she looked at Cam with fairly open curiosity. He seemed puzzled by the attention.

"I know that you've met Mark before but have you ever met Braden?" I asked, redirecting her attention before she got too curious.

"No, I haven't, but Gab's told me a lot about you." She smiled at him and her eyes seemed to involuntarily drop to his package but she quickly ripped them away and blushed. He shot me a rather irked look and I smiled innocently.

"And of course you and Adam know each other already," I added and both she and Adam cringed at the same time.

"Well, now we're all assembled, let's go check it out," Mark said.

We went through the archway where Kurt and Evan had come from. There were tables built into alcoves along two walls and a long bar stood in front of a third. There was a circular dance floor in the center of the room surrounding a round opening with a railing where people could stand to watch couples gyrate on the main dance floor below. Hanging above the opening was a huge saucer-shaped object with blinking lights that I took to be a UFO. We all slid into a long cushioned bench seat that wrapped around a table in one of the alcoves.

"Braden, Cam! It's Derek!" Drew said suddenly. Braden and Cam immediately followed his gaze to an exceptionally handsome guy at the bar who was presently feeling up a woman in a dress the size of a bikini. I could see the family resemblance right away. He was tall and he had classic good looks. His hair was a dark blonde, somewhere between Braden and Drew's blonde and Cameron's light brown. He had an air of confident sexuality and he surprised me. When Cam and Braden had spoken of Cousin Derek, the Larry Flint of the Main Line, I had pictured a greasy-looking guy, not this very sexy-looking guy. But then, he was their cousin, and they were both very sexy-looking guys.

"Oh shit!" Cam said and looked at Braden with panic.

"Just ignore him," Braden said. "He's busy. He probably won't even see us." We had only looked up at Derek for a moment, and now we were busy ourselves, staring at each other hotly and holding hands.

At that moment a bleach blonde waitress with boobs like watermelons spilling out of a skimpy silver space girl outfit came over to take our drink order. She looked like a cross between Dolly Parton and Barbarella. The second her eyes fastened on Braden I knew she recognized him. She gave him a flirtatious smile and licked her lips as she leaned down low to give him a good clear view of the melon match. He didn't avail himself of her offer though. In fact, he turned nearly sideways to face me.

"So baby, I was thinking about having another beer."

"Okay. Did you want me to order it for you?" I wasn't sure where he was going with this.

"No, sweetheart, that's okay. Heineken in the bottle and whatever my girlfriend wants." He glanced up at the barmaid and returned his attention quickly to me.

"I'll have a white wine spritzer, thanks." Dollarella gave me an unfriendly look and then slithered off. I didn't know about anybody else, but I wasn't leaving her a big tip.

"Did you know that waitress?" I asked Braden curiously.

"She used to work at another place I used to go to. I think she kind of liked me." I had a feeling that was the understatement of the century but I didn't pursue it. I didn't have time to pursue it, truthfully. I looked up and saw Cousin Derek approaching our table.

Uh oh. Things were getting better and better. Maybe Braden had been right about the club thing not being a great idea.

"Hello, Braden," Derek said in a voice that sounded like he should have been saying "Hello Clarice" instead. It was kind of mesmerizing, though, and I found myself staring at him, almost fascinated. "I haven't seen you out and about in quite a while." His eyes traveled over to me. "And who is this lovely woman with you?" He gave me an almost boyish look, but with an obscene undertone, and then he raked his fingers through his hair in a very Braden-like way that surprised me and threw me off balance. He was almost like Braden's evil twin.

"This is my girlfriend, Gabrielle," Braden answered in a slightly menacing tone. "She's not only lovely, she's an intelligent, accomplished, fellow attorney, for whom I have the greatest respect. We're a very happy, *monogamous* couple."

"Uh, hi?" I said, trying to sound friendly. After all, he was a relative even if he did have some obscene tendencies. Every family had a black sheep. In my case it was my grandmother.

"A pleasure," Derek replied. "And a surprise. It's been some time since Braden was half of a 'monogamous couple'. I'm not sure that he's ever been part of a 'happy' one."

"Gabrielle is exceptional," Braden responded coldly.

"She does seem rather extraordinary. And not only beautiful but brilliant and accomplished too. I must confess that I'm jealous." His voice was silky and his gaze was hot. He was looking at me rather like that snake from *The Jungle Book*. I half expected to see those little swirly things in his eyes.

"Well, we're enjoying the, uh, monogamy. And happiness! We're happy too. Happily monogamous! And stuff," I said. True, it was rather an awkward thing to say, but my tone was upbeat! At least I was a friendly weirdo! His eyes raked over me unashamedly and then he moved on and I released the breath that I hadn't realized I had been holding. I wondered if *my* eyes had those little swirly things now.

"And Cameron is here too. You, I have seen recently. Good thing you decided not to go to that party after all. Things didn't turn out too well for the guests, as I'm sure you've heard. I must confess that I wasn't heartbroken. They're not my favorite people, even though I'm obviously a patron. And, is this lovely lady your ..." He shifted his leer to Jess.

"Friend," Cam answered. Derek was looking at Jess like he might want to devour her. Jess looked like a deer in the headlights. A brave little deer, but no match for a Buick. Then Derek gave her a cute grin that looked a lot like Cameron's cute grin and I became convinced that he had evil superpowers and could morph into every woman's dream guy. "Very close friend," Cam added with a warning tone in his voice, grabbing her hand in his. Jess seemed to snap out of it then and looked at Cam with a smile. Derek nodded and then his eyes fixed on Lily with distinct interest – even beyond interest in getting her naked.

"I recognize you," he said, making it sound dirty. A slow Grinch-like smile spread across his face. Uh oh.

"You do?" she asked dubiously. She gave him a thoughtful expression, like she was trying to place him. I wondered what Lily had been doing to research those steamy novels.

"From a book signing event in New York. Many women who I've known find your novels very stimulating." I was pretty certain he meant women he had 'known' in the Biblical sense, and 'stimulating' in the, well you know, stimulating sense.

"Legal thrillers?" Adam, who had wound up sitting next to Lily, asked with a smile. I have to admit that I almost laughed out loud at the way he said it. I had a sneaking suspicion that Adam didn't like Derek very much. I can't imagine why not. Without answering, Derek shifted his gaze to him.

"Is she your girlfriend?" I could see that Lily was annoyed with how he had asked that question. It sounded kind of like he was asking him, "Is this your car?"

"Arch nemesis," Adam said with a smile and I felt Jess kick him under the table. "Just kidding, Lily and I are very close," he said, putting his arm around her. At least it was true in a literal sense. Derek gave Adam a look that seemed almost like a challenge but he moved on.

"And is this *your* close friend, Drew?" he asked, looking at Mark. Drew and Mark looked at each other and then quickly back at Derek as understanding of his implication dawned.

"Good buddy," Drew answered in a deeper voice than usual, slapping Mark on the back. "Just hanging out here. Doing guy stuff."

"Talking about women. And sports. And beer. And uh ..." Mark added.

"Condoms," Drew added and I rolled my eyes. Brilliant.

"I see," Derek said. "Well, I left a good friend of my own at the bar and she'll be rather annoyed with me if I keep her waiting too long. Fun chatting with all of you. Ladies ... perhaps I'll see you on the dance floor." And with that he left and everyone breathed a sigh of relief. I saw Adam let go of Lily. Was it my imagination or did he look a little reluctant to do it? Cam held on to Jess's hand for a couple more minutes which was very promising. The waitress came back with our drinks and Braden suddenly dropped a coaster under the table until she left again.

"Did you know her *well*?" I asked a little tensely, wondering if she was someone he had actually hooked up with.

"No!" Braden answered reappearing from beneath the table. "She flirted with me a lot but I always got a weird vibe from her." He got a weird vibe from her. Because, you know, *he* wasn't acting weird at all at the moment. People hid under tables all the time in these places.

"So Derek seems kind of ... alarming," Jess said with a smile.

"It would be best if you ladies stayed close to us when he's around," Cam said, glancing in Derek's direction. I followed his gaze and saw that Derek had his hand up his 'friend's' miniscule dress and she was grinding against him. Charming.

"Looks like you and Lily are a couple," Mark said with a smile to Adam.

"And so are you and Drew," Adam replied with a smile of his own. Mark and Drew both looked at him menacingly and I suspected that they wanted to grab the first club chick who walked by and demonstrate their raging heterosexuality right here on the table.

We decided to split up and look around a little to check the place out. Braden and I went exploring with Adam. Lily, Cam and Jess headed off together and Drew hung out with Mark - as buddies – and fellow sports fans, beer drinkers and condom consumers. Finally we all made it back to our table, without anything very interesting to report. It was a club. Kind of a cool one, but just a club. I wasn't really sure what I had expected to find here. Obviously, the cocktail napkin was just some drunken fireman's forgotten trash.

"Let's dance," Lily said and I got up to join her and Jess out on the dance floor. You know, alcohol did really seem to improve my coordination and balance. Or more likely it just made me think it did. We danced to a fast song, and looking to my right I noticed Derek dancing with the woman from the bar, who had been joined by another one who looked amazingly similar. They both had big hair and were dressed in very skimpy outfits. Actually, I would classify what the women were wearing more as fabric swatches than outfits and what they were doing more as writhing than dancing. Derek himself had plenty of good moves. He seemed to have natural rhythm and he moved his hips well. What a surprise.

He must have sensed someone watching because he looked in my direction and smiled when he saw me. I looked away quickly. Oh fuck! I hadn't been checking Derek out! He was just interesting to me because he was Braden's cousin and apparently the black sheep of their family. It was too late though. The damage was done. Derek started subtly dancing the trashy twins over in our direction. Great!

I made sure not to look at him again. That's what Braden had said and I think I had seen that in a wildlife documentary somewhere too. Never make direct eye contact with the deadly panther/poisonous snake/wild rutting pig/Derek. Unfortunately, that meant that I didn't have any idea where he was or what he was doing. Too late I realized that "where he was," was right behind me, and "what he was doing" was moving his hips against me. Derek was as tall and well-built as Braden and he felt disconcertingly similar but I knew it wasn't Braden behind me. I would have just known anyway but it was a dead giveaway when Derek leaned down and spoke into my ear and he was all Derek-sounding.

"Gabrielle, you really know how to *move*." Jesus, he made that sound so obscene! But then I had a feeling that he could make "pass the salt" sound obscene. I gave him what I hoped was a friendly (*just a friendly!*) smile and began moving *away*. Unfortunately, the floor was a bit slippery and I was a tipsy uncoordinated woman wearing six inch heels. My foot slipped out from underneath me and I went flying backward with one leg high in the air, landing squarely against Derek who caught me in what must have looked like some kind of fancy backward dip, because immediately the dancers around us backed up into a circle to watch.

With a sinking feeling, I recalled the surprise I had planned for Braden. I had decided to really go without panties and I had just flashed a portion of the crowd, including Jess and Lily, who were giving me an astonished look. I panicked, and attempting to right myself, I overshot and wound up pitching forward. I put my hands out to catch myself and landed in a push-up position, flipping over, landing on my butt and lower back, and spinning around in a circle with my legs in the air. The crowd started cheering! Holy shit, they thought I was break dancing!

Derek, who I was pretty sure I had also just flashed, apparently took this as an invitation. He came over and hauled me up and then spun me around, picking me up in the freaking air! The lights and the alcohol and the spinning combined to make me dizzy and when he set me down again I tumbled sideways and started flailing my arms in an attempt to catch my balance, first in one direction and then in the other. Derek followed right along and matched me move for move. I had a feeling that a new dance craze had just been born, The Flail, invented at Club 51 in Philadelphia. The crowd ate it up. Just when I was sure that I had reached the seventh ring of Hell the cavalry rode in to save me. Braden "cut in" on Derek, who gracefully stepped aside.

"What are you doing, Gabrielle?" he asked, speaking directly into my ear so I could hear him over the music. The crowd, including Jess and Lily, went back to what they were doing before Derek and I got jiggy. Derek himself had gone back to the Trash Twins, who I noted were now doing The Flail too.

"I was trying to move away from Derek and I slipped," I answered back into his ear. I saw him try to stifle a laugh.

"That was pretty impressive. I think you and Derek could probably go pro if you wanted," he teased.

"I'm just lucky I survived."

Braden was a great dancer and he could even make me look good on the dance floor. I relaxed against him and let him guide me with his hands and legs and hips and soon I started really enjoying myself. We had slow danced but this was the first time we had danced like this together. We were pressed up against each other, shaking our booties, and bumping and grinding in complete synchronicity. But then we had a lot of practice with doing those moves horizontally. We weren't actually simulating sex on the dance floor like Derek's new friends were now doing with him - simultaneously I might add - but the way we were moving was most definitely very hot. The night was improving. I even saw a few more adventurous souls in the crowd doing The Flail. At one point, though, I looked over toward the bar and I saw Dollarella glaring at me and leering at Braden. I leaned up to shout into his ear.

"You never hooked up with that waitress?" I asked suspiciously.

"No! I swear. She always kind of creeped me out. I pegged her as a crazy stalker girl. Come to think of it, I don't know if I trust her to serve you alcohol."

"Maybe I'll have Derek taste my drink first," I joked.

"Good idea." He laughed and dropped his hand to my bottom. "Are you wearing a thong?" he asked with a hot look. Apparently, he had missed the earlier part of the floor show.

"No. Actually I'm not wearing anything," I answered and gave him my best bad girl smile. The hot look he was giving me became scorching.

"Naughty girl. If I had known that I would have occupied myself better under that table."

Eventually Derek and the two women left together. Braden leaned down and kissed me deeply. Pulling back, he told me that he was going back to rejoin the other guys.

"Dance with your friends a little more. I'll talk to the guys a bit and then I say we get out of here and go have a more private party."

"That sounds good to me!" He left the dance floor and I moved back over to dance with Jess and Lily. The three of us kept dancing as another song came on and I watched the guys get involved in an animated conversation about something. Then I looked over toward the doorway arch and saw a woman with dark hair dressed in black who had her back to me. When she turned around I was surprised to see that I recognized her.

∽ CHAPTER EIGHT ᧽

Jess and Lily were paying attention to the DJ at the far end of the room and didn't see me leave but Felicity Mason was waving to me so I headed for the lobby.

"Gabrielle. Good to see you," she said, actually looking like she might be expressing something close to an emotion.

"Felicity. Um, nice to see you too." She looked just like she had when I met her at the Pierce Foundation fundraiser. She was dressed all in black but I could see her clothes were expensive. Her skin looked pallid, and her hair was dyed an inky color. She looked like a rich Goth chick. There was something odd in her tone. I have to tell you, though, 'odd' wasn't exactly a shock when it came to Felicity or her family. Her mother reminded me of Cruella de Vil but not as warm. Her father was so nondescript that he would be easy to lose in the snow.

"You look good in black," she said sullenly. I didn't take it personally. Felicity said pretty much everything sullenly. "Come on. We should talk."

"Talk? I have to tell my friends where I am then or they'll worry," I said, looking back toward the lounge. Braden would probably have the place raided by a SWAT team if he discovered I was missing. She ignored me, though, and turned around and headed down another hallway. Curiosity got the best of me and against my better judgment, I followed. She led me to a small private room with a couple of couches. I walked in and she closed the door behind us and sat down, waiting for me to join her.

"You and Braden are still together," she said as she stared at me gloomily.

"We're very happy together." I wondered if I should explain what "happy" meant. I sat down on the couch opposite her, crossed my legs and tried to make myself as comfortable as one could be having a private tête-à-tête with Elvira, Queen of the Night in a back room at a conspiracy club.

"You should be careful. There are people who might find that threatening," she replied in that flat-sounding voice of hers.

"Why?" I asked suspiciously, eyeing up my exit path to the door. I was starting to wonder if she might be a little nutty. I couldn't figure out why anyone would find my love life threatening.

"Because of your fathers."

"What are you talking about?" I turned back to her in confusion.

"There was an article in the paper ..."

"What, that Kingmaker thing in the New York Times?" I interrupted, feeling impatient. I wished that she would get to whatever her point was.

"Uh, I guess," she said, looking uncertain. "I didn't read it. I just overheard some people talking about it. They didn't want your dads to work together."

"And who are these people? Give me some names."

"I don't really know," she said, avoiding my eyes. "It was at the fundraiser and I didn't get a good look." I had a feeling that she did know but that she just wasn't going to tell me.

"And what did these people say exactly?"

"A guy said, 'You read that article. If Ben Ginsberg and Tyler Pierce get together it could ruin everything.' Then another guy said, 'We need to take her out of the picture so that they never do'. Then a woman said, 'Leave it to me. I'll handle it'."

"Someone's been sending me anonymous notes and following me around everywhere. Do you know anything about that?"

"What? No! " She looked shocked … and then she looked scared. "I've got to go. I have somewhere I have to be." She got up and quickly headed for the door. She seemed freaked out.

"Wait a minute! Did you leave the napkin?" I wanted some answers now and I stood up, preparing to go after her if necessary.

"Yes, I left it, the napkin that is. And I asked you to meet me *here* at *this* club for a very specific reason. I don't know anything else, though, so please don't ask me any more questions." With that she took off out the door and by the time I got there she was gone.

Okay, that was *really* weird. I wasn't sure that I even believed her. That story about overhearing someone at the fundraiser was just so crazy. Speaking of crazy, I headed back to the lounge and when I got there I found everybody going nuts.

"Gabrielle!" Braden called out with obvious relief. He rushed over toward me and pulled me into his arms tightly. Great, I had managed to make him worry about me more than he usually did.

"Where did you go?" Jess demanded, sounding stressed and stalking over to me with her hands on her hips. Apparently, I had worried everyone.

"Braden, honey! Air," I gasped. He was still clutching me so hard that I was starting to feel lightheaded. He loosened his hold but he didn't let go of me. I had a feeling that between him and my dad I was going to have to start wearing a homing beacon soon.

"I'm sorry. I didn't mean to scare everyone. I just had a very strange conversation with Felicity Mason. I saw her out in the lobby and she waved me over, then told me she wanted to talk, but she took off before I could tell anybody, so I just followed her to see what she wanted."

"Felicity?" Cameron asked, sounding surprised. It wasn't exactly shocking that she would be hanging out at a weird club but I guess it was kind of surprising that she would actually converse.

"Let's sit down, okay?" I asked and we all headed back to our table. Braden kept his arm around me and held me tightly by his side.

This was much more than a nestle. He had a grip on me like a vise. I quickly summarized the high points of our little chat.

"What in the hell was she talking about?" Drew asked, sounding confused.

"There was an article in the New York Times," Mark explained. "It suggested that Gab's dad might be powerful enough to pick the next president and that he seemed to be showing an interest in politics lately. Especially in backing politicians with views a lot like your dad's."

"There are so many nutty people out there," I pointed out. "It's *possible* somebody took that article in the Times too seriously. My dad even mentioned something like that once himself. And she said she wanted to meet me *here* for a specific reason. This place is all about conspiracies."

"Okay, so say it's some conspiracy theorist who's harassing you, *who* would it threaten if a powerful businessman backed a moderate Republican for president?" Mark asked.

"Extremists," Lily answered. "And Gabrielle's Jewish too. You've heard of all of those crazy conspiracy theories about the Elders of Zion, and Rothschilds and all that garbage."

"What, some far-right anti-Semitic hate group is investing their time trying to get Gabrielle and Braden to break up?" Adam asked sarcastically. "Don't they have anything better to do, like bring about the Rise of the Fourth Reich?"

"Remember that she said she overhead someone talking at the fundraiser," I reminded Lily. "It would be kind of hard to picture Senator and Mrs. Pierce inviting a Klansman or Neo-Nazi to their party. Although, I guess it's possible it could be someone who secretly holds those views."

"I have a thought. Maybe she's nuts," Cam said, looking disgusted.

"Yeah or just lying," Mark agreed. "She could be making the whole thing up because she's bored or jealous or something. Hell, maybe she sent you those notes herself. She admitted that she left you the napkin."

"Well, I know one thing. She wasn't the person I thought I saw staring at us on the night of the fire alarm, and I thought I saw that same guy following me that day when we went to the prison, Mark. I just didn't realize it until later. And her reaction to me telling her about it looked like genuine fear. I've never seen this woman express an emotion before."

"Okay, well I guess it wouldn't hurt to share it with the police, although I'm pretty sure they're not going to be able to do much," Braden said. "Maybe they'll at least question her."

"She won't tell them anything. In fact, she'll probably deny that we had this conversation. She didn't want to be involved any further; so all we have is what sounds like a warning for me to watch out for conspiracy theorists who don't want our families to get together. Take it for what it's worth."

"Well, I certainly hope that you're enjoying your courtship so far, Gabrielle," Adam said with a smile. "Now you can add breakdancing with Cousin Derek and having private meetings with creepy Goth chicks to your list of romantic memories."

"So have we done the Club 51 experience?" Cam asked.

"Yes," Braden answered. "Let's get out of here." We headed out and called cabs to come and pick us up, making plans to meet up the next day in Bryn Mawr.

ᴄᴏ CHAPTER NINE ᴄᴏ

We went to my apartment to get Bruno and then started off on the two block trip back to Braden's place. I noticed Braden looking around a lot as we walked and I had to wonder if maybe he had the same weird feeling that I had often gotten lately. Finally, something seemed to catch his eye and I saw him squint like he was trying to make something out in the distance.

"Something wrong?" I asked hesitantly.

"I think all the talk about being followed and conspiracy theorists and all that has made me paranoid. Now I have that weird feeling like somebody's watching us but I think it's just my imagination. I don't see anybody."

"I didn't notice it before but now that you've mentioned it I do. That's probably just the power of suggestion though. I'm sorry if I got us both feeling paranoid." I glanced around us nervously. There were still plenty of people out and about even though it was late, but again, nobody seemed particularly interested in us.

"Don't be sorry, baby. I'm glad that you're not keeping anything from me anymore. I would rather you told me everything, no matter how strange it sounds. If something's bothering you, I want to know about it."

Less than two minutes later we were greeting his doorman and hopping on the elevator. Braden looked deep in thought as we headed for his apartment and he dug out his keys and unlocked the door. When Bruno scampered off to check everything out as usual, he came over and pulled me into his arms.

"So Gabrielle, time to unwind. Did we forget to wear our panties tonight?"

"No, we didn't forget. We didn't wear them on purpose," I said with a naughty smile.

He gave me a cocky grin, nudged my legs apart and sank to his knees in front of me. He looked up at me as he slid his hands up my bare thighs and slid the skirt of my dress up over my hips. Then he looked down again, groaned softly, and began trailing light little kisses across my lower tummy. I felt intense heat between my legs at the same time as I felt chills that hardened my nipples, and I started reeling with all of the sensations bombarding me at once. He moved his mouth over and nipped gently at my hip, and I began urging his head lower with my hips and hands. I really was a demanding little hussy, wasn't I?

"I thought that patience was a virtue," he mumbled against my hyper-sensitized skin. He sounded very amused.

"Well, I'm not very virtuous either," I replied throatily, swallowing hard.

I felt his warm breath on me right where I wanted it, and I tensed, because I anticipated the feeling of his tongue against my clit, but then he pulled back and moved down to lick my inner thigh instead. I almost beat him. He was never ever going to forget those fucking dishes!

"Gabrielle, you're even wet down here," he murmured as he continued licking my slick thighs. He was driving me wild. I was a bundle of shivering heat and tingling ache, reacting in a dozen different ways to what he was doing to me with that sinful tongue of his.

"Braden," I whimpered and tried again to urge him with my hands and my hips to go where I wanted to feel that tongue the most.

"Do you want my mouth somewhere else, baby?" he purred against me.

"Yes!" I bit out. My legs were starting to feel weak.

"Tell me what you want me to do." Oh Jesus. He was going to make me say it! Okay, was it really such a big deal? I had asked him to fuck me. I had even ordered him to fuck me. Was this really so different? No! It wasn't!

"I want you to eat my pussy, Braden!" I demanded impatiently. There, I said it! Don't judge me. You would have said it too.

He groaned and moved up, breathing in deeply and releasing it slowly. I felt his warm breath on me again just before I felt his hot tongue drag across my clit. I gasped and grabbed onto his head as much for support as anything else. He held my hips still as he licked me slowly up and down along my wet swollen lady bits and made appreciative "mmm" noises, like he was tasting something wonderful. I started panting as I watched him tongue me and I knew that I would never be able to watch him eat anything ever again without getting turned on. When he actually started sucking on my clit my legs began to shake and I didn't think I could remain on my feet much longer.

"Please," I gasped.

"Please what, baby?" he mumbled and his breath blowing against me made me even more desperate. I couldn't think straight and I searched for something, anything …

"Please, I need some lovin' and I need it bad." It was all I could think of! He stopped in mid-lick.

"Okay, baby, how about if we don't say anything that would bring any of your clients to mind during our intimate moments?" he suggested, pausing and looking up at me.

"Okay." I panted. "Uh. Please … fuck me?" After all, it worked that time in the kitchen. And it was still a winner! He stood up quickly, fixed my skirt, grabbed my hand and pulled me with him to the bedroom where he untied my dress, slipped it off and threw it on a chair. I stood there naked except for my high heels and he took a step back to take in the sight, letting his eyes travel up and down my body slowly.

"I really like that look on you," he said thickly. "Lie down on the bed but leave the shoes on." I was good with that plan. I hit the bed so fast I almost bounced back off. He went over to his closet and came back with a couple of silk scarves. "Purchased just for you, Gabrielle," he said with a smile that liquefied me. And with that Braden tied my hands to his bedposts and I swear the only thing keeping me conscious at that point was the ache between my legs. Then he left the room. Where in the hell was he going?

"While you're out there, give Bruno a bunch of treats to keep him busy! He might find this confusing!" I called out. Silence. "Braden? Honey? You're not leaving, are you?" He came back in with a bottle of white wine and a sexy smile.

"What do *you* think?" he asked with laughter in his voice. He stopped just to look at me, laying there naked and panting in nine hundred dollar shoes and tied to a bed with Hermes scarves. We were kinky but we were stylish.

"I think that it's an odd moment for a toast." He opened the bottle, knelt down beside me, and gently dripped a little wine onto one of my nipples, which got even harder when I discovered the wine was properly chilled. Then he leaned down and began licking and sucking it off. The combination of the cold wine and his hot mouth launched me into orbit and I moaned and bucked my hips like I was doing a horizontal Twerk. My nerves were lit up. My body was on fire and I knew that I was soaking wet and ready to rumble. He did the same thing on the other side and I went half out of my mind. Okay, all the way out of my mind. I was already half out of my mind.

"Oh ga!" I panted. He dripped wine into my bellybutton and began to suck it out as my volume continued to rise and my coherence continued to dissolve. I sounded like I was speaking in Klingon at that point. Make that screaming in Klingon.

"You know I think this is a good year," he said, checking out the label while I tried to collect my scrambled thoughts. I *needed* him to understand me. And so. I forced. Myself. To enunciate. Clearly.

"Please! Fuck! Me!" I shouted with perfect elocution in the way that a lot of people speak to foreigners and half-deaf octogenarians.

He gave me a naughty smile and looked into my eyes as he peeled off his clothes.

"Since you asked so nicely," he said seductively. When he finally pulled off his boxers I made a very happy sound. He knelt on the bed between my legs, positioned his cock at my entrance and hooked my knees over his arms.

"Wait," I gasped. He looked up at me expectantly. "When it's time, pull out." I looked down at my boobs and then back up at him. Understanding dawned and his breath hitched a little. We had found another winner for the boob man! He nodded, pushed his hips forward and sank into me slowly and deeply, expelling a ragged breath.

"Ah!" He groaned. "There's my happy place."

Feeling him take me almost gave me an instantaneous orgasm and I felt my muscles clenching involuntarily.

"Oh yeah!" he bit out. "I love it when you grab me like that!" He pulled back and thrust into me deeply again and again, picking up his pace as I made happy sex noises to express my joy at having him inside me. "Oh, Gabrielle! You look *so* sexy!" Soon we were going hard with him pounding into me and me bucking my hips back against him, my hands still secured to the bedpost. I could hear our bodies slapping together and feel the slickness of our sweat. I watched as he slid into me over and over and I even smelled sex, so this was truly an extravaganza for the senses. There was something else that I wanted too, though.

"Tell me how good it feels," I cried out. I loved it when he talked dirty to me.

"So good," he groaned. "So hot. So tight," he ground out and I realized that he was having difficulty speaking at the moment too. That just turned me on more and I bucked my hips even harder. We were both completely covered in sweat now, and sliding against each other. I felt my orgasm beginning to build and I wanted it so badly.

"Braden!" I whimpered. He was breathing hard and groaning loudly, flushed, gleaming and beautiful with his wet hair plastered to his forehead, his eyes glazed over with ecstasy. "Don't stop! So close!" I pleaded. I could see that he was barely holding on, but I knew that I was almost ready too.

"Let go, baby." He gasped and adjusted his angle so he was rubbing against my clit more directly. Okay, that was the spot!

"Braden!" I screamed as I rapidly scaled Mt. Orgasm. I was fairly sure the folks in the lobby knew his name by now. I moaned loudly and went writhing and flailing over the edge, my inner muscles clenching and unclenching around him, grabbing his cock tightly in waves. My body shuddered hard and relief flooded over me like a warm bath. My muscles finally stopped pulsing and I lay there dazed as Braden kept thrusting into me.

"Going to come," he said hoarsely and pulled out. Kneeling over me, he stroked himself rapidly for a few seconds, his eyes fixed on my rising and falling breasts and then with a rapturous look he came hard. He just stared for a couple of minutes. I honestly think he was speechless. Finally, he said something.

"I've never seen anything so hot in my entire life." With that he collapsed next to me for a minute before he pulled himself up and untied my hands. He went into the bathroom and came back with a warm damp towel and then tenderly washed me off. He returned to bed and cuddled me into his arms, stroking my hair for a while. Eventually, we sat up and drank some more of the wine straight from the bottle and shared some very loving but sort of sloppy wine kisses. I was about to take off my shoes when he stopped me.

"Leave them on," he said, giving me that blue flame look I recognized. I looked down at his lap and found a happy surprise. My Energizer Bunny was still going.

I left the shoes on. I had them on when he had me bent over with my hands flat against the wall as he held onto my hips and pounded into me fast and hard from behind. I still had them on later when he had me laying on my back on the dining room table, with my ankles on his shoulders, slowly rolling his hips while he groaned and told me how he wanted to bury himself inside me forever. In fact, it wasn't until after he had me against the wall with my leg wrapped tightly around him, thrusting into me until we both came one last time that I finally took them off. I have to say, I definitely got a lot of wear out of those shoes.

$\backsim$ CHAPTER TEN $\backsim$

The next morning after showering and getting ready for our trip to his parents' house I quickly called my parents to check in and say "hi". My father grilled me for a while to make sure that I was remembering to triple lock my doors and carry a rape whistle, and that I knew what to do in case of a terrorist attack. And then my mother got on the phone and talked about how twenty-six was a great age to get married and reminded me that she and my dad loved Braden and would be thrilled to have grandchildren someday. I was going to need to tell them about our plans soon so that my father could stop worrying and my mother could stop hinting.

Finally, I got them off of the phone and we left. Mark and Adam were driving together and Jess and Lily were getting a ride with Cam so we just packed our bags and our Chihuahua, (and his bag), and headed for Bryn Mawr on the Philadelphia main line where the Pierces had a gorgeous Georgian home with a large in ground swimming pool and a Jacuzzi that I was looking forward to visiting with Braden alone later.

We got there at about eleven, greeted Drew and unpacked our stuff into Braden's room while Drew took Bruno on a tour of the house, showed him where his food and water were, and introduced him to Theresa, the live-in housekeeper and cook, who he reportedly took to immediately. The Pierce's property was enclosed with a large fence which meant that Bruno could run free outside. He was in doggy heaven.

Adam and Mark arrived half an hour later and Cam, Jess, and Lily pulled in at noon. Drew showed everyone to guest rooms and while they got settled in Braden went down to ask Theresa about lunch. She put a deli buffet spread out on the patio overlooking the pool and Jacuzzi and we all met outside to eat and relax. It was a gorgeous day with not a cloud in the sky. After spending a week under florescent lights and in subarctic air conditioning, the warm sun felt wonderful on my skin. We all got our food and made ourselves comfortable around the tables we had pushed together. Now that our trip to Club 51 was history we were able to laugh about it.

"I almost lost it when that barmaid came back with our drinks and Braden dove under the table," Cam said, sitting down across from Jess and biting into a ginormous sandwich.

"I was picking up a coaster!" Braden said defensively. "And avoiding any interaction that might have made Gabrielle unhappy." He brought over a pitcher of fresh lemonade for us to share and settled down in a chair next to me.

"You were down there so long I thought you were involved in an interaction that would have made her *very* happy," Adam joked. I felt myself blush thinking about how happy he made me down on his knees later that night.

"There's an idea for one of your novels," I said to Lily. "The hero disappears under the table at a club to hide from somebody and does naughty things to the heroine while he's down there."

"That doesn't sound like a scene from a legal thriller," Braden said suspiciously.

"Yeah, what was that Derek was saying last night? That he likes your books because women find them stimulating?" Drew asked Lily. "I can't see the chicks he hangs out with being John Grisham fans." He gave her an amused but intrigued smile.

"She also writes romance novels, erotic ones," I explained, snapping out the lustful fantasies I had just been having about Braden doing naughty things to me secretly.

"You're kidding!" Adam said, looking like he didn't believe it.

"Her books are very popular!" Jess said. "She's developing quite a following."

"*Romance novels*? Yeah, probably with sad lonely women who want to dream about Fabio sweeping them off their feet," Adam joked.

"Fabio? What decade are you living in?" I asked scornfully. "Lily's books are seriously hot. Girlfriend here writes mommy porn." I fanned myself as a visual aid.

"They're not *that* steamy," Lily said dismissively, laughing and rolling her eyes.

"Are you kidding? You need potholders to read them." Jess laughed. I noticed that Cam was giving Jess some very interested looks. He seemed to like her literary side and I had a feeling that he might want to form a little book club of two.

"Derek likes them," I added, giving Lily a significant look. "That should tell you something."

"That scene in the last one with that you know …" Jess began, and she actually blushed. Cam was starting to look a little flushed himself. I was pretty sure that Lily had a future fan in him, as long as he could read her books with Jess.

"I know exactly which one you mean!" I laughed. "I never really thought that was sexy until I read that scene! Now, I might want to try that myself."

"Wait! Try what?" Braden asked, suddenly looking extremely interested. "Maybe I need to check this out," he said, taking out his phone. Actually, she might have a whole fan club!

"You won't find them online under my real name. I write those books under a pen name. One that my friends won't disclose!" Lily said, giving Jess and I a threatening look.

"Oh come on!" Cam said with a laugh. "You girls can't say all that stuff and then tell us we can't read it ourselves!"

"Yeah!" Braden agreed. "That's not fair."

"How hot could they really be?" Adam scoffed, rolling his eyes. "How do you research your naughty books, Scheherazade?" he asked with a sarcastic smile.

"Why?" she asked, glaring at him.

"Just curious. After all, you write books about lawyers even though you've never practiced law. I assume that you haven't done all of these sexy things you supposedly write about either. How do you even know you're getting it right then?" he asked, holding her gaze.

"Why are you so fascinated?" I asked.

"Maybe he wants to help her with her research," Jess teased.

"At least then her knowledge would be authentic," he said in a slightly seductive tone, never taking his eyes off of Lily. Jess and I shared a surprised look and I noticed that Mark and Braden did too. Was he teasing her or was he actually flirting? I had a feeling he might not know himself.

"What makes you think it's not authentic now?" she asked, fixing him with a steady gaze. That stopped him. The two of them shared a look that was seriously charged and he looked away first! Wow. If they ever got together I had a feeling it would be explosive. Jess and Cam broke the tension when they started joking around about all of our attempts to thwart Derek.

"I loved it when Drew and Mark got all defensive and started trying to be as heterosexual as possible," Jess said with a laugh.

"You know it's funny, but I don't recall ever discussing condoms with my male friends," Cam joked and Drew sunk down in his chair and covered his eyes.

"Yeah, well I *didn't* love it when I looked over at Derek when we were dancing and he thought I was checking him out! I wanted to run and hide," I said, feeling mortified.

"What in the Hell was that dance you were doing with him, Gabrielle?!" Jess asked, shaking her head in disbelief.

"It wasn't a dance!" I said emphatically. "I slipped and my foot flew out from under me and shot into the air. I lost my balance and fell backward."

"The next time you go out you might want to wear, uh, more layers," Lily said tactfully.

"That high kick didn't leave a whole lot to the imagination," Jess added.

"Oh my God," Braden said, burying his face in his hands.

"Oh shit," Drew said with a laugh and winced. Adam and Mark completely lost it. To his credit, Cameron managed to contain himself, although I could see that it was difficult.

"Thanks for sharing, girls," I said in a deadly tone of voice, feeling my face turn Harvard crimson and accidentally stabbing my hand with a fork. Luckily, it didn't break the skin.

"Braden didn't love seeing crazy stalker girl again," Adam noted, wiping tears from his eyes. "I wouldn't be surprised if she were the one who was following you."

"No, the guy following me didn't have boobs like watermelons," I pointed out.

"Are you really sure there's somebody following you?" Mark asked. "I mean, you saw somebody outside in a crowd at night who may have been looking at you and you saw somebody for a couple of seconds on a busy sidewalk. Other than that it's just weird feelings you've been having. And there's a lot of power behind suggestion when it comes to this stuff, as we all know."

"I'm not sure," I admitted with a sigh. "Maybe Felicity did leave the notes for whatever reason and when I said someone was following me for real it just freaked her out. Maybe this really is nothing."

"Well, she might be easy to freak out right now," Jess said. "She's probably got a lot on her mind lately with her mom being busted for running sex parties and all."

"Oh, I heard something about that," Adam offered. "Looks like all three of your friends are going to get off, no pun intended, with a slap on the wrist. Probation deals and misdemeanor charges all around, even for the Main Line Madame."

"I knew it," Braden said cynically. "In another year nobody will even remember it."

"I would think that Cole's political career might be somewhat shortened though," I said.

"He's got business investments on the side. I'm sure he'll be able to survive," Cam put in. "In fact, they all do, I think. I heard them discussing it at the fundraiser before Marla got expelled."

"If she had business investments why was she a call girl?" I asked.

"Who knows?" Braden said scathingly. "Probably because she can never have enough money. If Cole also had an inheritance, she would probably be after him."

◌ CHAPTER ELEVEN ◌

After lunch we all headed toward our rooms to get ready to hang out by the swimming pool. Braden looked yummy in his swimsuit. More importantly, though, he looked relaxed and content. We didn't make it downstairs immediately.

"Braden, you're looking mighty happy lately," Mark said knowingly when we eventually arrived down at the pool.

"I am happy," he said, giving me a warm look and lightly brushing a thumb over my lips. In fact, my lips had just made him very happy.

I grabbed his hand and kissed it and then went off to join Lily who was enjoying the water. She and I hung out together and chatted and eventually Drew came in and joined us. He spent some time joking around with us for a little while and then went off to swim a couple of laps. I glanced up at Braden and smiled.

He and Adam were involved in some kind of animated discussion. The two of them really did make a nice contrast aesthetically. Braden was all blonde beach boy and Adam was all tall dark and handsome. Not that I was looking, but he was built pretty nicely too. He was about six two himself and he obviously worked out. I wouldn't blame Lily for being attracted to him, and something told me that deep down she was.

"So what was that with Adam earlier?" I asked her quietly, returning my attention to her.

"What was what?" she asked innocently.

"Him saying that if he helped you research, your books would be authentic? That almost sounded like an offer." She looked away and turned a little red.

"It sounded like his usual brand of arrogance to me," she said dismissively. She wasn't going to admit it. Either that or she didn't realize that the feeling was probably mutual.

"Where does all this animosity between you two come from anyway? I know that you grew up together but did he pull your braids or steal your bike or something?"

"No!" She laughed. "Although he did lock me in the boys' bathroom once. He just used to tease me, along with a bunch of other girls. And then we all got older and they eventually started giggling and flirting when he did it. I, on the other hand, eventually started giving it right back to him. He just doesn't know what to do with a woman who doesn't worship the ground he walks on."

"Well, I could see how that might be disconcerting for him." Privately I thought that it could also be rather intriguing for him which may have been *why* it was disconcerting.

"There was one incident that really seemed to escalate things. I accidentally walked in on him making out with, and feeling up, Shari Edelstein at his Bar Mitzvah."

"Who?"

"Shari was the popular girl who all the guys wanted. When I walked in and caught them together in the stairwell, she slapped him. Apparently, he recovered. It didn't stop him from being lowered from the ceiling in the Las Vegas style review he put on at the party."

"Oh my God!" I laughed. "You're kidding me, right?"

"He sang 'I Did It My Way.' Complete with showgirls!"

"You know, I could see Adam doing that."

I looked around more carefully at the others. Mark, Cam and Jess seemed to be engrossed in some funny conversation while giving Bruno lots of love and tossing his ball to him. Braden was still talking to Adam while occasionally watching me with what looked like a combination of amusement, affection, and lust. Adam, in turn, frequently stole glances at Lily, who was looking very good in her hot pink bikini. *Wait – did she say showgirls?*

Eventually the rest of them decided to join us in the pool and Drew and Braden set up a net so that we could play water volleyball. Let's just say none of us is ready for serious water volleyball competition. It quickly became a contact sport, the way we played it.

At one point I smacked into Drew who caught me in his arms and then asked me if it was good for me, earning him a glare from Braden. Jess jumped up to hit the ball and wound up on top of Cameron who was also going for it. It was rather humorous watching them try to extricate their slippery limbs from each other while laughing their asses off. I had a feeling that Cameron would be going for something else very soon. He seemed to be enjoying the extrication process immensely.

Then Lily jumped back quickly and crashed into Adam who instinctively put his arms around her to catch her, and after a tense moment they retreated to opposite sides of the pool like oil and water. Yeah, that one was just a matter of time too. I hoped that they both survived. I had a feeling that it would soon just be Mark and Drew, with some scantily clad club girls, the Phillies, a case of Bud and a box of Trojans.

Later we sat and dried out in lounge chairs, listening to music while Braden and Drew brought out cold beer for everyone. The male majority voted for classic rock and so we were listening to the Rolling Stones. Braden had put out a soft towel especially for Bruno next to his water bowl and he was blissfully napping in the shade. This was good, very good. No crazy shoplifters or elderly potheads or naked drunk drivers, just my good friends, my beautiful Braden and my dog.

"So, Lily, why won't you tell us your pen name?" Mark asked with a cute smile.

"Because I don't think you're true fans of the genre," she answered.

"Fans of romance novels or fans of real erotica?" Adam asked, giving her an intense look that seemed to hit her like a wave of heat.

"She's not talking about porn, Adam," Jess said, rolling her eyes.

"Did I say porn? I was just asking her if she was referring to novels by Nora Roberts or novels by Nabokov." He took a swig of his beer. He could even manage to look cocky sitting in a lounge chair. He was like the King of Swagger.

"Adam's a big Nora Roberts fan," Mark deadpanned which made Braden and Cam laugh out loud. Adam glared at them malevolently.

"She's obviously embarrassed by her own writing. Must be some great works of literature that she's produced," Adam said.

With that Lily turned to him with her eyes blazing. "You think I'm embarrassed just because I have a pen name? Has it ever occurred to you that a single woman living alone who happens to write erotic books may want to protect her privacy? Plenty of novelists much greater than me have had pen names. In fact, V. Sirin was the pen name of …."

"Vladimir Nabokov," Adam finished for her. "I'm not illiterate, you know. In fact, I majored in English, for your information." He was still looking at Lily as he got up and headed for the house. "I'm going to take a nap before dinner," he added and shot her a backward glance that I could have *sworn* held an invitation. I saw her let out a deep breath, put her head back and close her eyes.

"Is there something going on between you and Adam?" Drew asked her suggestively.

"Yeah, an epic battle," she answered. She went in herself a few minutes later, though, and I wondered if she might be taking him up on that invitation.

Eventually the rest of us decided to go in to shower and get out of the sun. When I went up to our room, for a second I thought I heard quiet voices around the corner, but whoever it was stopped talking when I made it to the top of the stairs. Braden had gone to check with Theresa and he let everyone know that dinner would be at six. It was four at that point so we settled in to wash off and change our clothes.

"I'm looking forward to hearing all of the different kinds of music tonight," I said, laying down on the bed and stretching out to pet

Bruno who was lying on his back asking for a belly rub again. So far Bruno was enjoying this weekend immensely.

"Yeah, there are a couple of performers in particular I'd like to check out," Braden said, joining me. "There's a violinist I want to see playing later and there's a blues group playing that you would probably like."

"Sounds good." I smiled. Bruno flipped back over and went to nuzzle Braden's hand. I didn't blame him. Braden had talented hands. I wondered if that would work for me.

"Then we'll come home and check out the Jacuzzi when all of them turn in."

"Mmm." I sighed. "That sounds *very* good." We were lying on our sides with our heads propped on one hand facing each other and he looked deeply into my eyes.

"Don't worry about anything, Gabrielle. It'll be okay."

"I won't worry if you'll stop worrying about me so much at work."

"I've been trying to think of a plan for us like you said. The thought of you being locked in a cell with a killer scares the hell out of me. I just wish you didn't have to do that."

"But it's part of my job and not all of my clients are killers or naked drunk drivers, Braden. I help homeless people who get busted for trying to keep warm. I help poor single mothers busted for stealing diapers. That means something to me. I was so lucky to be born into a happy and wealthy family. This way I feel like I'm giving something back in a very real way."

"I feel the same way when I help an elderly person who got ripped off in some scam or some guy who got beaten up just for trying to walk to work in a bad neighborhood. That's one of the reasons I fell in love with you so quickly. Because I saw that inside you and I recognized it."

"So, we both want to make a difference. What else can we do besides what we're doing?"

"Like I said, I've been giving it some thought. We both have money of our own and together we have a lot of money. Maybe we should start our own non-profit and you and I could run it. We could work together. We could help people who really needed us to defend them but we could choose the cases we thought were most important and that we wanted to handle. We wouldn't represent anyone violent."

"That's not a bad idea! You would be willing to do defense work?"

"If it were a just cause – like a case where we thought an innocent person was being prosecuted. Or even if maybe it were just a poor homeless person busted for trying to keep warm – like your friend Stan."

"You knew that he had been one of my clients?"

"Yeah, I recognized him. And I also recognized the waitress at the kabob place too. I'm glad to see she's got a job now. I hope her baby's okay."

"Yeah, he's doing really well. He's getting big. And Stan has a regular gig at The Blue Moon too now, you know. He's a hit," I said and my voice caught.

"I love you so much, Gabrielle," he said and his voice was filled with emotion too.

"I love you too, Braden and I think this might be the answer we've been looking for." I yawned. The swimming and the sun and alcohol, not to mention all the sex we had the night before, had tired us out and we fell asleep like that, content in the knowledge that we would figure it out together.

Sometime later there was a knock on the door that woke us up and I heard a familiar voice call out to tell us that it was almost time for dinner. I sat up and jumped out of bed.

"Hi, Beth! I thought you weren't coming home until Sunday!" I said throwing the door open to Braden's beautiful blonde younger sister who gave me a big hug.

"I came home early because I want to spend time with you guys and meet your friends." Braden got up and came over to hug his sister too. The Pierces were huggers. Bruno yipped and jumped down to greet her and she immediately fawned all over him which, of course, made her very popular, very quickly, with Bruno.

"Have you met them yet?" I asked.

"Well, I already knew Mark and Adam," she said, smiling up at me from where she was crouched lavishing Bruno with affection, "but I've met Jess and Lily too now and I love them."

We caught up with her for a few minutes and then we all went downstairs to join the others for dinner. Theresa had made some terrific paella and we had a lively meal trading stories and filling Beth in on everything that had been happening. She was intrigued to find out that Lily was an author and it turned out that she too was a fan of spicy romance novels. She begged Lily to tell her what her pen name was and when Lily whispered it in her ear, Beth got all excited.

"Oh wow! You're kidding, right? I can't believe you're sitting right here at my parents' dining room table." I saw Adam roll his eyes, but mercifully, he didn't comment. The tension between them seemed to be escalating. No way was that all based on bad bar Mitzvah memories.

"Thank you but I'm no great novelist," Lily said and glanced over at Adam like she was expecting him to agree. "Although I would love to become a great mystery or thriller writer someday."

"Well I like the hot romance novels! I'm learning all kinds of new things!" Beth said with a laugh. She blushed a little which made her look even prettier.

"I don't want to hear this!" Braden cut in, looking distinctly uncomfortable.

"Me neither!" Drew agreed looking equally uncomfortable, which I found kind of ironic considering how comfortable he had been teasing Braden and me about our sex life.

"I do," Mark said with a flirty smile which earned him deadly looks from both Braden and Drew and a laugh from Adam. Beth glanced up at him and blushed even deeper.

"I have to ask, how do you come up with these ideas? I mean that scene in the last one with the ..." Beth went on. Apparently we had *all* read *that* scene.

"Not listening!" Braden cut in urgently.

"Yeah, come on, *Beth!*" Drew said. "It's one thing to make fun of your brother and his girlfriend for knocking down a wall but hearing your *sister* talk about sex is just wrong."

"I was just talking about her *books*! It's not like I was going to give you play by play from my last date," Beth said, rolling her eyes. "I'll talk to you later," she said conspiratorially to Lily. So, this is what it was like to have siblings.

After dinner we headed out to the festival, leaving Bruno at home with Theresa to guard the house. We arrived at about seven and I saw that the whole center of town was shut down for the event. After parking we walked around for a while. The summer air was warm and fragrant with the smells of fried foods and lemonade. There were tents and pavilions set up in various locations where musical groups of many varieties performed. We went from location to location listening to musical styles ranging from Australian Aboriginal to Zydeco with performers playing everything in between, including Bavarian guys in lederhosen playing huge horns, a barbershop quartet and a doo-wop group. As I walked along, though, after a while, I got that now familiar feeling. The back of my neck started to prickle and the hair on my arms stood up. It just felt like somebody was watching me and I casually looked behind us several times.

"What's the matter?" Braden asked after the third time I did it. I guess I wasn't that casual.

"Nothing. Just looking around," I answered with a smile, not wanting to worry him. After all, it was probably just my imagination. Like Mark said, the power of suggestion was very strong and now it was almost like I expected to get that feeling.

We went to see the blues act that he had mentioned and they were quite good but still not like my friend Stan, who was the real deal. While we sat watching the group play the feeling of being watched got stronger. I glanced around again and out of the corner of my eye I thought I saw Evan, the guy I had met the other night. He was talking to another man whose back was to me, but he seemed to be occasionally glancing over his shoulder in our direction. Still, he wasn't staring directly at us and it wasn't odd to see him here since he grew up in this area. I was losing it. I needed to get a grip.

I settled back in to try to enjoy the music but the feeling didn't go away. I looked off to my left and something else caught my eye, a figure standing off in the distance in a baseball cap whose attention seemed to be focused right on us. I waited a couple of minutes and then checked again. He was still staring in our direction. I wanted to go see who it was who was so interested in what we were doing but I wasn't about to get up and wander off on my own again.

"Braden," I whispered in his ear. "Don't look but there's someone over to the left in a baseball cap and I think that he's watching us. I'm not positive but I think it's the guy I saw before."

"Are you sure he's not watching the band?"

"I'm pretty sure it's us."

"I'll ask Adam and Mark to go check it out." He leaned over to grab Adam's attention and whispered something to him. Then Adam whispered something to Mark, they got up and walked off to the right. I tried not to look, even though I was very curious. The band finished up the last song a few minutes later and we stood up to get ready to go. There was no sign of Adam and Mark and when I turned toward where the figure had been standing I saw that he was gone too. We decided to walk in that direction to try to find our friends. Not long after, we saw them walking around searching the crowd.

"What's going on?" Braden asked as we approached them.

"You were right. Somebody was watching you. At least it seemed like it," Mark answered.

"We didn't get a good look at his face. He had a hat pulled down pretty low and never looked directly at us," Adam said. "He was a white guy, though, and he seemed like maybe he was in his twenties or thirties, average height, average weight, average."

"We came up behind him and asked him what he was looking at and he turned part-way around and mumbled something about 'the band' but he was looking at where we were sitting," Mark added. "He started walking off really fast. We tried to stay with him but we lost him in the crowd."

"Well, there's nothing we can do about it right now," Braden said. "I'll tell the police about it on Monday and I'll pass along what Felicity said, too, for what it's worth." I saw him glance at his watch.

"That reggae band is probably still playing," Adam spoke up. "I think we should go check it out. Wasn't there a violinist you wanted to see though, Braden?"

"Yeah, there was. Should we meet up at the theater afterward?"

"Sounds good," Mark said. Braden took my hand to lead me off in the other direction.

We walked for about five minutes until we reached a small wooden pavilion off to a side. It was strung with lights that were twinkling in the rapidly darkening night. A lone violinist stood at one end playing Beethoven's Moonlight Sonata while two couples danced to the sweet romantic music. We stood listening until the song ended and then he squeezed my hand and asked me if I would dance the next one with him. We went up the stairs as the other two couples descended. It was getting late and I knew this would likely be the last song.

Braden took me into his arms gently and smiled down at me as the violinist began to play Clair de Lune and we started to dance. Feeling him lead me around the floor to the strains of the beautiful song while lights twinkled around us and the moon shone overhead seemed like a moment that couldn't possibly be more romantic. I knew that I would remember this dance for the rest of my life. At that moment no anonymous letter writer, conspiracy nut, kinky politician, or naked drunk driver mattered. It was like Braden and that violinist and I were alone in the universe. As the last few notes faded we slowly stopped dancing. I was about to turn to leave when Braden got down on one knee. Oh my God! I would *definitely* remember this dance for the rest of my life! I held my breath as I looked down into his eyes.

"Gabrielle, will you marry me?" he asked softly.

"Yes, I will," I answered with tears in my eyes. And with that he slid the most beautiful diamond ring I had ever seen on to my finger. It was a square-cut center stone on a band embedded with smaller diamonds that sparkled in the moonlight like the city lights that I loved.

∽ Chapter Twelve ∽

AUGUST

IN THE COURT OF COMMON PLEAS OF PHILADELPHIA COUNTY, PENNSYLVANIA

<u>Commonwealth v. Petrillo</u>

"So Ms. Robbins, you're saying that Mr. Petrillo is your ex-boyfriend?" Adam asked the buxom redhead on the stand. I was kind of surprised. I thought he would be acting like Mr. Suave with this chick but he actually seemed kind of annoyed with her.

"Yeah, he's my ex and he's harassing me." She shot an angry glance at my client, who flinched and hung his head. I had a feeling that this was a lovers' spat turned into criminal case, which was probably why Adam seemed so unmotivated to impress Big Red up there.

"What do you mean by that?" Adam asked, sounding like he could care less.

"I mean whenever I see him out he says nasty things to me. He calls me names."

"What kind of names does he call you?"

"Nasty ones." She pouted and shot another unfriendly look at my client. I was waiting for her to stick her tongue out at him. What grade was she in?

"What *kind* of nasty ones?" Adam asked, actually starting to sound irritated.

"He called me a shallow b-i-t-c-h!" She sneered at my client like she thought he was lower than a piece of dirt. I couldn't imagine why anyone would call her a nasty name. She was a real sweetie pie. Who in the hell was she spelling for, anyway? The stenographer?

"He called you a bitch?" Adam asked just a little too sarcastically, proving that he could, in fact, spell. I actually winced. Ms. Robbins obviously didn't pick up on the fact that he wasn't really being sympathetic, though. She was a smart one too!

"Yeah! Can you believe that! And he's one to criticize anybody! He's got a beer gut!" I had to admit that I didn't really see the connection between having a beer gut and being a bitch, or the relevance for that matter, but no way was I going to object and cut *this* off! I expected Adam to get her quieted down but instead he egged her on!

"And he's calling *you* names?" What the fuck was he doing?! Was he nuts? I looked up at Judge Channing, who was starting to give Adam some very angry looks. Then the judge gave me angry looks for not objecting. I just smiled.

"I know! Seriously! You know, he doesn't have a decent job either. He's a stock boy at a supermarket! And he doesn't even have a car! I don't know why I wasted my time with him!"

"She's right!" My client yelled out. "I am a loser!" Oh shit! I knew that it was going too well. I started trying to get him to shut up, but of course, he wasn't going to listen. "I never deserved her and since she left me I've been a broken man!"

"Well, Goddamn, Tony!" Ms. Robbins responded. "If you would just spend less money on pizza and beer you could save up to buy *some* kind of vehicle!"

"I would go without food if it meant you would give me another chance, Vera!"

"Be a man, for crying out loud!" She appeared to be thinking about it, though. The rest of us all just kind of hung out, since it didn't seem like we were needed for anything.

"I'm begging you, Vera!" My client actually dove out of his chair and kneeled down on the floor. I put my head down on the defense table and banged it a few times. Suddenly, some guy in the crowd yelled out:

"Take him back, Vera! The man's a mess!"

"Why does he want her back? She really is a b-i-t-c-h!" A female voice from among the spectators chimed in.

"Order! I want order in this courtroom!" Judge Channing yelled, banging his gavel, looking apoplectic. "This is a court of law, not daytime television! Mr. Roth, Ms. Ginsberg, I suggest that you work this case out between you and get it out of my courtroom!"

You know, I would just like to point out for the record that I didn't bring this case; I didn't put that woman on the witness stand, and I didn't tell my client to act like an asshole. Yet, for some reason, I was being yelled at. Sometimes I just loved my job. Judge Channing basically kicked us out of the courtroom at that point so I grabbed my stuff and met Adam outside where he was waiting with Braden. Jess had already gone back to the office. She would be so sorry that she missed this very special episode of Dr. Phil.

"So, tell me, Adam," I said with a smile, "when you were at law school dreaming about bringing justice to those who had been wronged, did *you* imagine Vera?"

"Stick around, Braden, you might be needed to defend your fiancée's life," he said in a deadly voice. He actually looked rather homicidal at the moment, if I must say so myself.

"What? You can dish it out but you can't take it? Well, don't blame me for this bullshit case, counselor. So is Vera going to take Tony back or not?" I asked impatiently.

"Who the fuck knows?" Adam bit out. "Who the fuck cares? I'm withdrawing the charges." He sounded *really* angry. In fact, I didn't think I had ever seen him this angry. He had been really cranky in general lately though.

"All right then. Thank you," I said, trying to placate him a little. I wondered if something was up with him. I said goodbye to Braden and headed out.

It was nearly Labor Day, and as I made my way back to my office, I thought about all that had happened in the month and a half since Braden had officially proposed. Even though we still had two different apartments we spent every night together. We would pick up Bruno, grab some take-out and go home to relax and have dinner. We would talk, play with our dog, watch PBS and usually make love. It was very domestic and very nice. As we predicted, our parents were thrilled about our engagement but did recommend we not rush the wedding. That was fine by us. We hadn't even really discussed a date. Actually, we really hadn't discussed any details. We were just happy being together at the moment.

The only bump in the road was the fact that we still sometimes felt like somebody was following us. Braden had felt it too a few times, so it wasn't just me. We did tell the police about our mysterious shadow but since the information was so tenuous there really wasn't much they could do. So every now and then my neck felt prickly and it just felt like someone was watching. A couple of times I even thought that I had seen an actual shadow around a corner that made me feel suspicious but at least there had been no more notes or paper products on our doorstep and nobody seemed particularly worried that our parents had met and gotten along fabulously.

When I got back to the office, Jess was still out but Cameron was there. I sensed immediately that he wanted to talk about something. He looked up like he had been waiting for me to come back. I tossed my briefcase on the floor and, thankfully, it didn't crash through to the floor below despite the fact that it weighed three tons.

"So, what's up, Cam?" I asked, spinning my desk chair to face him, opening up the bottom drawer of my desk and putting my feet up. I folded my hands on my lap and tilted my head to the side. I was in my "I'm listening" pose.

"I'm going to be going back to my firm," he answered, turning toward me. "The thing is, that I like criminal law so my dad is giving me the opportunity to coordinate their pro bono program if I want to. I would take our associates and teach them how to do preliminary hearings and I would schedule them and supervise them."

"That sounds great! You'll get to do something you like and stay with your firm. I know that your great-grandfather was a founding partner and everything."

"Yeah, even though it's a two hundred lawyer firm it's still pretty much the family business. Anyway, since I'll probably be leaving soon, I was thinking, I might ask Jessica to have a drink with me after work if she's free."

"She's free!" I sat up so quickly that I went flying out of the chair but because one heel caught on the drawer, I wound up in a heap on the floor. I got up quickly and straightened my skirt, glaring at my chair like it had been a mechanical malfunction.

"Are you okay?" he asked, rising to see if I needed help.

"Oh, yeah, I'm good. Uh, what I meant was that she's probably free. If she's not, you, know, busy." Brilliant! I was smiling and nodding like a bobble-head doll.

"Okay! Great!" He smiled and turned back to his work, probably thanking the good Lord that Braden had been the lucky guy to snag me. Why was I so freaking awkward? Later that day Jess stopped me in the hall.

"Cameron asked me if I would go out for a drink after work with him," she said in a quiet voice, sounding very excited. I so wanted to make a girlie SQUEE noise but I managed to control myself. I looked around quickly to make sure that we weren't being overheard. Although, I'm not really sure why.

"Okay, I'm going to need a debriefing. Braden and I will stay at our apartment tonight instead of at his. You can tell me about it then."

"I can't tell you with Braden there! It's a girl talk thing!" she objected, looking up and down the hallway nervously, toward our office.

"I'll make him go in the bedroom and wait for me."

"You're going to lock your fiancé away in your bedroom?" she asked giving me a look somewhere between amused and incredulous.

"I'll crack a window and make sure he has food and water. Besides, I've got a TV in there and Bruno will keep him company."

"Okay. We're going to O'Malley's. I'm not sure when I'll be home but it probably won't be late. I'm not getting my hopes up though. We've gone out before and nothing has happened."

"I have a feeling this is different. He mentioned going back to his firm so he may realize that it's time to act."

"I'll meet you in the ladies' room at five minutes to six so you can reassure me that I don't look haggardly."

"I'll be there!" We went our separate ways and I tried to look casual. Although nobody was actually in the hallway so it probably didn't matter.

∽ CHAPTER THIRTEEN ∾

I met Jess in the ladies' room at the designated time and did a stall check to make sure we were alone. I made sure to open every door in case anyone was standing on the toilet. You never know. People are weird. I was getting much better at this covert stuff.

"You look great," I told her as soon as I was done. "Not in the least bit haggardly."

"It's just drinks. So I'm not going to worry about the fact that I haven't shaved my legs in two days and I'm wearing underwear that comes up to my chin."

"There'll be alcohol involved. It's going to be fine. Tell me everything when you get home. If you get home."

"I'll get home. We have court tomorrow!"

"Okay, remember what you told me."

"Never trust a guy who brings a roll of quarters on a date?"

"No! It's okay to want him to bang you until you can't walk straight."

"I never told you that." She looked confused.

"Oh, I must have imagined it. Anyway, good luck!" I patted her on the back. She gave me a slightly baffled look, shook her head and left to go back to our office. We heard Cam and Braden talking as we got closer and we gave each other a silent nod. It was Go Time. We walked into that office like we were walking the catwalk in Paris. At least Jess did. I accidently slammed my shoulder in the doorframe but I recovered quickly.

"Hey gorgeous," Braden said, making me feel all fluttery as usual. "Are you okay?" He winced.

"I'm good! No worries! Hey Jess, look there's a sexy guy sitting in my chair." I was *so* glad that he hadn't seen the incident with the chair earlier.

"Hello, Braden. She's all yours. Are you ready to go, Cam?" she asked with a smile. How did she manage to be so cool like that?

"I am. See you tomorrow, Gabrielle. Talk to you soon, Braden." With that the two of them left to go have drinks. I watched them walk down the hall together and get on the elevator then I turned back to Braden.

"Are you happy now?" he asked, getting up and coming over to put one arm around my waist and gently rub my injured shoulder with the other. He looked down at me with a smile.

"What do you mean?" I asked innocently.

"You wanted them to get together, didn't you? You've certainly had them on enough stakeouts together looking for our shadow." I couldn't hide anything from this man anymore.

"Yes, I want them to get together because I know that they're attracted to each other and they have fun together. I think they would make a great couple but I'm not positive that anything will happen just because he asked her out for drinks. They've gone out for drinks before and nothing did."

"I'll let you in on a little family secret. Cameron does more soul searching than fucking Hamlet, but he's finally done dicking around. He's going to ask her out this time." I had definitely wound up with the right cousin for me. I didn't have Jess's patience.

"He is? That's great!" I looked up at him with barely contained excitement. "She'll be so happy! They really do make a nice couple. And then you won't worry anymore!"

"Gabrielle." He gave me a look that seemed like a combination of amusement and affection. "I haven't been worried in quite a while. You and I belong together and nobody's going to get in the way of that." He pushed a loose strand of my hair behind my ear. "I suppose you want us to stay at your place tonight so you can hear all about it when she gets home?"

"You know me so well."

"I know you intimately," he said with a naughty look, squeezing my bottom. There was a reason I kept him locked in my bedroom, you know.

That evening I finally convinced Braden to watch the first couple of episodes of Downton Abbey with me. I owned all the previous seasons so far. Even though he was kind of grumbly at first he actually started getting into it.

"You know, you're right, this show's pretty good."

"I knew you would like it! It's kind of hot too, all that repressed sexuality."

"Yeah, maybe we should play rakish aristocrat and sexually curious daughter of a wealthy landowner," he joked, and raised his eyebrows provocatively.

"Braden, we play that all the time. That's us you're describing."

"Oh yeah." He laughed. I heard the front door open. Bruno raised his head and yipped.

"Don't worry, Bruno, it's just Jess. Now Mommy's going into the other room to beat information out of her, so you hang out with Daddy."

"I'm going to read. Is that okay or do you want me to leave the TV on?" Braden asked tactfully.

"No, honey. We'll be in the next room. Do whatever you want and I'll be back shortly."

I went out to get the scoop. Cool collected Jess was gone. This Jess was so happy that she was almost vibrating. Immediately, easily excitable Gabrielle showed up to keep her company.

"Gabrielle! He asked me out!" She looked like she wanted to jump up and down. Hell, I wanted to jump up and down. And I was home now and no longer wearing heels. So I did! I jumped! Up and down!

"Tell me everything!" I demanded, grabbing her by the arms and shaking her as I hopped up and down like a crazed bunny rabbit.

"Okay, stop assaulting me and sit down," she instructed. We went over and threw ourselves down into a couple of armchairs and sat forward in full attention information sharing poses.

"Tell me what he said word for word or I'll have to hurt you."

"Okay, he told me that he found me very attractive and that he felt like the two of us had a lot of chemistry," she began.

"Yes!" I interrupted her and pumped my fist in the air. Then I rubbed my shoulder, because it was still kind of sore from the door thing already and I might have just dislocated it.

"He said that at first he worried that if it didn't work out he would wind up making you and Braden all pissed off at him again because you and I are such good friends but that now he was pretty sure that it *would* work out!"

"Oh Jess! That's so great! I'm getting all verklempt," I said, feeling teary-eyed. I loved it when a plan came together.

"I don't know what that means," she said.

"Don't worry about it. Neither do most people who aren't Jewish and over the age of sixty. Just keep talking."

"Um, he also admitted that at first he was jealous of Braden being with you. He realized, though, as time went on that the two of you were developing really deep feelings for each other and you just seemed right together. He's been thinking about asking me out for a while."

"Oh Jess! I'm so happy!" I gushed.

"Me too!" she squealed.

"Me too!" Braden called out from the other room. "The walls are really thin in here, by the way." Bruno yipped in agreement.

Drew had gone back to D.C. to finish his last year of law school but Beth, who lived with her parents and worked at the art museum, was still around. She and Lily, both being artistic had hit it off particularly well. Beth was a painter and she was really talented. Lily encouraged her to enter her work in various art shows and Beth encouraged Lily to do more author events. We also frequently had a girls' night with all four of us on Sunday while the guys were doing Game Night, which was exactly what we were doing at that moment.

"What's the status with the big engagement party?" Lily asked.

"Our parents are making a formal announcement this week and then invitations will go out. It's going to be in the Grand Ballroom of the Ritz-Carlton," I answered, feeling a little queasy, which didn't stop me from loading up a Triscuit with port wine cheese.

"Wow that should be quite a guest list," Jess said. "Senators and CEO's." She popped the cork on a bottle of Chianti and filled all of our glasses.

"You know, Braden and I are actually allowed to invite our friends too," I pointed out.

"I'll bet the media will all be picking it up," Lily, who was sitting on the floor, pointed out, popping a grape into her mouth.

"Great. Maybe they can capture me tripping down a flight of stairs or making a corny joke to a national leader." What was I going to do with no cat, no kid, and no laundry?

"Braden will make sure everything's okay, Gabrielle. He's used to stuff like this." Beth was such a sweet person. I was really going to like having her as a sister-in-law, and having grown up with Drew, I probably wouldn't even embarrass her much.

"Does he get engaged a lot?" Lily joked.

"No!" Beth laughed. "My mother almost fainted when she found out."

"With happiness, right?" I asked nervously.

"Of course! She was so thrilled that she called every human being on the planet who she knew and some who she didn't!" Beth said with a laugh. "Our mailman knew that you were engaged by the end of the day."

"Well, Braden made my mom so happy that I think she made her employees' yearly bonuses dependent on naming a child after him. Even if they already had another name," I said, dunking a baby carrot in some unidentified dip-like stuff.

"So, everyone is happy, and nothing weird has happened lately, right?" Lily asked.

"Well, no more notes or napkins. Sometimes, though, we do feel like maybe somebody's watching or following us, and I have to admit, it's starting to get to me a little."

"The chances are that you guys are imagining it. Nobody's following you, Gab," Jess said reassuringly. "It's probably just nerves from everything that's happened in the past few months."

"Yeah. You're right – just nerves. That's probably all it is."

That week Senator and Mrs. Tyler Pierce and Mr. and Mrs. Benjamin Ginsberg formally announced the engagement of their children, Braden Tyler, and Gabrielle Sarah. Within days of the announcement, which was picked up in several national and local newspapers, and on various websites, the feeling of being followed and watched became more than occasional. Now it was almost daily, and Gabrielle Sarah, for one, was getting mighty tired of it. If the police couldn't do anything then we would just have to try to figure it out ourselves. Unfortunately, we didn't have much to go on other than the possibility that our shadow was some kind of conspiracy theorist.

∽ CHAPTER FOURTEEN ↺

SEPTEMBER

Wednesday

IN THE COURT OF COMMON PLEAS OF PHILADELPHIA COUNTY, PENNSYLVANIA

<u>Commonwealth v. McLaughlin</u>

"Counselor, this is a very serious case," Judge Channing admonished. I held my temper in check. Did I look like I was laughing? "Your client was carrying an unlicensed deadly weapon concealed in her clothing in a highly populated area. She refused to turn it over to law enforcement. In fact, she became verbally abusive to Officer Wilkins. I'm quite aware that she is employed and does not have a record but this was outrageously dangerous and unnecessary. Furthermore, what kind of example was she setting?" he chastised. Breathe, Gabrielle!

"Your Honor, Sister Mary Catherine works in a very dangerous part of the city. That nine millimeter semi-automatic pistol was for her personal protection. She couldn't get a carry permit because the diocese frowns on sisters arming themselves, but I don't see the Bishop hanging out in North Philly." Uh oh, the anger was slipping into my voice and I had a feeling that I was starting to turn red in the face. "She is trained in how to use the gun safely. Officer Wilkins *lectured her in a very condescending way* and threatened to strip search her! Saying 'young man, you should have better manners' is *not* verbal abuse. And finally, with all due respect, allow me to point out that she's a *nun*! Um, thank you."

There was a moment of silence. Oh shit. I had gone too far. He was going to put me in jail for contempt, wasn't he?" I sighed. At least I could interview some clients while I was there. Finally, he cleared his throat and spoke.

"Perhaps Ms. Ginsberg has a point." *Huh?* "Sister Mary Catherine isn't a hardened criminal. You can't do this anymore though, Sister. Do you understand?"

"Yes, Your Honor," she answered sweetly. "I do want to assure you that I believe that every life is sacred. I wouldn't have smoked anybody unless I were in fear for my own."

"Er, that's good. And I know North Philly is dangerous but if the diocese has a problem with you getting a carry permit, you need to take it up with them."

"Yes, Your Honor," she said again with a gentle smile. "I'm sure that God will provide me with another solution so that I won't have to bust a cap in anyone's ass."

"Mr. Pierce, find some community service project she can do so that the Commonwealth can withdraw the charge." He gave Sister Mary Catherine an odd look.

"Yes, Your Honor," Braden said with a nod.

"Court adjourned." He left the bench shaking his head and muttering something to himself. That man had to be close to retirement. Even though Sister Mary Catherine's entire life was a community service project I was very happy with the result. Gun charges were serious and let's face it, she was guilty as sin. (No pun intended. Oh, okay. I did intend that one.)

Jess had already gone back to the office and Adam had gone off to talk to a cop. Braden came over to talk to me. I was busy tossing papers into my briefcase.

"You look tense," he said with classic understatement and a note of concern in his voice.

"Why does he have to lecture me for doing my job?" I slammed down a file and turned to face my gorgeous fiancé. I had finally gotten used to calling him that. "Is it my fault that Sister Badass is packing heat?" I knew that I was starting to sound like I was on automatic loop with this whine but I was practically on my last nerve.

"He backed down when he saw that he was pushing you too hard. I actually think that Judge Channing really likes you a lot."

Braden leaned against the defense table and gave me a sympathetic look. I didn't want sympathy at the moment, though. I wanted to kick somebody. Not Braden. Somebody else. I had to admit it. Work was really starting to get to me. Ever since we had discussed the idea of starting our own foundation I had been thinking about leaving all of this glamor behind.

"Okay, well, he has a strange way of demonstrating it, but whatever you say, Braden." I didn't believe him but I appreciated the effort.

"So, you want to cook tonight?" he suggested, and I must confess, that made me pause. I put down the file I was holding and turned to face him again.

"We cook? That's news to me."

"Well, more like heating. I had an idea for a dessert." He was leaning against the defense table giving me his boyish look and despite everything, I felt a smile coming on.

"You want to stay at my place? Jess might have some food there. She cooks. She had parents who did that." Unlike ours. Braden's family had servants and my family had a stack of take-out menus the size of the Manhattan phone book. "She and Cam are going out tonight anyway."

"Sure. She probably won't have what we need, though, so we'll stop off at a market before we get Bruno."

"Wow! You know where we can buy uncooked food? You're like a survivalist!" I joked. "So, any ideas for relieving my tension?" I asked lasciviously. Against the odds the smile had broken through and I went back to packing files much more gently.

"Chocolate."

"Chocolate? That's your only suggestion?" I asked, looking up at him quizzically.

"You'll see," he said with a naughty smile.

That evening, after eating our usual take-out and giving Bruno his supper and a bacon flavored chewy treat, Braden gathered together the ingredients he had picked up for dessert. We were going to dip strawberries in melted chocolate, which seemed to be easy enough even for people with our limited cooking experience. I personally thought it sounded quite yummy too. That probably really would cheer me up. It turned out to be very yummy indeed. We sat down at the table with a couple of plates, bowl of strawberries and a pan of melted chocolate. I went first and dipped my strawberry but I got chocolate on my fingers. I licked it off so it wouldn't drip all over the place.

"Mmm! This is good!" I looked up at Braden who was watching me intently. It was starting to dawn on me why he had suddenly felt the culinary urge.

"It looks good," he said in a slightly husky voice. "You missed some, though." He took my hand and licked the rest of the chocolate off of my finger. My breath hitched and I swallowed hard. He dipped his own strawberry and bit into it while giving me a really hot look. He started to lick the chocolate off of his own fingers but I took his hand, popped his finger into my mouth, swirled my tongue around and pulled it out slowly, never taking my eyes off him. I saw his breathing get heavier and his eyes get darker.

"You taste really good." I smiled and raised my eyebrows provocatively. I picked up another strawberry, dipped it in the chocolate and bit into it.

"Uh oh. You got a little bit right there..." he leaned over and licked chocolate from the corner of my mouth. You can probably figure out where this was going. "You're delicious," he said seductively. "I wonder how this would taste on other parts of you."

He pulled me up and guided me over to stand in front of him. He pushed my top up to expose my tummy and I held it there. Then he dipped one of his fingers in the chocolate and swirled around my belly button. I started feeling flushed and breathing faster. He leaned in and began licking the chocolate off of me, which incidentally, felt incredibly good and looked amazingly erotic. Suddenly Bruno gave a yip and headed for the door, which was already opening as Cam and Jess came in.

∾ Chapter Fifteen ∾

"We can go to my place!" Cam said, immediately assessing the situation, and preparing to vacate the premises. Jess had a slightly surprised and very amused look on her face.

"No! You don't have to leave," I said, pulling down my shirt and desperately trying to reclaim a shred of dignity. "I just got some chocolate on me and Braden was helping me get it off," I said, as if it were completely normal that someone would get chocolate on their stomach and their companion would help them clean it up with his tongue.

"Just let us quickly clean up in here," Braden said. "Don't let us get in your way and don't leave on our account. We're just planning to hang out tonight." I guess he meant as opposed to having chocolate-covered sex in the kitchen.

"Okay," Jess said, looking like she was trying not to laugh. "We were going to go for a drink after dinner but we changed our minds. I probably should have called."

"That's okay. It's no big deal," Braden reassured her.

"We were just going to hang out too," Cam added. "Do you mind if …"

"No! Of course not," I said, smiling in what I imagined was probably a rather maniacal way. I probably looked like a crazed Oompa Loompa.

They headed off to Jess's room while she changed out of her work clothes. As soon as they were out of earshot Braden and I turned to each other.

"Good thing they weren't a few minutes later." He smiled.

"Yeah, or they might have seen chocolate with nuts."

"Oh, that was bad," he said, but he still laughed.

Later, the four of us sat in the living room talking and snuggling on opposite couches. Bruno was contentedly nestled with Braden and me as I petted him and Braden scratched him behind the ears. Incidentally, that was Chihuahua paradise. He kept sniffing at my tummy though, which was rather disconcerting. Not to mention an embarrassing reminder of earlier events. I kept subtly shooing him away.

"So what's up with Adam lately?" Jess asked.

"I know. He seems distracted and cranky," I agreed.

"He might just be a little stressed out," Braden offered. "Mark mentioned that he wasn't going out as much lately for some reason, so I guess he's not unwinding a lot." That would make sense. Adam was cranky because he wasn't getting laid. The question was why.

"Maybe he needs a vacation," Cam suggested.

"Oh wait! I almost forgot," I said excitedly, sitting up and dashing into the other room. I came back holding the Metro, a little free newspaper that people picked up from stacks all over the city. "Look!" I handed the paper to Jess and she looked at the page I had opened it to.

"September is a popular month at Overbrook Lodge," she read and then started skimming the article. "On the 28th of this month every year they have a conference for a group called The Truth Seekers. It says that 'some may call them conspiracy theorists but they consider themselves people who have opened their minds to the fact that not everything is as it seems. They are most well known for their belief that politicians and powerful businessmen have been working together for decades to cover up evidence of extraterrestrial visitation'." She read silently again for a moment and then summarized. "A flying saucer was allegedly spotted near there one September back in the forties and the aliens supposedly made contact and said they would return on that day in … 'an upcoming year'," she said.

"Well, that narrows it down," Braden said with a laugh.

"Did you hear that? This is a group of local conspiracy theorists who specifically think that *politicians* and *businessmen* are working together to cover up the truth about UFO's!" I looked around at the faces staring back at me blankly. Okay, they weren't getting it.

"So?" Cameron asked finally.

"Politicians and businessmen. Working together. Conspiracy theorists?" Did I have to spell it out? How much clearer could it be? "Look, Braden and I both feel like someone is following us and watching us, and it's gotten worse since our parents announced our engagement. Felicity said that someone was threatened by the idea of our fathers working together. I think maybe this guy may be a Truth Seeker!"

"What would he hope to gain by following you?" Cam asked.

"I don't know. Maybe he thinks we'll slip up and show him where the alien autopsies are done. These people have their own sense of reality."

"Okay, so say you're right and whoever is following you is part of this group. What are you going to do about it?" Jess asked.

"We're going to go and confront him once and for all," I answered emphatically.

"We?" Jess asked, looking like she already knew the answer to that question.

"Well, I think we should all go but you don't have to, of course. It could be a fun trip though! It's out in rural Bucks County, PA."

"Oh perfect," Braden said. "Out in the middle of the woods with UFO enthusiasts. Maybe we should save that trip for our honeymoon, sweetheart."

"Gabrielle, don't you think that maybe this is pretty far-fetched?" Jess asked. "I mean, just because these people are conspiracy theorists, and Felicity *may* have been warning you to watch out for conspiracy theorists …"

"And they believe that businessmen, like my father, and politicians, like Braden's father, are plotting together. And someone is *following* me and it's starting to drive me nuts," I answered, feeling exasperated. "I don't have any other ideas, Jess. I'm desperate, and anything seems worth a shot. It's pretty late notice, though. I wonder if they're booked up."

"Somehow I doubt it," Cam said.

"So what do we need?" I asked, going over and firing up my laptop. "A bedroom for you guys and one for us and we'll need to take Adam or Mark or both."

"What would possibly make you think they would be willing to go to a gathering of UFO Enthusiasts in rural Bucks County?" Cam asked me.

"Yeah, I'm not sure *I'm* willing to go to this," Braden added.

"Aren't you curious?" I asked him.

"About what? Felicity's conspiracy theorist, or whether the Mother-ship will finally be returning this year?" Braden asked with a smile.

"Both," I said. "Come on, it'll be fun. Oh hey! It says there's also legends about ghosts at the Lodge! This place is haunted!"

"Oh great!" Braden laughed. "This just gets better and better."

"Is Jack Nicholson the caretaker?" Cam asked, which made Braden crack up even more.

"That hotel was called the Overlook," I pointed out. Although I had to admit that in the picture I was looking at it did resemble the hotel in The Shining a little.

"Gabrielle, not to rain on your parade, honey," Jess said, "but if there really is a conspiracy theorist, who isn't too psyched about your wedding plans, couldn't it be dangerous to go hang out with him in the middle of the woods?"

"Yeah, if there really is some crazy guy watching you and following you around maybe it's not a great idea to go socialize with him and all of his friends."

"And what are we going to do if we find him, Gabrielle?" Braden asked. "Ask him to take us to his leader? Cross-examine him?"

"I'm tired of us being spied on and followed, honey. I want to confront this guy once and for all and tell him to leave us the hell alone. We'll tell him that our dads aren't hiding any spaceships or little green men so he should go find Elvis or something instead."

"You should be excited, Braden!" Jess teased. "You've never been included in one of Gabrielle's crazy schemes before. Well, other than Club 51, and that was tame by her standards."

"Yeah, wait, is Ricky allowed to come along on Lucy's adventures?" Cam asked.

"Are Fred and Ethel definitely coming?" Braden asked.

"We wouldn't miss it, honey." Jess laughed. "I want to see a UFO!"

"I'm just in it for the ghosts," Cam said.

"Hey wait," Braden said looking at me, "hotel sex. Okay, I'm in."

"So we definitely need at least three rooms then, maybe four."

"I think Mark's ten year high school reunion is this weekend," Cam said.

"Yeah, it is," Braden agreed. "He's been talking about it for a while. No way will he miss that to go to a UFO gathering."

"Well that leaves Adam. Like Cam said, maybe he needs a little vacation."

"I was thinking more like a trip to the Caribbean, not to a haunted lodge in the middle of the woods," Cam noted.

"Everybody goes to the Caribbean. It'll give him something different to do."

"There's a reason everybody goes to the Caribbean, baby," Braden said. "The Caribbean is fun. Rural Bucks County? Not so much."

"And speaking of doing something different," I went on, ignoring them, "Jess you've been saying that Lily should get out more often. Maybe we should invite her too."

"I meant go out on a date or something. Not go hunt UFOs," she said.

"Maybe it will give her some ideas for a thriller. I would ask Beth too, but I know she's going out of town this weekend," I said distractedly.

"If Lily goes does that mean that Adam won't?" Jess asked.

"We won't tell him." Braden laughed.

"He's getting sneaky," Jess teased. "Gabrielle's definitely rubbing off on him."

I checked out the accommodations at Overbrook and found out that while the Lodge itself was full there was still one last four bedroom "luxury cabin" available.

"Um, I don't know," Cam responded when I shared that news. "I'm not sure that the words 'luxury' and 'cabin' actually belong together."

"Yeah, I agree, Gabrielle," Braden chimed in. "It's kind of like saying 'luxury tent' or 'luxury cot'."

"The cabins have private hot tubs!" I said, ignoring them.

"On the other hand ..." Braden said.

"And a fireplace, and big screen TV, and a bar ..."

"Okay, maybe that's luxurious enough." Cam came around too.

I reserved the last luxury cabin for Friday and Saturday night. We decided that if everyone agreed we would drive up after work. Jess had been searching for something on her own computer while I was checking out the digs and booking our accommodations.

"Ah ha! I found something we can watch tonight to get in the mood for our romantic weekend getaway."

She went over to the TV and set up the computer stream. I came back over curiously and resumed my snuggle position. I saw the logo for the History Channel and then the name of the show – The UFO Conspiracy. Great.

∽ Chapter Sixteen ∾

Friday

IN THE COURT OF COMMON PLEAS OF PHILADELPHIA COUNTY, PENNYSLVANIA

Commonwealth v. Jennings

"Mr. Mickley, would you please tell the court what happened outside the Bucket O' Chicken restaurant that you manage on September third?" Braden asked.

"Yes sir," Mr. Mickley, who bore a striking resemblance to Orville Redenbacher, answered politely. "I hired the defendant, Mr. Jennings, to hand out flyers on the sidewalk outside the restaurant. One of my employees let me know there was a disturbance and I went out to see what going on. I saw Mr. Jennings arguing with another man and it became physical."

"What do you mean by that?" Braden asked. I knew that this was another one of "those" cases and I had prepared myself mentally as best I could.

"I saw Mr. Jennings start pecking the other man." Yes, he did really just say "pecking".

"Would you explain what you mean by pecking?" Braden asked.

"He was wearing a chicken suit and it had a plastic beak attached to the headpiece. Mr. Jennings began vigorously nodding at the other man in a manner that looked like a chicken pecking."

"What did the other man do?"

"He turned and started to run and Mr. Jennings pursued him."

"What happened then?"

"The man attempted to cross the street and Mr. Jennings followed, which caused several cars to slam on their brakes. Then one of the drivers got out and yelled something and Mr. Jennings attempted to peck him too but several bystanders intervened."

"No further questions," Braden said and glanced at me. I stood up and walked over to question Orville.

"You didn't hear the exchange between Mr. Jennings and the man on the sidewalk. Correct?"

"That's correct, ma'am."

"It is possible that Mr. Jennings was actually nodding, as in agreeing?"

"Well, technically, yes ..."

"And the other man did shove Mr. Jennings after the nodding?"

"He did, but it looked like he was trying to keep Mr. Jennings back."

"But you don't know that was his intention, correct?"

"Well, no."

"You also didn't overhear the conversation between Mr. Jennings and the driver of the car that stopped. Right?"

"No, I didn't."

"So, again, he could have been agreeing with something the driver said, correct?"

"I suppose it's possible, but it looked like ..."

"Thank you. No further questions."

"Redirect?"

"No, Your Honor. The Commonwealth rests but Mr. Robbins, the man from the sidewalk and Mr. Thomas, the driver would both be available to testify at trial."

"Okay, Ms. Ginsburg, I assume you don't have any evidence to present."

"Wait a minute!" my client stood up and announced in a very loud voice. *Oh Jesus Christ no!* We had *discussed* this. I had explained the difference between a preliminary hearing like this one and a trial. I had also explained what a *bad* choice it would be to testify. I tried to talk to him but he wasn't listening. "I have a right to be heard!" he boomed in an exceedingly dramatic manner. *Shit.*

"Ms. Ginsburg," Judge Channing said with a warning tone. What did he want me to do, wrestle Tweety Bird to the ground? I tried threatening and pleading with my client to no avail. Why did nobody ever listen to me?

"I wish to testify!" he cried as if he were making a declaration of war.

"I'm sure that Ms. Ginsburg informed you that it would not be in your interest to testify, Mr. Jennings," the judge announced in a scathing tone, "However, if you *insist* then take the stand. Swear him in, Wayne."

I had a feeling that Braden was going to see me drunk for a second time soon. I got up to do my duty.

"Mr. Jennings, would you please *briefly* explain what happened on the day in question," I asked resignedly.

"Well, first of all, hello, I'm Lance Jennings and I'm an actor," he explained to the judge, sounding like he was doing a public service announcement. "I was hired to do promotional work for the Bucket O' Chicken restaurant. I was *not* informed that I might be verbally abused and attacked in the street!"

"Objection. Nonresponsive," Braden interrupted.

"Get to the point, Mr. Jennings!" Judge Channing admonished.

"I was simply playing my role out on the sidewalk when a cretin with dreadlocks began calling me a murderer. Like I killed the damned chickens myself! I don't even *like* chicken!"

"He called you a 'murderer'. Did he threaten you in any way?" I asked with a glimmer of hope. Maybe I could at least build a record to support a defense for trial.

"Yes! He asked me how I would like it if someone lopped off my leg and served it with gravy! I was in fear for my life!" There went the glimmer. The chicken was a ham.

"Did he make any aggressive moves?" I tried another tactic. Maybe Orville had missed something. His glasses were about six inches thick, after all.

"Objection! Calls for interpretation," Braden said.

"Overruled. You can answer," the judge replied.

"He *jabbed* me!" He said it like someone would say "I'm hit!"

"He jabbed you?"

"With his finger!" He looked traumatized.

"Did that place you in fear?"

"Objection! Leading in effect if not in form. She's telling him what to say, Your Honor," Braden correctly pointed out.

"Sustained," Judge Channing ruled. "Don't answer that, Mr. Jennings."

"How did it make you feel?" I tried again.

"I was in fear of course! God only knows where that finger had been! He looked like he hadn't bathed in about a decade. I'll probably get a disease!"

Curiosity got the better of me then and I glanced at Braden, who, as I suspected, was biting his own finger trying desperately not to laugh. He looked away so that he wouldn't lose it.

"So what happened then?"

"I defended myself by the only means available to me! I *pecked* him!" Braden suddenly had a coughing fit behind me.

"So the pecking was a defensive move?"

"Yes!"

"Why did you chase after him?"

"I don't know," he said, shaking his head and looking like he was searching for an answer in the very depths of his very soul. "I can only assume that it was temporary insanity brought on by emotional anguish." Oh, wasn't *that* special? Now the chicken was a lawyer too.

"And what happened with the driver of the car?"

"He tried to kill me! That vehicle was a deadly weapon in his hands and then he got out of it and yelled at me very rudely! I knew that someone that uncivilized had to be violent. I did what I *had* to do."

"No further questions." I sat down and thanked the good Lord for creating vodka.

"Mr. Pierce?" Judge Channing asked in a falsely cheerful voice. Braden stood up and approached Mr. Jennings cautiously. I didn't blame him. Mr. Jennings did seem like kind of a volatile guy even peckerless like today.

"Just to be clear here, Mr. Jennings, you were not actually nodding in agreement with either the man on the sidewalk or the driver of the car at any time. Correct?"

"Agreement?! With those Philistines?! No!"

"You freely admit that you did, in fact, peck the man on the sidewalk and attempt to peck the driver of the car?"

"And I would do it again," he said in a dramatically hushed tone. I half expected him to stand up and do a sweeping bow.

"No further questions," Braden said.

"Defense rests."

"Argument?" Judge Channing was being so calm that I got a little worried. I cleared my throat, stood, and with as much dignity as I could muster did my best to make a professional-sounding legal argument. Or at least one that was less asinine than my client's testimony.

"Your Honor, my client, Mr. Jennings, has testified that he was in fear for his safety,and not thinking clearly due to the ... emotional anguish ... he was suffering. I would argue that he lacked the necessary intent to commit simple assault."

"Mr. Pierce?" the judge asked with a smile. I was getting really worried now.

"Your Honor, I'm pretty sure that he just confessed to assault under oath."

"That would be *my* interpretation as well, Mr. Pierce," Judge Channing said. "Mr. Jennings, from now on I would seriously consider listening to your attorney. I'm going to advise the Commonwealth to add the charges of reckless endangerment and aggravated assault. I'm holding all of the other charges for trial. Schedule it, Wayne! Court adjourned!" He banged his gavel so hard I thought he might break it and then he got up and stalked off the bench.

"This is a miscarriage of justice!" Mr. Jennings cried as the deputy led him away. Wow, what an exit. I turned slowly to face Braden who was sitting at the prosecution table. I saw Adam and Jess approaching from opposite sides of the courtroom.

"Go ahead," I said to Braden.

"Oh, baby, I just don't even know what to say." He was trying *really* hard not to laugh.

"I'm sure *you* can think of something," I said to Adam.

"Too easy," he said, also obviously trying to contain his mirth. Hey, at least I had cheered him up!

"What do you mean?" I asked, confused.

"Just what I said. Too easy, and too easy is getting boring."

"Gabrielle, honey, that was just bizarre," Jess said sympathetically.

"I *told* that pecker not to testify," I said through gritted teeth and Braden snorted with laughter and covered his face with his hands, trying not to completely lose it.

Adam started humming the Foghorn Leghorn song, filling in the "doo-dah, doo-dah," and Braden almost choked.

ᖇᐧᓄ CHAPTER SEVENTEEN ᐧᓄᖇ

We had all left work a bit early that day and met in the parking garage of Braden's building. I had insisted that we rent a minivan. If there was one thing I remembered from the hellish experience of Girl Scout camp (other than the fact that mosquitoes the size of small poodles existed on Earth), it was that out in the woods it was best to do everything in groups. I might add we needed a large vehicle anyway since we had brought enough alcohol to guarantee that we would all being seeing UFOs by the end of the weekend. Adam thought that the image of Braden driving a Dodge Grand Caravan was extremely amusing, though.

"Dude, six months ago if I had suggested you would be driving this fine piece of machinery you would have told me to go fuck myself," Adam said, laughing. I might add that Braden normally drove a BMW M6 convertible.

"Go fuck yourself," Braden answered.

"I feel like we should be dropping somebody's kids off at soccer practice," Jess said.

"Or transporting a soccer league," Lily added. Adam had seemed to take Lily's presence in stride. In fact, I almost thought that he might have secretly been happy she was going. I was pretty sure that Adam really was getting bored with things that were too easy.

The trip would only take about forty-five minutes so we would be there in plenty of time for the opening get-together of the UFO gathering that I had also booked us into. I brought along plenty of information to supplement that fine documentary Jess had made us watch the other night. I wanted us to sound like well-informed conspiracy theorists, as I felt it was important to blend. God knows, we didn't want to seem odd.

Bruno was being doggie-sat this weekend by Aunt Beth and Grandma and Grandpa Pierce. Beth had just taken him with her (along with a few thousand dollars' worth of doggie accessories and gourmet kibble) after an emotional goodbye. I thought Braden might actually cry. We both came from very close families. Cam and Jess climbed into the rear seats and Adam and Lily took the middle. I, of course, rode shotgun.

"Now I want you kids to behave back there. No fighting or kicking the seats," I joked.

"Yeah, don't make me turn this minivan around," Braden added.

About fifteen minutes later we had made it out of the city and we were on the open road headed for rural Bucks County, PA with Lily, Jess and I belting out the lyrics to Southern Cross along with Crosby, Stills, & Nash. It was getting darker earlier now and by the time we were close to our destination the atmosphere had definitely changed.

"Nice location," Cam called out from the back. "Very Blair Witch Project."

"You know if I were driving a spaceship I'm not sure I'd want to land here," Lily said, peering out the window.

"It's better than the Ozarks, or the Mojave desert or any other places that they land. I mean at least they have hot tubs and a bar here," I noted.

"It's probably really pretty in the daytime," Jess said optimistically.

"Maybe tomorrow when it's light out they'll plan a fall foliage nature hike and dead alien recon mission," Adam added.

We arrived about fifteen minutes later. We pulled into a long drive bordered by trees and at the end I saw a large historic-looking white building that was actually quite lovely. Ha! The main lodge was in the center and two other wings connected to it on each side. The drive continued on around a small lake to the rear of the hotel and I could see the lights of cabins along the perimeter nestled amongst the trees and backed by forest.

"Hey!" Jess called out. "Are you sure you're in the right place?"

"This is it. Overbrook Lodge," Braden called back. "Must be for a better class of UFO hunters and conspiracy theorists."

We parked the van and went into the main lodge where a huge stone fireplace formed the centerpiece and the hardwood floors gleamed. A bellman directed us to the antique-looking front desk where we checked in and got the lay of the land. There was a restaurant, saloon and gift shop, along with conference rooms, located in one wing and there were bedrooms and suites in the other. The front desk clerk gave us a schedule for the UFO conference, the keys to our luxury cabin, and instructions on how to get there. The restaurant did deliver to the cabins so we grabbed menus, placed an order, and left to go settle in.

The cabin was really nice too. We went in and quickly looked around. The floor plan was similar to that of the main building, as there was a central stone fireplace. A big screen TV was fixed to the wall behind it in lieu of artwork and it was surrounded by comfy-looking sofas. A tall bookshelf filled with novels, magazines and board games stood to one side. Behind the central fireplace area there was a modern kitchen, a small bar, and a table that seated eight. Sliding doors at the back led out to a deck that, as promised, housed a hot tub. To each side of the central area there were two bedrooms, and every bedroom had its own small private bathroom. Even though it was rather spacious, it had a cozy atmosphere. It also smelled like spiced cider, which, combined with the rust and gold décor created an autumn-like feel.

"This is pretty!" Lily said, sounding surprised.

"How much did you pay for this, baby?" Braden asked me suspiciously.

"Um, two or three thousand?"

"Two *or* three thousand?" Cam laughed. He was a former financial planner, by the way.

"For two nights?!" Jess asked. She was just a person who had a better grasp of money matters than I did. I was never good at that stuff.

"I think so," I replied. "I just paid for it out of my trust fund."

"I suspect that Braden will be handling their finances as a couple," Adam said as Braden laughed and shook his head.

"So should we pick bedrooms?" I asked excitedly. I might have actually enjoyed Girl Scout camp much more if this had been my cabin. Nobody really had any preference about bedrooms as they were pretty much exactly alike so Cam and Jess went to the left along with Lily and Adam and Braden and I wound up in the two bedrooms to the right.

Braden and I took a few minutes to check everything out. Our room had a nice queen size bed with a very soft-looking comforter in a rich red color. The décor in there was also warm and rustic and so, like the rest of the place, it was very cozy. The private bathroom would make things easier. Our joint morning shower could be slightly more awkward with a line of people waiting outside. We started unpacking and putting our things away.

"I was thinking. After dinner and this get together, or whatever it is, we could come back here and have a drink and maybe enjoy the hot tub for a while," Braden said as he unpacked. I had a feeling that was just the beginning of his plan for the evening.

"That sounds nice." I smiled.

"And then later, we could come back in here and I know a position we haven't tried that I think you would really like. I've been saving it for a special occasion," he said happily.

"Well, actually, I have a surprise for you later too," I said, feeling myself blush a little.

"What kind of surprise?" he asked, sounding very intrigued.

"I'm not telling." I giggled. "Then it wouldn't be a surprise."

"Oh come on!" He stopped packing and came over to me. "If you don't tell I'll be forced to get the information out of you by other means."

"What other means?" I giggled more and found out as he started tickling me. "I'm not telling!" I squealed and the two of us fell onto the bed where I squirmed, writhed, laughed and tried to get away. Soon I was bucking my hips underneath him and I quickly realized that he was becoming highly aroused.

"Gabrielle, I think it's time for a quickie," he said thickly and started kissing my neck. I moaned and wrapped my legs around him.

And then the knock on the door came. Because you *knew* that there had to be a knock on the door. Braden and I practiced coitus interruptus more often than most Catholics.

"Yes?!" Braden called out none too warmly.

"I'm sorry guys!" Cam answered sounding embarrassed. "The food's here, though, and everyone's waiting."

"Okay! We'll be right there!" I called out in what I hoped was a light cheerful voice and I heard him walk away.

"Does it seem like we don't get to have sex very often without a waiting period being involved?" Braden asked, rolling onto his back and staring at the ceiling blankly.

"It'll be worth the wait," I rolled onto my tummy, gently stroked his hair and leaned down to kiss him softly on the forehead. He looked up at me for a second and smiled and then got up silently and went to go splash cold water on his face and pace around to reestablish the blood flow. Five minutes later we sat down at the table to dig in to our Italian cuisine. Braden was still not looking very jolly though.

"Oh, I think someone's a Gloomy Gus," Adam said with barely suppressed mirth.

"I'm sorry I bothered you guys," Cameron said, looking a bit more contrite but also rather amused. "We're running kind of late though." He shrugged and pointed at his watch helplessly.

"Your fiancée there has us scheduled for drinks with the X-Files gang tonight," Adam, who obviously had a death wish, went on. "Wouldn't want to be late for that."

"I was looking at the schedule," Lily chimed in. "They've got a local historian coming to tell the stories of both the UFO sighting and the ghosts that supposedly haunt this place."

"I'm sure that's *much* more fun than whatever you had planned, Brade." Adam smiled.

"Keep it up and you'll be the next ghost haunting this place," Braden said, which just made Adam laugh more.

"So, we listen to the historian and...?" Jess asked Lily who was still reading the schedule.

"And there's a 'meet and greet' and then some folks will be heading out to the woods to see if they spot any UFOs," Lily answered.

"How about instead of searching for aliens and sitting in a forest at night we come back here and search for some alcohol and sit in the hot tub?" Jess suggested.

"Ah! Come on! I wanted to hunt the aliens!" Cam laughed.

"How long do the lecture and the meet and greet last?" Braden asked. I had a feeling he was mentally counting down the minutes until we could go to bed.

"Um, well it runs from eight until ten," Lily answered. "And it's seven-thirty now so we'll have just enough time to clean up and head over to the Lodge."

We finished up and while Jess and I cleaned up and Lily stocked the kitchen with the few groceries we had brought along, Cam and Adam stocked the bar with the large supply of alcohol we had brought. Braden, meanwhile, checked to make sure that the hot tub was working and to quickly finish our unpacking. Twenty minutes later we headed to the Lodge on foot. It took less than five minutes to get there but the darkness and woods made it feel kind of spooky. When we arrived we followed signs to the saloon where the 'meet and greet' was taking place. As soon as we got in the door we saw a table with "Hello" badges and went over to fill them out. The ink had barely dried when we were approached by a positively exuberant couple with badges indicating that they were Earl and Marge.

"Hello there!" Earl said enthusiastically. "Earl Samuels, and my better half, Marge." He reached out a hand and vigorously pumped all of our arms a few times.

"Nice to meet you!" The woman, who resembled a codfish, said in a slightly manic voice. Marge looked like she had drunk about sixteen pots of coffee.

We introduced ourselves and they shared that they had been attending this conference for several years. We also learned that Earl sold insurance and Marge was a service desk manager at K-Mart and that they both firmly believed that aliens walked among us. Yeah, this was going to be a long night. We finally managed to extricate ourselves and make it to the bar.

"Did you think that Earl could be the shadow?" I asked Adam.

"It's hard to tell. Like I said, I didn't get a great look at his face. I thought he might have been a little younger, but Earl seems to be in decent shape and he's about the right size. It's possible."

"They didn't act like they recognized us, though," Braden commented.

"Marge seemed pretty nervous," I pointed out.

"Honey, I get the feeling that Marge is nervous a lot," Jess put in.

After fortifying ourselves with alcohol we decided to work the room a little more. The next couple to approach looked like former hippies. They appeared to be in their sixties and it seemed like they hadn't had a haircut since then either. The woman was dressed like a gypsy and the man was dressed like Tonto.

"Hello," said the woman pleasantly. "I'm Rain and this is my lover Forrest." I laughed loudly. Nobody else laughed at all, loudly or otherwise.

"Oh!" I said. "You weren't kidding." Braden quickly pulled me to his side and reached out to shake their hands.

"I'm Braden, my fiancée Gabrielle, our friends Cameron, Jessica, Adam and Lily." They all smiled and waved to Rain and Forrest.

"Wow man, it's really cool to have new people here!" Forrest said. "We want to share your thoughts so I hope that you'll take some time and rap with us."

"Well, personally, I don't really like rap, but I do like the blues," I assured him.

"What he means is that we want the information to flow freely. We are all here to explore the possibilities and expand our minds," Rain added helpfully.

"Oh, okay. Well, I'm good with flowing and expanding," I answered, nodding like I understood what in the hell she was talking about.

"Far out," Forrest said. "We'll catch you later." With that they wandered off.

"I think that Braden will also be handling most of the speaking for them as a couple." Adam laughed and I glared at him.

"Forrest is too old and too skinny. Do you agree?" I asked him irritably.

"Yeah, absolutely. It's not Forrest and it's not Rain even though she's pretty tall for a woman," Adam agreed.

"Well, the room is packed with white guys of average height and weight, do you see him anywhere?" I asked.

"I don't think so but it's kind of hard to tell," he answered, looking around. "There are *so many* average-looking guys here, which just makes it all the scarier." I saw someone else on the move, coming in our direction.

"Greetings!" said a short skinny guy with black-framed glasses and wild red hair that stuck up in several places. He was wearing a T-shirt with a Star Trek insignia on it. "I'm Stew Morrison and I'm an organizer of this conference. We're so happy to have you with us. Are you here because you've made contact or just because you want to learn the truth?"

"Well ..." I started but Braden cut me off tactfully.

"We're open-minded and curious people," he said with a smile.

"I see! Well, that's wonderful!" Stew was looking at Braden carefully. "You look a little familiar. What do you do?"

"I'm a lawyer," Braden answered in a friendly tone. "We all are actually." We introduced ourselves to Stew and he turned his attention to me. "You look familiar too. I could almost swear that I've seen you two somewhere recently." I was about to explain that he might have seen a picture of us together in the engagement announcement but Adam jumped in.

"So, Stew! Is this the whole gang assembled here?" he asked.

"Oh, no. There'll be more people arriving tomorrow and even more still tomorrow night when we all go out on the watch. Stella, who's also a group member, has psychic abilities and she has a strong feeling that this is the year that our visitors will return. Here, let me introduce you." He looked over and waved at a woman standing near the bar who looked like she was having a conversation with the air beside her. She looked over at Stew and began walking in our direction.

"Stella, let me introduce you to …"

"She's psychic. Maybe she already knows our names," I joked.

"What's that?" Stella asked the chair to her left. Nobody was actually sitting in the chair at the moment so I thought she meant literally.

"That's a chair," I said helpfully.

"Her name is Gabrielle," Stella continued.

"Do you name all of your furniture?" Adam asked with a smile.

"She's speaking with Emily," Stew explained. "One of our resident ghosts."

"Uh *huh*," Cam said. "I take it that you and Emily have met, Gabrielle?"

"I don't think so," I said. "I know some Emmas …"

"Hang on a second!" Lily jumped in. "You're saying that there's a ghost sitting in that chair and the ghost knew Gabrielle's name?"

"Yes, Emily knows *many things*," Stella said with dramatic flair. She should meet the pecker. She seemed to be glancing back and forth between Lily and Adam though. That actually made me wonder …

"Emily must read the Philadelphia Inquirer," Jess said with a smile.

"I sense skepticism," Stella said a bit reproachfully. "There's too much negative energy here now. We must be moving on." With that she and Emily left.

"She's a bit touchy," Stew explained. "Let me know if you need anything." He smiled and moved on.

"Don't be snarky with the crazy ghost lady," I said to Jess as soon as Stew was out of earshot. "We need to get in good with these people."

"You guys were messing around with her too," Jess said with a smile.

"I don't think that you should openly share who your relatives are with these people, Gabrielle," Adam warned.

"He's right, Gab," Cam agreed. "A senator's son and the daughter of a powerful CEO might not be the most popular folks in a room filled with conspiracy theorists." Three more people started moving our way.

"How nice to see some new blood here this year!" said a squat, middle-aged guy who reminded me of an accountant "Stephen Jebson!" He shook our hands. "I'm an accountant." Hey! Did I call it?

"Mathew Sinclair. I work in the hospitality industry," said a second man, who reminded me of Liberace but more flamboyant. He had tinted hair, a hot pink shirt and a diamond earring.

"I am Raoul," said the third man, like that meant something. He had jet black hair with enough grease in it to lube the entire parking lot. He also had a shirt unbuttoned halfway to his navel and about fifty gold chains. Sexy. We introduced ourselves yet again to the newest arrivals.

"We haven't had anyone new at the conference in a while," Mathew offered.

"Well, we're kind of new to the UFO world," I explained.

"You have picked a good year to come," Raoul said. "Some believe that de ship, she ees coming at last. You have met Stella? Yes?"

"*And* Emily!" Adam said with a smile.

"Have you met Rain and Forrest too?" Stephen asked.

"They were abducted back in the sixties!" Mathew volunteered, sounding very excited. "Forrest was anally probed!"

Just then Rain stepped behind a small podium that had been set up at one end of the room. She tapped on a microphone a couple of times, creating a sound loud enough and shrill enough to pierce my brain, and then proceeded to get the ball rolling.

"If you would all please have a seat. My friends, it's wonderful to see you all here again this year, and we're fortunate enough to welcome some new attendees." Every eye in the room turned to us. We shared a friendly wave. "As most of you know, Overbrook Lodge is located in what is considered a 'hot spot' for paranormal activity and it's probably that which drew our visitors from space here in the first place. As is our tradition, we've invited local historian Leland Harding to get the flow of information going. So, for those of you who are familiar with the fascinating tale, just sit back and relax and for our newcomers, we are very happy to be able to enlighten you and open your minds to the truth and the mysteries that surround us." She did something with her arms that looked vaguely hula-like. "Without further ado, Leland Harding."

A guy who looked like an undertaker, make that the Crypt-Keeper, stepped up to the sound of polite applause. I half expected to hear a wolf howl a bloodcurdling scream. He cleared his throat, said "Good evening," in a creepy Dracula-like way and proceeded to tell us enough freaky shit to guarantee that we wouldn't sleep all weekend.

∽ Chapter Eighteen ∾

An hour later we were walking back to the cabin, feeling pretty anxious and looking kind of like Marge. An owl flew by us and we almost hit the ground.

"Just so we're on the same page," Cam said. "I'm not up for the anal probing."

"I think you should discuss that with Jess," I replied numbly.

"So, how many people died horrible tragic deaths at this place?" Lily asked.

"A lot," Braden answered.

"And apparently they're all still here," Adam added.

"Maybe they'll scare off the aliens," Cam suggested.

We made it back to the cabin alive and without being abducted or probed. Braden made a fire in the fireplace while Jess put together snacks and Cam played bartender. We had decided to save the hot tub for the following night as nobody really felt like being outside near the woods after that fun little lecture. We all settled in and made ourselves comfortable in front of the fire, sipping our cocktails.

"So, do you think that maybe Rain and Forrest did some drugs back in the sixties?" Adam asked.

"No! What would give you that idea?" Braden replied.

"More importantly," I said. "What drugs do you think Marge is on right now?"

"Psychotropic ones," Cam answered.

"I think Mathew *wants* to be abducted," Lily put in.

"I'm pretty sure he's already being anally probed, honey," Jess noted dryly.

"You didn't see the guy from the music festival?" I asked Adam with a sigh.

"I don't think so. Sorry," he replied. "Although I guess that either Mathew or Raoul could possibly be him. Stew is too short and skinny and the accountant guy is too short and fat. Nobody else in the room really jumped out at me either and nobody was acting weird. Well, nobody was acting *suspiciously*."

"Well, according to Stew, there are supposed to be more people coming tomorrow," Lily offered. "There's a lecture and then there are some breakout groups afterward."

"Where do you think they broke out of?" Braden asked with a laugh, cracking Adam and Cam up.

"How do you think that Stella knew Gabrielle's name?" Lily asked. "You don't think she's really psychic? I mean, there wasn't really a ghost there, right?"

"She probably saw their engagement picture. That's what I meant by saying that Emily reads the paper," Jess said. "Stew probably saw it too but Stella has a better memory."

"I hope there's no Emily," I said. "Isn't she the one who got hacked up?"

"No, she's the one who got mauled by the bear," Cam answered.

"Oh God!" Lily winced.

"I thought you wrote thrillers," Adam said scornfully.

"Legal thrillers! Nobody gets mauled by a bear in court!"

"So should we check out the lecture and breakout groups?" I asked.

"The lecture is an overview of all the truths that the Truth Seekers are seeking," Jess said. "And the breakout groups are about assassinations, secret societies, and extraterrestrials."

"You had better make sure that nobody mentions Senator Tyler Pierce or CEO Ben Ginsberg by name in the free flow of information and mind expanding tomorrow," Cam said.

"I guess we're breaking out," I agreed. "Why don't we just pair up and each take a group."

"I think that assassinations might freak me out considering my dad's line of work," Braden said, sipping a vodka and tonic.

"Okay, why don't you and I take extraterrestrials?" I suggested. "Jess and Cam can take secret societies and Adam and Lily can take assassinations."

"Adam and I are a team?" Lily asked dubiously.

"Are you afraid to spend time alone with me?" Adam asked with a smirk.

"Why in the hell would I be afraid to spend time alone with you?" Lily asked, looking at him like he was nuts.

"Maybe you're worried you wouldn't be able to control yourself," he said suggestively.

"Yeah! I might kill you and then we would be haunting this place together forever."

"You're not going to be alone," I reminded them. "You'll be in a group."

"Okay, fine. You realize you're stuck with me now, Mr. Funny Guy," she said to Adam.

"Who wants another drink?" Cam, the bartender, asked. We had another drink. I was feeling pretty good. Cam was generous with the booze.

"What kinds of cases have you been handling lately, Cameron?" Braden asked changing the subject. That led into a general discussion of some of the other cases we all had been handling lately, some courthouse gossip and some talk about the upcoming election. Braden had begun stroking my leg, and I was starting to feel rather aroused.

"So, honey, are you ready for bed?" I asked hopefully.

"Uh oh, Braden. I think Gabrielle's trying to lure you away," Jess teased.

"You know what it's like when a woman's been drinkin'." I laughed.

"Oh Jesus, baby! I told you not to put that image in my head before we go to bed," Braden said and Adam lost it.

"I'll explain later," Jess said to Cam and Lily.

"Goodnight everyone!" Braden called out as he grabbed my hand and pulled me back to our room like we were exiting a burning building.

When we got to our room he shut and locked the door and pulled the curtains closed while I put the bedside lamp on low and pulled back the covers on the bed.

"Why don't you get undressed and wait for me in bed with your eyes closed and then I'll show you my surprise," I said with a smile.

"I like the sound of that," he answered, giving me a hot look of anticipation. When he wasn't looking I grabbed his shirt which I had packed and ducked into the bathroom. I undressed and slipped it on, along with a pair of skimpy black lacy panties and another pair of very high heels. I rubbed a little oil onto my skin, spritzed perfume between my breasts, put on some fresh lipstick and tousled my hair to make it sort of wild. After three vodka and cranberries I was feeling sort of wild myself. When I came back out Braden was sitting in bed, with his eyes closed as promised. He was looking all deliciously gorgeous and muscly. As usual he was also already semi-erect, which was a beautiful sight to see. I went to stand about five feet away from him.

"Okay, open your eyes," I said seductively. He did and his breath hitched. It didn't take very long before it wasn't a semi he was sporting anymore.

"Oh baby," he said huskily. "That shirt has never looked that good on me."

"I beg to differ but I'm glad that you like it," I said, feeling very coquettish.

"I love it. Turn around for me." I did a flirty little strut and pirouette for him. Too bad I didn't have a pole to work with here.

"You're gorgeous. What do you have on under there?" He began stroking himself while he watched me. Oh my! That was really hot! I realized suddenly that I was just standing there staring. Some stripper I would make!

"Uh, well," I swallowed. "Let's find out." I reached down and started slowly unbuttoning. He started to look dazed. When I got to the last button I let it just hang open in the front so it was still covering my breasts but he could see that all I was wearing underneath were my tiny black lace panties.

"Come sit on my lap," he said huskily. I looked at him intently and gave him my best sexy smile. I stalked toward him, and thankfully, did not catch my heel on the rug. I once pitched down a whole flight of stairs that way. Catching my heel. Not stalking toward a hot naked guy. When I reached him I crawled onto his lap, straddling him, but being careful not to crush anything we needed. Don't ask me how I had learned that lesson!

"Well, hello handsome," I said teasingly.

"Hello gorgeous." His breath sounded labored as he slid his hands inside the sides of the shirt and ran them down from my waist over my hips and around to squeeze my bottom.

"Ooh, I like that," I said as I wiggled around and ground my hips into him.

"I like *that*," he said in a husky voice. His hands left my ass and went to my boobs. He cupped them under the shirt and then he urged me up onto my knees, pushed the shirt aside and leaned in to gently bite, lick and suck one nipple. I whimpered with pleasure and buried my fingers in his hair, my hips moving of their own accord. He moved to the other side and a small moan escaped my throat. His tongue felt so hot.

"Mmm, Braden," I panted. I knew that he would be reaching lower any second and I still had something else to show him, so I pulled back, eased off of his lap, and stood beside the bed again. "This wasn't the surprise."

"Oh?" He was looking flushed and breathing hard.

I let the shirt fall to the floor, stepped out of my heels, and moved my hands to the edge of my little black panties, hooking my thumbs under the sides and wiggling my hips flirtatiously. I was starting to feel lightheaded. I eased them down and let them fall to my ankles and then I stepped out of them and threw them aside. I was now completely bare down there. And I do mean completely *bare*. He was surprised all right! His eyes dropped and he groaned.

"Oh, I *really* like that!" he bit out and slid down onto his back. "Come here and kneel over me."

I crawled up to straddle him again, thinking he wanted me to be on top, but he put his hands on my hips and urged me higher. Then he positioned me over his mouth and I started to feel faint. He grabbed my hips and gently lowered me until I felt his tongue penetrate me and I gasped and whimpered at the incredible feeling. He pulled it out, flattened it against me and dragged it slowly up to my clit. From there it just got better. He proceeded to give me the best oral sex I had ever experienced in my life. Even with him.

"Oh my God!" I gasped as he did things to me with his tongue that were probably illegal in several States.

"Baby, you taste so good and I love you bare like this. I could eat you all night," he said as he licked my clit like a lollipop. Three orgasms later I had to stop because I couldn't support myself anymore and I was afraid of what could happen if my legs gave out. "Senator's Son Smothered by Snatch."

"Come on, we'll try our new position," he urged as I half collapsed onto the bed.

"I don't know how much more she can take, Cap'n," I whispered in a very bad Scottish accent. Stew's Star Trek shirt had made an impression on me.

"Oh baby, we haven't even engaged the thrust yet. I'm planning to send you into hyperspace." He was still lying on his back with his legs about a foot apart and he bent one knee. "Sit facing away from me and straddle my leg so when you take me your clit is rubbing up against it. Okay?"

"Aye Aye," I responded, and did what he said as he helped me ease down and take him inside me. "Oh!" I moaned quietly, as I felt him fill me completely.

"Squeeze your thighs together, Old McDonald," he said thickly. I did it and heard his breath catch. "Okay, baby, here we go. Bounce." He pushed on my bottom and I used my legs to push up and down on his cock. Immediately, the tight fit and the friction blew my mind. This position was incredible! Bouncing was good! So *very* good! I started bouncing hard and trying desperately to swallow my moans as I came down on him deeply again and again.

"Does this? Feel? Incredible? To you too?!" I gasped as I bounced.

"Fuck yes!" he ground out.

Soon I was bouncing like a low rider on Cinco de Mayo. My gleeful sex sounds were getting louder and our bed was starting to make a lot of noise but I didn't think that Adam had come back to his room yet. At least if he had, I hadn't heard him, but then I was kind of distracted at the moment.

Thanks to all that wonderful friction I very soon felt myself slip over the edge and I moaned and whimpered as Braden held my hips still while my inner muscles contracted around him in waves of pleasure. As soon as the last wave passed, he started pushing my hips up again.

"More, baby!" I started bouncing, and once again, within minutes, I was tumbling over the edge but we kept going. Eventually, he started thrusting his hips beneath me, gave a final deep thrust, and with a low groan froze and shuddered as he let go. I sat there panting for a minute and then climbed off of him and cuddled into his arms.

"Braden, you made me come like five times."

"Six," he corrected.

"Six," I acknowledged. "I liked that new position. A lot. I think we should bounce more often. Like daily. A few times."

"I like your new look too," he said, gliding a hand over my now bald girl parts. "Not in a perverted 'I'm into little girls' way, just in a 'holy shit that's hot' way."

"Did I make a lot of noise?" I asked, wondering if I had provided entertainment for the rest of the group.

"Compared to how much noise you usually make? No. Compared to quiet – well."

"God, I'm wiped out. Do you think we can sleep in tomorrow?"

"Hell, yeah. Today I prosecuted a pecker, drove fifty miles in a minivan, went to a meet and greet for UFO enthusiasts and made my fiancée come six times. I think that I deserve a break, baby."

"Goodnight, honey," I said and I was out within minutes. I was woken out of a deep sleep some time later, though, by the sound of Lily screaming Adam's name. I had a feeling it wasn't for the same reason that I usually screamed Braden's name.

∽ CHAPTER NINETEEN ↷

I shot up to a sitting position and Braden woke up too. I heard a crashing sound downstairs, and Lily, sounding further away, still calling Adam's name. Braden and I flew out of bed and threw our robes on, heading out to the hall. Cameron and Jessica had just come out of their bedroom too at the other end of the cabin.

"What's going on?" Braden demanded.

"I don't know!" Cam replied. "We heard Lily calling Adam's name and a crash."

We met in the middle, looked up and saw the sliding doors at the back of the cabin open. Braden ordered Jess and I to stay put while he and Cam went to go check it out. I had brought my cell with me and I prepared to call nine one one if necessary. About five minutes later, though, Braden and Cam came back with Adam and Lily in tow. Lily was dressed in her night shirt. She had been running outside barefoot and she was freezing. Jess and I pulled her over to the couch and wrapped a blanket around her.

"What happened?" I asked.

"Why can you *never* listen?!" Adam yelled at Lily, ignoring the question. "I told you to wait here!"

"I wasn't going to just wait here while you went after him!" she yelled back.

"Why in the hell not?!" he shouted angrily.

"Because you were alone and I was afraid he would hurt you!" she screamed. That stopped him. He looked at her silently for a moment and I saw all kinds of emotions flit across his face. Finally, I saw that he was biting back a smile.

"And what? You were going to protect me?" he asked with amusement. "What would you have done? Given him a stern lecture? Put him in your next book and killed him off?"

"Made him sit and listen to your jokes all night! He would have killed himself!" she said, shivering. They looked at each other then and I could see the two of them were trying not to laugh.

"Nutty broad," he mumbled, shaking his head.

"What *happened*?!" Jessica repeated.

"Lily and I were in the living room together, uh, talking," Adam said in kind of a funny way, "and we thought we heard somebody out on the deck. We snuck back there to the doors and we saw somebody out there by the hot tub. I flicked on the outside light and he stood up and turned around. It looked like the guy from the music festival. He didn't look armed, so I opened up the door and yelled, 'Hey, what are you doing?' He took off, and I took off after him, and told her to *stay here*!"

"I wasn't going to let him just run off into the night after some crazy guy by himself," Lily jumped in. "So I ran after them. I found Adam, but the guy had gotten away."

"Because I stopped to make sure you were okay!"

"You wanted to make sure I was okay?" she asked, sounding surprised.

"What were you talking about at three a.m?" Jess asked suspiciously. Adam and Lily gave each other a slightly guilty look.

"Uh, I don't know. General stuff," Adam answered.

"I couldn't sleep and I came to get a book," Lily explained.

"I was in here reading already," Adam said, looking away. "That's not important. What's important is that schmuck is still following you two around. If he were just here for the UFOs he wouldn't have known which cabin was yours."

"He's right," Braden agreed. "He may have been coming here, or been here already anyway, but at some point he must have been watching us too."

"Should we sit up and watch for the rest of the night?" Cam asked.

"I doubt he'll be back tonight after all this," Braden said, going over to check the locks on the doors.

"I don't think I'm going to be able to sleep anyway," Lily said. "Ghost stories, UFOs and now a stalker. I'll just sit and hold onto my cell phone for the rest of the night."

"You won't be any use tomorrow if you don't sleep," Adam said, picking up a book. "Come on. I'll go with you."

"What do you mean, you'll go with me?" Lily asked.

"I'll go and sit with you until you fall asleep. Now, for once in your life don't argue with me!" He pushed her gently toward her room and to my surprise she actually went quietly.

After breakfast the next day, we headed for the lectures and subsequent breakout sessions. We all met up for lunch in the restaurant and upon comparing notes we discovered that if our guy had been present that morning, he wasn't doing anything obvious to make himself known to us. Nobody seemed to be staring at or following Braden and me. Adam and Lily didn't see anyone who looked familiar to them, and not many people in Cam and Jess's group even fit the description.

"It makes sense," Cam said. "I mean, he knows that at least one of us has seen him, so I don't know why he would want to take a chance at getting caught by going to a lecture."

"I wonder if anyone who was registered was a no show," I pondered.

"No, everybody was present and accounted for," Lily answered. "I checked the sign-in sheets."

"Good thinking, honey!" Jess said, sounding impressed. "We should have had her on the garbage can mission."

"You know, I have to admit, that overview lecture was kind of interesting," Braden said. "I've got to ask my dad about some of this stuff. I'm starting to wonder if he knows any aliens."

"I think my Uncle Ira might be an alien," I said. "No *human* could be that into dry cleaning."

"Felicity's dad could be an alien," Cam suggested and Braden and I agreed.

"So, what's the plan from here, kids?" Adam broke in.

"If your stalker is really into this conspiracy stuff, maybe he'll still go on the UFO watch tonight," Jess suggested. "It would seem like that would be kind of important."

"I say that we hold our own UFO vigil from the hot tub," Cam suggested.

"The chances that we would be able to recognize him in the woods in the dark are pretty slim. Maybe we should just decide later whether we think it's worth it," I said.

After the later lecture, wherein we discovered that certain celebrities might be aliens, which explained a lot about Miley Cyrus, we went back to the cabin. Everyone decided to retire to their rooms to relax and nap, since we might be having a late night. At around five, we started assembling again. The guys wanted to watch sports, so we ordered dinner and watched football for a couple of hours. After we ate, we decided to play one of the board games called "Say My Name." It involved giving your partner clues to try to get them to identify the person or character on your card, but you couldn't say the "forbidden words" as clues. Adam wound up paired with Lily again and the two of them were hysterical. And so were we most of the time watching them.

"Okay, this is a fictional character," Lily began. "And he's like a human."

"What?" Adam asked her, looking befuddled. "What the fuck does that mean? He's *like* a human?" He shook his head and scowled at her.

"He wears clothes!" she said frantically. I had feeling that this game had Lily on the verge of a nervous breakdown.

"He wears clothes. Great. Well, that narrows it down." The sands of the hourglass were pouring away and Braden, Cam, Jess and I, were laughing our asses off at this exchange already.

"And he walks upright!" she added, waving her hands frantically.

"I would hope that most of the people in this game walk upright! Give me a real fucking clue already!" Adam had that homicidal look again.

"Duh huh!" she said desperately.

"Hey! All you've told me is that he's a fictional character who wears clothes and walks upright. Don't duh huh me!" he spit out angrily.

"No! No! He says that!" Suddenly she started making barking noises.

"Are you okay?" he asked looking at her like she was nuts.

"Has a place in Florida..." She looked seriously stressed out. I was starting to worry.

"He's retired?" Adam asked, still looking confused.

"He wears bright colored clothes. He tells jokes."

"It sounds like you're describing my Uncle Murray," Adam was shaking his head.

"Time!" I yelled almost peeing myself I was laughing so hard.

"Goofy! The answer was Goofy!" Lily said with disgust.

"Goofy?! That was the best you could come up with for Goofy?!"

"I couldn't say Disney or dog or cartoon or *anything* because they were forbidden words!" She pointed to the card.

"Oh now now kids! Play nicely!" Jess said.

"What do you say we do one more round and then hit the hot tub," Cam suggested after a while. That idea received universal support.

Adam and Lily went last. I had a feeling this would be a Grand Finale.

"Okay," Adam began, "Now concentrate! This was a real person. White suit!"

"Colonel Sanders!" Lily replied quickly.

"Colonel Sanders? I said it was a real person, not a logo for a chicken joint!"

"He *was* a real person! If you don't believe me look it up!"

"Whatever! Not Colonel Sanders though. Humor!" he said urgently.

"Steve Martin!" She clapped her hands with joy, obviously believing that they had finally gotten one right.

"No, uh ..." He searched for another clue.

"Wait! White suit and humor but *not* Steve Martin?" She looked crushed.

"I just said no!" He yelled. "Hannibal!"

"Um, uh, Dumbo ..." she said with a deeply pensive expression.

"Dumbo?! What the fuck?!"

"Hannibal! Elephants! And before you say it he was real too, you schmuck!"

"Guess again goddamnit!"

"Anthony Hopkins!" Adam threw down the card and looked like he was going to cry.

"Halley's Comet!" he growled.

"Halley's Comet?! What in hell do you mean Halley's Comet?"

"Time!" Braden informed them gleefully, wiping tears of laughter out of his eyes.

"Mark Twain! You're an author Christ's sake!" Adam bit out.

"Oh, right! He was from Hannibal, Missouri! What in the hell did Halley's Comet have to do with Mark Twain?!"

"It appeared on the day he was born and the day he died! Duh huh!" Adam said.

"This isn't Trivial fucking Pursuit!" Lily shot back. "Why didn't you say Mississippi or riverboat or frog jumping contest or something besides Halley's Motherfucking Comet?!

"Because they're all forbidden motherfucking words! Miss 'like a human'!" he yelled. I could just picture them as an old Jewish couple for some reason. Okay, maybe with fewer uses of the word "motherfucker."

"Okay guys! Let's hit the hot tub!" Cam interrupted. Adam and Lily stood up and promptly crashed into each other while attempting to walk in opposite directions. They were stuck between a couch and a coffee table and neither was willing to back up so they literally climbed over one another and headed for their rooms. They really were very entertaining.

∽ CHAPTER TWENTY ↶

We were back downstairs and in the hot tub with cocktails and music in fifteen minutes. Let me point out that none of us were really heavy drinkers. It was an occasional thing we did to let loose, like visiting conspiracy clubs and going on UFO hunts.

Our group had varied musical tastes but most of us were eclectic. The guys all preferred classic rock but we girls liked our 80s music and it was our turn. While they weren't thrilled about it, they sat there tolerantly listening to us do our really bad sing-along Karaoke versions of Blue Jean by David Bowie and A- ha's Take On Me. Somewhere in the middle of Tonight is What it Means to be Young I looked up and saw something weird. It was a light. Up in the sky. Oh, *no way,* man!

"Look!" I pointed and mentally tried to calculate how many vodka and cranberries I had drunk. Everyone turned to look up in the direction I was pointing.

"What is that?" Cam asked, squinting.

"It looks like it's just hovering over the trees," I said.

"Wait, it's moving!" Braden joined in.

"It looks kind of like a cigar-shaped object," Lily said, sounding awed.

"How in the hell can you tell at this distance, Agent Mulder?" Adam asked derisively.

"Because I can!" she retorted and splashed him. As Braden mentioned, the object had begun to move and then suddenly it seemed to dart off and soon it was out of sight.

"Whoa. That was wild!" Cam said excitedly.

"You don't think it was …" Jess said, not finishing that thought.

"Well what was it then? A weather balloon?" Lily asked. Lily had been taking notes during the afternoon lecture about Roswell. She wanted to believe.

"It could have been a lot of things. Willow Grove army air force base is somewhere around here. Maybe it was something they're testing," Adam said.

"Or chasing," Cam muttered. "You know, after those lectures …"

"Yeah," I agreed. "It was probably some kind of plane or helicopter though."

"Yeah!" Adam seconded. "That's all it was." Cam started whistling the X-Files theme and we all laughed nervously.

"Did it look like it was trying to land?" Jess asked, sounding rather apprehensive.

"We're in the middle of the woods," Braden reminded her.

"It supposedly landed here before," Lily pointed out. "They must be pretty good drivers if they made it here from another planet."

"Yeah, but landing in the woods would be harder than parallel parking in Center City on Saturday night," I threw in.

"Maybe they have autopilot," Cam suggested. "They must have kick-ass GPS."

"Maybe we can ask the little green men if they saw your stalker," Adam said.

"Gray, they're gray," Lily corrected. "Weren't you listening this afternoon?"

"You seem to know an awful lot about this. I'm starting to think that you've been anally probed," Adam said with a suggestive smile.

"It's interesting!" she replied, giving him a fierce look. Adam's sarcastic expression melted and for one second I saw a much softer humor underneath it. I started to suspect that he liked pushing her buttons sometimes because he thought she was cute when she got mad. He actually shifted a little closer to her under the pretense of getting a better view of where the object had been.

Just then I heard voices somewhere in the distance and they sounded like they were getting closer. They seemed to be coming from the woods. Eventually, I could make them out better and Raoul's accent and Mathew's high-pitched voice came through clearly.

"Uh oh, I think the hunt is coming this way," Braden noted. And indeed it was. Earl and Stew came crashing out of the woods followed by the rest of the Not Ready for Sanity Players.

"Hello there!" Earl called out. "You guys had better run in and get ready or you'll miss all the fun!" They came tramping over to where the six of us sat in our hot tub sipping our cocktails and listening to Michael Jackson sing Thriller. Appropriately.

"Come on! Did you see the light?" Mathew enthused and he came running over excitedly. "Maybe we'll make contact!" Personally, I thought that Mathew should make contact with a psychiatrist. We looked at each other, realizing that the decision had been made for us. We were going on a UFO hunt.

After determining where we were supposed to meet up and setting our GPS we changed into warm dry clothes and sturdy shoes, grabbed some flashlights and set out to meet up with the rest of the Truth Seeker gang. We had been tramping through the woods for several minutes when Cam stopped.

"Okay, it should *not* be taking us this long to find them. Check the GPS," he said.

"Uh oh," I said, taking it out of my bag. "It's not working. It mustn't be able to get a signal out here."

"Oh great!" Adam laughed. "We're in the middle of the woods in the dark and we have no way to figure out where we're going?"

"It's not like we're in the middle of the Pine Barons or anything," Braden said. "Most of this area is developed. If we keep walking in any direction we should run into civilization before too long."

"We haven't gone very far. Maybe we should just turn around," Lily suggested. That sounded like a plan so we all turned around and started back but it wasn't really clear that we were, in fact, headed back toward the lodge. After another fifteen minutes or so I thought I heard something in the distance.

"Listen! It's like a humming sound, coming from that direction." I pointed. We altered our course and started walking toward the hum. In a few minutes we saw lights, but they looked strange. They seemed to be up in the air. There were several in a row and one above that was blinking on and off. They were stationary, above the treetops.

"Do you see that?" Lily asked excitedly.

"Obviously we see it. We're standing right next to you," Adam answered.

"What is it? It looks like it's floating," Jess said.

"Maybe we should go closer," I suggested. Nobody moved.

"I'm sure it's not a UFO," Braden said finally. Five voices agreed with him enthusiastically. "So what is it?" Silence.

"It just seems to be hovering. What kind of aircraft can hover?" Lily asked.

"Helicopters," Cam answered.

"It wouldn't be that still though," I said. "Okay I think we need to do it. We need to go and see what that is. On three. One. Two. Two and a half..."

"Three!" Braden said and started walking forward. The rest of us followed our leader. The lights looked brighter as we got closer and we could make out what looked like a triangle shape attached to them. Like a pyramid maybe! I could feel my heart pounding as we got closer.

"There's a clearing up ahead," Adam said, sounding tense.

"Let's hold hands, everyone!" Jess said, sounding panicked. We all reached out and formed a human chain. We kept walking like that together, closer and closer until finally we broke through the bush to the clearing and looked up silently at the sight before us.

"Well folks, looks like we've had a close encounter with a radio tower," Cam said.

"This has been such a fun trip," Adam chimed in. "We really have to do this more often." Just then we heard voices somewhere close by.

"Hello!" Braden shouted. "We're over in the clearing. Anybody there?"

"Hey there! It's Forrest, man! I'm with Rain and a few of the others. We'll be right there." And that's how we were rescued from the woods by two aging hippies, a pudgy accountant, a gay waiter, and Raoul.

We were all back by noon the next day and since both Mark and Beth were curious to hear about the weekend, Game Night and Girls' Night were both a go. Tonight Bruno was hanging with the boys, so it was just Jess, Lily, Beth and me along with various varieties of crackers, cheeses, and a couple bottles of wine. For the rest of my life, that combination would remind me of Mr. Hughes with the shopping cart pants. Clearly, I was emotionally scarred.

"So after all that you didn't get to confront him?" Beth asked, taking a bite of her brie-covered Melba toast and washing it down with a sip of Chianti.

"Nope. But we did confirm that Braden and I are not just imagining things. Some schmuck is actually following us," I answered, biting into my Triscuit.

"I learned some fascinating things about political assassinations," Lily added.

"Yeah, and she talked about them all the way home. I now know way too much about what John Wilkes Booth was doing the day Lincoln got shot, and don't even mention the Grassy Knoll," I said, spraying crumbs in my general vicinity.

"The truth I'm seeking is what she and Adam were really doing when that intruder showed up," Jess said, giving Lily a suspicious look.

"Adam?" Beth asked, sounding intrigued, as she poured herself another glass of wine.

"Oh come on!" I agreed. "All that tension wasn't about Goofy."

"Goofy?" Beth asked, raising her eyebrows.

"We were playing that board game 'Say My Name'," Jess explained, cutting a piece of brie and spreading it on a cracker.

"I'm sorry I missed this!" Beth said with a big smile. "I want to know! What happened?"

"Nothing happened," Lily said, rolling her eyes and blushing furiously.

"You didn't sleep with him that night?" I asked, spearing an olive.

"Gabrielle!" Beth said with a laugh. "You sound like Drew."

"Drew and I are actually quite alike in many ways," I pointed out.

"If you mean did we have sex, then no we didn't. If you mean literally, as in did we sleep together in the same room, then yes." She explained to Beth how after the intruder freaked her out, Adam offered to just sit in her room until she fell asleep, but he fell asleep first.

"So you haven't had sex with him." I continued with my interrogation. "Have you kissed him?" Inquiring minds wanted to know. Now that Cam and Jess were a done deal, I might be in the market for another project.

"No," she answered, and after hesitating for a moment she went on, "but we came close that night you're talking about. We really were talking, but there seemed to be this tension, a different kind than usual. Anyway, I think he was going to kiss me. Well, I'm sure he was going to kiss me, but the intruder interrupted us." I started making squee noises and kicking my feet. I really had no shame.

"But he didn't kiss you later, when you two were alone in your bedroom?" Jess asked curiously.

"No. After all the adrenaline had left our systems, we were both exhausted. It was like four a.m. anyway. He sat on the other side of the bed and read, but I could see he was about to pass out. So was I for that matter. The fact that he and I were able to sleep in the same bed together should tell you how tired we were."

"But he didn't even mention the almost-kiss? Not at all?" I asked, surprised.

"He said something kind of weird right before he fell asleep. He said 'I'm not ready.' He could have meant anything though. His eyes were closed. He might even have *been* asleep."

"So, what are you going to do about all this?" I asked excitedly.

"What do you mean?" She looked confused.

"Don't you want to get together and turn the almost-kiss into something more?" I elaborated.

"He's a womanizer. I have nothing against casual hook-ups in general. I just couldn't be casual with him."

"I said the same about Braden!" I insisted. "No offense," I said glancing at Beth.

"He *was* a womanizer before he met you, Gabrielle!" she said with laugh.

"Well, see when we got together, he stopped being one."

"I had a feeling he had met somebody he at least liked even before you guys started dating though," Beth said, "because I hadn't seen him out nearly as much as I had in the past for a couple of months before you got together."

"Mark says that Adam hardly goes out clubbing anymore. He's been spending more time just hanging out with the other prosecutors than picking up chicks," Jess shared.

"Well, I'll bet that Braden has had girlfriends before," Lily argued. "I'm not sure, of course, since we didn't go to college or law school together, but I have a feeling that Adam's never been willing to limit himself to one woman."

"Braden has had girlfriends," Beth answered, "but those relationships didn't even come close to the one he has with Gabrielle. We've never seen him act like this before with anyone."

"And Adam acts differently with Lily than he does with any other woman," I pointed out. "Jess and I stand up to him too and there's not all that tension there."

"It still doesn't mean that he and I could be a couple. We've been arguing since we were four years old."

"What kind of stuff did he do when you were four?" Jess asked.

"Let's see, he locked me in the boys' bathroom. He put paste on my chair. He licked my fruit Roll-up and he stole my red crayon. And that was just the first day of pre-school. It went downhill from there."

"Mmm hmm!" Jess and I shared a knowing look.

"And what did he do when you were older?" she asked.

"Um, mostly he teased me. Like, for example, once in biology the teacher asked for an example of an asexual organism and he said Lily Adler. He used to say things like, I was only hostile because I wanted him. Actually, he still says shit like that."

"I think he's in love with you," Jess concluded.

"You *must* be kidding." Lily looked at her like she had two heads. "Torturing and teasing are indications of deep affection?"

"They are when you're four and when you're fourteen. And apparently in your twenties too if you don't know what else to do in a particular situation," Jess replied.

"And if he's never had a serious relationship then he wouldn't know what to do," I added.

"I agree," Beth said. "He's probably really attracted to you but you make him feel off balance because you don't throw yourself at him like so many other women. He doesn't know how to handle it."

"He's always laughed at me and made fun of me," Lily argued.

"Humor is often a defense mechanism," I pointed out. "I think he wields that sarcasm like a sword and uses it like a shield."

"Well, I'm not sure I'm up for *that* battle. I could become a casualty. I could just picture him yelling at me in bed, or worse, laughing at me!"

"I think neither one of them is ready yet," I said to Jess and Beth.

"So what's up with you romance-wise," Jess asked Beth, changing the subject. Beth told us about the guys she had been on dates with – none of whom she had found terribly impressive. Then talk turned again to my rapidly approaching engagement party.

"It's going to be gorgeous!" Beth gushed. "My mom and I just bought our gowns and we're so excited. We have family coming from all over!" Family. The word that struck terror into my heart.

"Are all of your relatives coming, Gab?" Lily asked.

"Yeah," I said weakly. "Unfortunately."

"Oh come on honey! They can't be that bad!" Jess laughed.

"If you don't believe me, ask Braden. Luckily, there aren't all that many of the weird ones. I mean, my dad's side of the family is pretty normal. It's my mom's side that worries me. Her brother Ira lives and breathes dry cleaning. He's got a chain of shops in Queens and Brooklyn and it's all that he thinks about, which is good in some ways, because whenever he talks about anything else he says the most tactless shit you've ever heard."

"More tactless than Drew?" Beth asked, sounding surprised.

"He makes Drew seem suave," I answered. "But even he is not as bad as my grandmother, who will be blessing me with her presence the day before the party too."

"Maybe this isn't the best time to mention this but my parents invited her along with your aunt and uncle and cousin Rachel for a house party on Friday night."

"What?!" I cried, spitting out a mouthful of Chianti onto Lily's white shirt. "I'll pay for that, by the way," I told her. "Are you nuts?!" I asked, turning my attention back to Beth. "You don't want to invite that woman into your home! You'll have to have to have it cleansed by a medicine man and blessed by a priest after she leaves!"

"Gabrielle!" Beth laughed, sounding shocked. "She's your grandmother!"

"Oh my God! Why? Why? What have I done?" I asked the ceiling imploringly.

"I'm sure it will be just fine, Gab," Lily said reassuringly.

"You've never met her!" I practically shouted. "Evil has a name and it's Rose Lipschitz!"

"Rose Lipschitz? You're kidding, right?" Jess asked, coming back into the room from the kitchen and handing Lily a damp cloth to wipe the Chianti off her shirt.

"Bubbe is no laughing matter. Please let me apologize in advance to your family, Beth."

"For what?" Beth laughed.

"For everything," I answered and chugged the rest of my wine.

∽ CHAPTER TWENTY-ONE ∾

OCTOBER

IN THE COURT OF COMMON PLEAS OF PHILADELPHIA COUNTY, PENNSYLVANIA

Commonwealth v. Durbin

"Ms. Holden, where are you employed?" Braden asked the witness, Britney Holden, who had big Jersey Girl hair, a big Jersey Girl accent and a wad of gum the size of Jersey lodged in her mouth.

"H&R Block." Incidentally, in addition to the accent she also had a voice that made you want to jump off a bridge. It sounded like someone had taken a screeching cat and dragged its nails across a blackboard.

"Were you employed there on September twelfth?"

"Yes. I was." I hoped that she wasn't the front desk person. Personally, I would rather risk an audit than go to that H&R Block if she was there. I felt like my ears might start bleeding.

"Was the defendant Mr. Durbin also employed there?"

"Yes."

"Did you work in the same area?"

"Yes. His cube was right next to my cube." Wait, who was the victim here?

"Did anything out of the ordinary happen on that day?"

"Yes. I was on the phone with a girlfriend of mine when suddenly he came crashing through the wall of my cube."

"Right through the wall?"

"Yes. Right through the wall. Then he grabbed my cell phone and beat it."

"Wait – you mean beat it, as in he left with it?" Judge Channing asked.

"No. He actually beat it. He threw it down on the floor and he stomped on it but it didn't break. So he picked it up and slammed it against my desk several times but it still didn't break, because, you know, I have one of those protective covers on it. Then he slammed a book down on it a few times and when it still didn't break, he screamed."

"He screamed? Did he say something?"

"Yes. He said, 'die die die motherfucker!' Then he went running outside, and while we all watched from the window, he ran over it with his car."

"How much was the phone worth?"

"One hundred and ninety dollars."

"Thank you. No more questions."

"Any questions, Ms. Ginsberg? Recall that this is just a preliminary hearing, not a trial, so whatever motivated your client won't be relevant. In fact, I'm sure it's no mystery at all what motivated him, and perhaps a jury will feel some sympathy, but this is neither the time nor place."

"Well then, I suppose I don't have any questions, Your Honor."

"Good choice Ms. Ginsberg. I'll hold it as a theft rather than as a robbery." I guess that was my gift for not annoying him by making him listen to Ms. Holden's voice any longer.

"Thank you, Your Honor."

"Mr. Roth, call the next case." Just then a deputy came in.

"Sorry to interrupt, Your Honor, but Judge Wilson is ordering Ms. Ginsberg downstairs to talk to a defendant."

"Tell him she's busy," Judge Channing snapped.

"It's kind of important, Your Honor. They brought in the defendants on that West Two Ten case for some kind of emergency hearing and there's a guy in there who she was representing. The PD he has now is out in the districts and since she was the last counsel of record and they have to do the hearing, he needs her to at least talk to him until his lawyer can get here."

"Alright then," Judge Channing conceded. "She can go down to talk to him and explain what's happening until his lawyer gets here. I'll take Mr. Roth and Ms. Albright's cases first. But I'm going to need her back here when they're done."

"That should be fine, Your Honor. Mark Patterson is the guy's lawyer now, and he called to say he's on his way in."

"Okay, Ms. Ginsberg. You're excused for now." I looked nervously at Braden. He did not look happy at all. Just what I did not need a few days before our huge engagement party. I sighed and grabbed my notebook.

"I'll be right back." Famous last words.

In retrospect, something felt off from the very beginning. I met up with two senior defenders, Tom and Rob, who filled me in quickly on the hearing. When the deputy buzzed us in he seemed distracted, and I heard raised voices somewhere within and what sounded like a scuffle. I tensed up instinctively but we kept walking toward the interview rooms because those sounds weren't exactly foreign in lock-up. We had just made it there when all hell broke loose. I was confused at first and I didn't understand what was happening. There was shouting and people were running and pushing. We turned and started back for the door but then I saw a blur of bodies in motion blocking it. I heard a gunshot and my heart almost stopped. Tom and Rob shoved me into an interview room. Holy shit! We weren't going to be getting out of there.

"What's going on?" I asked, feeling terrified.

"I don't know, Gab, but there wasn't any way we were going to get through that door with the fight that was going on there," Tom answered.

"Who was that fighting?"

"Looked like two deputies and two West Ten Sixers," Rob said.

"Oh my God." My stomach felt like it dropped to my feet. It was the gang members and they were out of their cells.

"Just stay calm Gabrielle," Tom said. "People had to have heard the gunshot and they're going to send reinforcements here really soon."

"What if they start a shoot-out? We're like sitting ducks in here." I wasn't handling this well.

"Only one deputy would be armed so there should only be one gun," Rob replied.

"Yeah, but who has it?" I was starting to shake. This had to be a nightmare. This kind of thing didn't really happen, did it?

The door burst open then and a guy in prison clothes ducked inside with us and slammed it again. He looked up at us and got startled. Putting his hand over his heart, he took a deep breath. If he was a gang member, he wasn't one of the braver ones.

"Ya'll scared the shit out of me! I didn't know this room was occupied, but it's gonna be a little more occupied, because I ain't goin' back out there!"

"What's going on out there?" Tom asked. I could still hear shouting and crashing sounds but thankfully there were no more gunshots.

"What the fuck you think's goin' on? Bunch gangbangers going fuckin' apeshit!"

"You're not West Six Ten?" Rob asked.

"Do I *look* like a motherfuckin' gangsta? That ain't even my part of town." I looked at him and I had to admit he didn't look like a motherfuckin' gangsta. At least he didn't have any tattoos and he didn't look very tough. He was kind of scrawny, to tell you the truth. Gang bangers came in all shapes and sizes though.

"Who are you?" Rob asked.

"Terrell Jones, and I'm only in here because I bought a bag of weed off the wrong guy. Shit ain't even illegal in Colorado and they dump me in here with a bunch of criminals." Terrell sounded seriously aggrieved. "Hey wait. You guys PDs?"

"Yeah, why?" Tom answered.

"Well, hallelujah, praise Jesus! It's about fuckin' time! I've been tryin' to get in touch with ya'll! That cop set me up, man!"

"Uh, Terrell, I don't think this is the time," Rob began. Out the window in the door I saw two people fly past and then I heard a crash.

"It's never the time, man! I'm tellin' ya I was entrapped goddamnit and I need defendin'!"

"Okay, uh, Gabrielle, why don't you talk to Terrell here and I'm going to take a quick look out there and see if I can find out what's going on," Tom said.

"What are you whack?!" Terrell cut in. "I'll tell you what's goin' on. Some fancy private defense lawyer with mo' money than brains came strollin' into a cell and ordered the guard to uncuff his gangsta client and the stupid ass guard did it. The dude went fuckin' nuts and grabbed his lawyer by the neck. In came Dudley Dooright deputy with his piece and another banga' took him down from behind. I don't know what happened then because the door was open and I was on my way out but it looked like a fight over the gun and now somebody out there is strapped up. I figure it must be one of the home-boys 'cause if it weren't we'd be out of here by now."

"Well, there's nothing we can do but wait then," Tom said.

"So, while we waitin' let me tell ya'll how I was set up!" I took a deep breath and tried to calm my nerves and focus. I sat down at the desk and started listening to Terrell's story about how he was the real victim in his case.

It wasn't lost on me that I was a woman trapped in a locked area with a bunch of loose, and possibly armed gang members. Who had probably been incarcerated for a while. Without access to women, but I tried not to think about it. It actually wasn't as hard as one would believe because I felt kind of numb at the time and everything seemed to be moving in slow motion. Looking back, I'm pretty sure that I was experiencing mild shock.

There were still the sounds of yelling and fighting outside but I kept taking notes on how Terrell believed that it was totally unacceptable that a cop would tell him that he was running a special on marijuana. After all, who could resist a buy one get one free deal?

I had no idea how much time had gone by, but finally, after what felt like an eternity, we heard a huge crash and loud voices. The door flew open and I saw officers in riot gear there. They ordered us out, and believe me, we weren't arguing! As soon I cleared the outside door I saw Mark, who ran over, grabbed me, and pulled me out of there and past a gauntlet of reporters yelling out questions. He yanked me into a stairwell, grabbed me by the arms and spoke to me frantically.

"Are you okay, Gab?"

"Yeah, I'm fine. There are reporters. How long were we in there?"

"Only about twenty minutes. They were probably in the building already."

"Twenty minutes! Oh God! Braden! Is Braden okay?"

"Is *Braden* okay?! You two really are in love."

"*Is* he? Where is he?"

"They're all in the courtroom waiting. They wouldn't let him come downstairs. In fact, it took Adam and two deputies to hold him back. He's pretty upset."

"Oh God. I feel so bad."

"Gabrielle, you were just in a hostage situation in lock-up. Cut yourself some slack. Come on though! We need to get upstairs. Judge Channing wants to see you too."

"Oh fuck! I was supposed to come back to do my cases. Am I in trouble?"

"Are you *nuts*? No, you're not in trouble! He wants to see for himself that you're okay."

We got to the courtroom door and Mark led me inside. Suddenly a cheer went up and a dozen public defenders, a few prosecutors who were Braden's friends, Judge Channing and various other members of courthouse personnel were waiting but I only focused on one person. I literally ran to Braden who pulled me into his arms tightly and wouldn't let go.

"Mr. Pierce! Take her back into my chambers," Judge Channing ordered. "Don't come out until you're ready." Braden kept his arms wrapped around me as he led me quickly up the stairs and behind the bench where we went through the door and back into the judge's chambers. He closed the door behind us and pulled me over to a sofa and onto his lap where we just held each other.

∾ Chapter Twenty-Two ∾

Eventually, I stopped shaking and eventually Braden was willing to loosen his grip. Our heart rates even started to slow down.

"I want to get married," he said. I sat back and looked at him with confusion. My brain was pretty scrambled at the moment.

"I know. You gave me this ring, remember?"

"Saturday, before the party."

"You want to get married *before* our engagement party?"

"Yeah. If we apply for the license today we'll get it on time. Judge Channing will marry us. I asked him."

"You did? In the middle of all this?"

"That deputy who came and got you earlier came back and interrupted court in the middle of the hearing. He said that there was a riot down in lock-up and that you were one of the public defenders trapped inside."

"Oh God, Braden! I'm so sorry about what you must have gone through."

"Me?! Baby … anyway, I tried to leave but they held me back. They said there was nothing I could do down there. They wouldn't even let me call you until they knew what was going on."

"I wouldn't have had much to tell you. I was holed up in an interview room with two other PDs and guy named Terrell who was only in for taking advantage of BOGO on some marijuana."

"I felt so powerless, Gabrielle. It made me realize that anything can happen and life is too short to waste. Whatever does happen, I want it to happen to us together as man and wife. So, I asked Judge Channing if he would marry us and he said yes. Now I know that ..."

"Okay," I interrupted.

"...we talked about ... Did you just say okay?"

"I agree. Life is short and whatever happens I want it to happen to us together." I didn't care about what anyone said. Even if it had only been a few months I knew that this relationship was the real deal. Braden looked elated.

"I was thinking that we could do it Saturday before the party!" he said with a huge grin filled with relief and love.

"Maybe the Ritz will let us have a smaller room too. Just a little private ceremony and the party can be our reception."

"Yeah! And we could see if your friend Stan is free to play us a song."

"Stan?" I smiled. "You would let Stan play at our wedding?"

"He played at our first date. And we can invite your friends from the kabob place too."

"Oh Braden!" Finally, I had tears in my eyes and they were tears of joy. Go figure.

"So how about if we get the hell out of here, and go apply for a marriage license. Then we'll go get our dog, go home, make plans, and make love."

"Yes to all of that."

"Come on, let's go."

That night we mostly held each other and talked. We discussed all the details we had left hanging including the plans for our non-profit. We tossed around some names and The Justice Project was our favorite so far. We agreed to talk to our parents as soon as possible to get their help with setting it up and we hoped to be able to start running it by the new year or at least by the spring. We decided that even though we would be working on the same team in the future, we would keep our skills sharp by arguing cases with each other privately. After all, we liked all that adrenaline, and arguing cases was much better than arguing about personal things.

Finally, after we were all talked out, he brushed a piece of hair that had come untucked behind my ear and then leaned in to kiss me slowly, lovingly, and sweetly. I responded, pouring all of my feelings and my desire into it. Finally, he pulled back, scooped me up into his arms and carried me into our bedroom. Bruno followed along but he was perfectly content to just lounge in his doggie bed with his chew toy. We really had trained him well.

Braden put me down and the two of us undressed each other slowly and walked hand-in-hand to our bed. Then we lay down next to each other and just stared into each other's eyes for a long time. There were no words at all to describe the intensity of emotion between us that night. It may have only been a few months, but we were deeply and passionately in love. I felt like our souls recognized each other. Like we had always been together and we always would be. We began to kiss and caress each other tenderly and when he finally slid slowly into me, he told me that he loved me and that he would love me for the rest of his life. I told him that he was my bashert – my destiny – and that I would love him forever. Later, we fell asleep in each other's arms.

The rest of the week was kind of a blur. My office gave me some time off, which I appreciated. Braden also took a couple of personal days and he enlisted his mom to organize the wedding, a project she performed with great talent and skill. She managed to secure the musical talent of Stanford Benson, (also known around Philly train stations as Stan the Bluesman) to play a special dedication for our first dance. She not only invited Ahmet and Damla, she put in a huge order for their special Turkish pastries. Their desserts would be sampled by senators, congressmen, judges and various other notables. Since they would all be joining us at the engagement party turned wedding reception later, Claire even made sure that they all had formal clothes to wear. She thought of everything.

Senator Pierce and my dad quickly assembled more security than the Pentagon had and arranged for us to have access to a private plane and a room at a lovely resort for a long weekend on St. Thomas the following week. My mom dedicated her energy to trying to get her relatives to behave themselves. She had the toughest job of them all. She also came into Philly several times that week, and took me shopping for my dress, veil, and shoes, out for mani/pedi, to have my hair trimmed and styled, all the good girlie stuff. She and I talked a lot about marriage, the ups and downs, the give and take. In case I haven't mentioned it, my mom is an incredible woman.

Braden and I spent our time mostly talking and planning. We took the first steps toward forming The Justice Project and found some nice Center City office space. The week flew by. Before I knew it, it was Friday evening. My parents, along with my aunt, uncle and cousin would be arriving any moment along with …Bubbe.

∽ CHAPTER TWENTY-THREE ∾

The Pierces had planned their house party carefully. Beth had conveyed my anxiety to Claire, who, in turn, had felt guilty. She didn't want me to be embarrassed, so she had purposely invited the most questionable relatives of theirs who she could find as well, which was how Derek came to be there. Braden and I went to Bryn Mawr together that evening. He was planning to stay overnight there with his family and I would return to the Ritz with my parents and stay with them in their suite there until the next day. He squeezed my hand as we saw the two limos pull into the drive.

"I love you, Gabrielle," he said solemnly.

"I love you too Braden," I replied, trying not to sound overly fearful.

The doors of the lead car opened and my parents stepped out looking fabulous. They came over and hugged Braden and I warmly. Then doors opened on the second car and my stomach dropped into my shoes.

"Oy vey! A cab to a train to a car! What are you going to put me in a rowboat next? I'm an elderly woman!" It was Bubbe.

"What are you complaining about?" My cousin, Rachel, exclaimed in her heavy New York accent. "You rode in luxury on the Acela and you were driven in style in a limo! It's not like your son-in-law tossed you in the trunk of a Chevy Nova!"

"Enough already!" My Aunt Ruth said, looking like she was on her last nerve. "The two of you have been arguing since we left Penn Station. You're giving me a headache!"

"Braden, you remember my relatives I'm sure," my mother said with a smile.

"I do, Judy." He laughed. "Hello everyone! Welcome to my family's home. Let me get you inside and introduce you to my parents, Tyler and Claire."

"This is a nice place!" My Uncle Ira said, looking the house over. "So your father's a senator, Braden!" As he passed by me he said, "Good job, Gabrielle!" in a whisper loud enough for half the house to hear. I rolled my eyes heavenward.

"You see this, Rachel?" Bubbe asked. "This is what you get when you keep a man happy! You make sure that when you're married you keep giving him whatever he asks for in bed, Gabrielle!"

"Oh, my God," I whimpered. Braden put his arm around me reassuringly.

"We'll have to introduce her to Derek," he suggested with a smile. We all went inside and we introduced my relatives to Braden's relatives. Claire had amazing hostess skills! She had found a second cousin who owned a string of tuxedo rental places in New York. He and Ira were talking some serious dry cleaning before long. My Aunt Ruth found a common interest in daytime television with a rather loud cousin with a heavy Boston accent. Rachel and Derek hit it off immediately. That was interesting. I would have imagined that she would have been more interested in Drew. Speaking of Drew, he and Bubbe and a couple of frat boy cousins were having a great time drinking, playing poker, telling dirty jokes and smoking cigars out on the patio. Which meant that Braden and I were able to relax and enjoy some time with our parents together.

"So Tyler, I understand that you popped the question after six weeks too," my dad said.

"I knew right away that young lady was right for me," he said, smiling at Claire lovingly. "I guess that Braden inherited my decisiveness *and* my impatience."

"Well, Gabrielle must have inherited my courage and adventurous spirit because I accepted his proposal after eight weeks of dating," my mom added, gesturing at my dad.

"*You're* courageous? Have you met her mother?" my dad joked. "Never question how much I love your mom, Gabrielle," he said looking at her adoringly.

"When Braden asked me I said he was the bravest man I knew besides you."

"I can't believe that at this time tomorrow you'll be my wife," he said looking at me in much the same way that Tyler had looked at Claire and my dad had looked at my mom. Seeing that look I knew that it would be okay.

We stayed until nine and then Braden and I hugged each other tightly and went to spend some private time with our parents. We knew that while they were thrilled, it also wasn't easy for them to see their babies grown up. After a lovely night full of laughter and tears with my parents I found myself getting ready for my wedding the following day in their suite, accompanied by Jess, Lily and Beth. They were acting as my bridesmaids and they had all bought very pretty matching dresses in a deep sapphire blue that looked great on all of them. I had bought a simple white (yeah, whatever!) bias-cut silk sheath wedding gown and I wore my diamond necklace and long sheer veil attached to the back of my head with a beautiful diamond clip that had belonged to Braden's great-grandmother.

My parents had reserved the entire floor for close friends and family. Braden's family had taken over the floor above. It was still only four when I was finished getting dressed and made up and I wanted to go walk to work off some nerves, so we set out to see who was around.

"You look so gorgeous, Gabrielle, I can't wait to see Braden's face when he sees you," Beth said, sounding emotional. She had told me that there had been plenty of laughter and tears at the Pierce home the night before as well.

"I can't wait to see him. I'll bet he looks amazing," I answered just as we turned a corner. I saw someone else who amazed me in the hall up ahead of us. I knew that bellman!

"It's him!" Lily suddenly cried out. The figure looked up quickly and took off down the hall. Without even really thinking about it, I hiked up my skirt and took off after him.

"Wait, Gabrielle!" Jess cried. When I didn't stop, my friends, loyal until the end, took off in pursuit with me. The bellman ran into a stairwell and I ran after him. I could hear him a flight below and I did everything in my power to follow and not break my neck. After two flights I heard him exit and I followed, yelling for him to stop. Jess. Lily, and Beth were not far behind me. He had exited onto a mezzanine that connected with the grand staircase. As I chased after him I heard a voice call to me from below.

"Gabrielle?! Baby, what are you doing now?!" Braden called out. I realized that this probably looked kind of odd, a bride and three bridesmaids chasing a bellman around a fancy hotel. We did seem to be attracting some attention. I hoped that they hadn't let the media in yet.

"Stop him, Braden! It's him! The stalker!" I saw five figures, Braden, Cam, Drew, Adam and Mark, all dressed in tuxedos, come bounding up the grand staircase with hotel guests scurrying to get out of their way. When they reached the mezzanine they took off after us and now all eight of us were in hot pursuit. The bellman dove onto an open elevator.

"Shit!" Braden swore. "Watch to see what floor he gets off on and call up to me on the stairs." With that the five guys took off for the stairwell.

We watched and saw that he had stopped at my family's floor again, which I called up to Braden and headed back up the two flights myself with my friends right behind me. When we got there we saw the guys knocking on doors and searching. Suddenly, I heard my cousin Rachel's voice scream out from around the corner. We all headed in that direction and threw open the door to find Rachel in bed … with Derek! We all came to a crashing stop, almost knocking one another over.

"He went that way!" Rachel screeched and pointed to an open door.

"Why did Sam Walker just run through here?" Derek asked much more calmly.

"Who?" Braden asked, bewildered.

"Sam Walker, that sleazy fuck who works for the Hill Group. He must be trying to get some dirt on somebody." I wondered how sleazy a person would actually have to be for Derek to call him sleazy.

"Hi, Gabrielle!" Rachel said. "You look gorgeous, darling! Mazel Tov!"

"Thanks. I see that you've met Braden's cousin, Derek."

"Get dressed! I may need you to identify him!" Braden demanded. Suddenly I heard a male voice yell out.

"Hey, lady! Back off! I didn't mean to barge in on you! Ouch! Cut it out!"

"Who in the hell are you?! I didn't call a bellman! Oy gevalt! What kind of crazy goddamned hotel is this?! The privacy of my own room and some meshugener bellman comes crashing in?!!"

"Oh my God! He's in Bubbe's room!" I cried out. "Nobody deserves that!" I ran toward the sounds and my posse followed me.

We ran through the door and back into the hall where we saw Sam Walker go flying out a door up ahead while being chased by my grandmother who was beating him with a handbag. She was a fast old bugger. I noted that she left her cane behind. She was slowing him down and we were making ground fast but as we rounded a corner I saw that he had a straight shot for another open elevator.

"Get him, Bubbe!" I yelled. Just then I heard a familiar yip. They had brought Bruno and he was in my parents' suite! I saw a teeny tiny head poke out of the doorway! "Bruno! Baby! Go get him! Go get the bad guy for Mommy and Daddy!" Like lighting Bruno shot out of the room and launched himself at the fleeing bellman, grabbing onto his ankles and sinking his teeth in. Walker screamed out in pain and fell to the floor where Bubbe overtook him and started beating him again with her handbag. We finally caught up and pulled Bubbe and Bruno off the beaten man on the floor. The guys continued to subdue him while we called security and the police.

They arrived shortly after and took Sam Walker, who was complaining loudly that he was being chased without reason by a bunch of crazy people, into custody and charged him with stalking and harassment. That was just for starters. We asked them to take him into a room for a few minutes first, though, before taking him to police headquarters, since Senator Pierce would probably like to speak to him.

Our parents had been alerted to what was going on and came up to meet us. Beth took Bruno with her to give him a special treat for being a hero. Drew took Bubbe down to buy her a martini as a reward for taking down a guy a foot taller and forty years younger than her. Someone had been sent to get Derek, who seemed to know this guy and he showed up five minutes later very calm, completely dressed and not at all disheveled.

"Well hello there, Sam," Derek said as he strode into the room. "Still working for the Hill Group? Or can't they afford you now that they're out of the kinky party business?"

"You've been to plenty of those parties yourself, Mr. Fuckin' High and Mighty."

"Yeah, but just as a guest. At least I'm not a pimp," Derek replied with a smile.

"What's the Hill Group?" Tyler asked.

"It's the group that owns Club 51. You know some of them already, Marla Benton, Veronica and Roland Mason, and Cole Stevenson."

"They own Club 51?" I asked. Felicity didn't want to meet there because it was a conspiracy club! She wanted us to figure out who owned it!

"Yeah and a few other legit businesses. I suspect they probably use them somehow to launder the proceeds from their less than legit enterprises."

"Hill Group? Like the Fanny Hill Club?" Cam asked.

"That's right," Derek said with a lascivious smile, "Like the Fanny Hill club and a very high-priced ring of society call girls. Veronica's not really the Madame – she just runs the parties. Marla's the Madame. Roland does the books and Cole, at least in the past, helped to smooth the path with the local politicos and made sure nobody bothered them with any pesky new regulations."

"So they would have been nervous if someone like Ben Ginsberg, who's helping legislators in New York to clean up crooked business practices, started giving Senator Pierce any ideas for similar legislation in his own constituency," Adam summarized.

"Yeah, if that happened it could shut them down," Cam added.

"So the question is, what were they going to try to do about it?" Braden asked.

"According to what we heard, they wanted to 'take Gabrielle out of the picture'." Adam said in his most intimidating prosecutorial voice. "I wonder if this is going to turn into a murder for hire investigation."

"What?!" My father looked apoplectic. "If I find out that you had any intention of harming my daughter you'll wish that a criminal prosecution was your worst problem." His voice was colder and more deadly than I had ever heard it. Wow.

"Homicide?! Are you people nuts?! Nobody wanted to kill her! They just wanted them to break up, that's all! Marla tried to get her pissed off at him by acting like the crazy ex-girlfriend and then Cole tried to seduce her away and when that didn't work they tried to get her to leave by freaking her out a little. They had me write and deliver a couple of anonymous notes. I even followed her all the way to her parents' place in New York. Not even that worked though! Finally, they just had me follow them around. Eventually, everybody does something dirty and I figured that I would just be there to witness it.

Then maybe they could get them to agree to keep their dads out of our business, you know?"

"In other words blackmail us," Braden said coldly.

"Semantics," Walker said with a sneer.

"They didn't realize that someone had overheard them, someone who may seem weird on the outside but is basically a decent person on the inside, and who appreciates it when people are nice to her," I added quietly. I had been too quick to judge Felicity. Her parents probably had all kinds of criminal associations. Trying to warn me took courage.

"Well, even if your story turns out to be true," Adam said, "sending someone anonymous threatening notes and following them around are enough for us to charge you."

"And I think that a thorough investigation of the Hill Group might be warranted," Senator Pierce said. "Don't you agree Ben?"

"Absolutely, Tyler. In fact I would be happy to help out. Perhaps it will even lead to some new legislation regulating business reporting practices."

"Which I would be happy to help out with," Tyler replied with a smile. It looked like the kingmaker and the senator would be working together. Who knew, maybe it would even lead to the White House someday.

"I think that maybe Marla, Cole and the Masons may wind up with a bit more than just probation after all," Braden said with satisfaction. The cops took Walker away and checking our watches we realized that we were five minutes late for our own wedding so we all headed downstairs.

"I guess you were right after all, Gabrielle," Braden said. "You had those three pegged from the beginning."

"Yeah, but I didn't realize everything that was behind it, and I didn't realize it was all of them working together. Very Agatha Christie." I smiled.

∽ CHAPTER TWENTY-FOUR ᴄ

I went in to freshen up quickly and then we went downstairs. Judge Channing was waiting patiently for us. It was only our parents, Braden's brother and sister and our closest friends who were with us. That was the way we had wanted it. Before we started Judge Channing asked to make a few remarks. He cleared his throat and spoke, mostly to our parents.

"Several months ago," he began, "we started assigning lawyers to specific courtrooms and Mr. Pierce and Ms. Ginsberg were assigned to mine. I could see right away that there was a spark between them. They were always stealing looks at each other." He smiled as if remembering. "I often wondered if they would eventually get together and I knew right away when they had, because they both looked really happy. Criminal law is a tough job and it can really get to you. I'm glad that these two have had each other to lean on. They're both first-class lawyers and it's been an honor to work with them." He actually sounded a little emotional. I couldn't believe it.

"Thank you, Your Honor," I said and then I went over and I shook his hand. What the hell. Braden got up and did the same.

"So, now, let's get you two married before any other crazy stuff happens," he said, back to his gruff self. We went through the simple civil ceremony and Braden and I took our vows. We promised to love, honor and cherish each other, to always be faithful and to remain together through sickness and health until death did us part. Finally the judge pronounced us man and wife, and my beautiful blonde Braden, my husband, kissed me. I was lost in that romantic dreamy moment when I heard a yip. Bruno had hopped off of Aunt Beth's lap and came over to beg to be picked up. At least he wasn't trying to play the humping game anymore.

The guests had assembled in the Grand Ballroom and our dads went in to make the happy announcement that we had just been married. I heard surprised murmurs and then applause. Then I heard Braden's dad introduce us for the first time in public as Mr. and Mrs. Braden Pierce and with tears in my eyes I let my husband escort us into the ballroom. The applause got much louder. He guided me to the middle of the dance floor, in front of a stage where a lone guitarist stood. And then Stan began to play Louis Armstrong's *What A Wonderful World* and as we danced, I have to say that I agreed.

The End

Continue reading for a sneek peek of N.M. Silber's next book.

LEGAL BRIEFS

Coming 2014

CHAPTER ONE

I sat staring at my friend Bruce over my drink. The lights and pounding music of the club combined with the alcohol to make my head feel a little fuzzy. It was just as well, though, since I was bored out of my mind and numbness seemed like a desirable goal. Our co-worker, Marilyn's, boyfriend, who she had been dating for a million years, had finally popped the question and we were out "celebrating". So to speak. Librarians weren't generally known as wild party animals.

Bruce and I were considered the "risqué ones" of the bunch, which was a big joke to us. He was only "risqué" because his partner of seven years, with whom he had a happily monogamous relationship and contented home life, just happened to be of the same sex he was. I, on the other hand, was "risqué" because I wrote erotic romance novels or "dirty books" as my co-workers would say. It didn't matter that my own love life was dryer than the Sahara at the moment. They considered me raunchy and possibly a little dangerous. Right.

Marilyn, Jane, and Rochelle, sat around and watched in scandalized astonishment as the "playas" around us picked up women on the make. I don't know what the library gang had expected to experience here; tea and crumpets with the Queen? This club was the new "hot spot" in the city, and thus, it was the most fertile hunting grounds for young and beautiful Philadelphians searching for relationships of extremely short duration. The other librarians thought this club was cool, and hip, and sexy. Bruce and I realized, of course, that it was just trendy. It was Junior High School with a liquor license. Even though we were unimpressed, though, we were both basically kind people, so we pretended that this was all very exciting.

"Did you see that?!" Jane asked sounding like she had just witnessed someone commit a crime. "The way they were dancing, they might as well have been having intercourse." And yes, she really did just say "intercourse". Jane had derived her sexual vocabulary from her sixth grade health class. I could just imagine her in the throes of passion. 'Don't stop inserting your penis into my vagina! I'm going to achieve orgasm'!

"The guy doesn't have any rhythm," Bruce commented. "He's probably a lousy lay." He was just noting it idly, and I agreed without giving it much thought, but the other three broke into blushes and giggles. It was all I could do not to roll my eyes. These girls were the types who would blush and giggle reading a Victoria's Secret catalogue. I tried to remember again why I was there. Celebrating. We're celebrating. Yippee. I slurped my drink.

I shouldn't be complaining. It's not like I had anything better to do on a Saturday night. I worked every day as a research librarian and then went home and wrote books. On Sunday evenings I got together with some girlfriends of mine, and Bruce and his partner, Jason, had been inviting me over for dinner more often lately. Sometimes I even went out on dates. The guys were nice; some were even charming, but let's just say that the Earth didn't move for me. Truthfully, I wasn't even sure that I wanted nice. Not that I wanted to date some guy who treated me badly either. I just want someone who sparked some kind of … reaction. It was November and getting colder in more ways than one. That summer and early fall had been more interesting. A guy who I had being doing battle with since childhood seemed to suddenly start looking at me like a desirable woman and that had, most definitely, created a reaction!

It certainly inspired my writing! I wrote some really spicy love scenes with him in mind. In fact, the book that I had just published had a tall, well-built hero with dark brown hair, laughing brown eyes and just a touch of five o'clock shadow. The heroine had voluminous brown locks, big brown eyes and long lashes. It didn't take Sigmund Freud to figure out that I was describing Adam and me, and oh boy, did *they* get down and dirty! Let's face it, I had written my sexual fantasies into a romance novel. Hell, if I couldn't have a real "happily ever after" at least I could make one up.

Although we had been mortal enemies since the first day of preschool, the minute that Adam Roth had begun to direct his over-abundant sexual energy my way, it had felt like a tsunami rolling over me. The tension between us had built and finally one night he had almost kissed me and I had almost let him. We were interrupted though. And the next time we were alone together it was at the wedding of our close friends. He seemed distracted and we went our separate ways without a word about our "almost kiss" and with no plans to see each other again.

Even if we had seen each other, though, it wouldn't have mattered. Adam was a womanizer so I didn't expect anything to ever develop. His friend Braden, the groom in said wedding, had been too, but not like Adam, I suspected. As if to underscore that fact, when I was on my third Martini Bruce's gaze became riveted by something over my left shoulder.

"Uh oh," he mouthed. Our three co-workers were engrossed in conversation about the way some of the women in this place were (shockingly!) aggressively flirting with the men. In any event, the ladies' sewing circle wasn't paying us any attention so Bruce and I spoke freely, or more like shouted freely.

"Uh oh what?" I asked.

"Your boy is here." I knew immediately who he meant and I tensed up. I had unburdened myself to Bruce one night over too much wine. He assured me that telling secrets to a gay man over wine didn't count as a confession, but rather, was just the natural order of things. One day, not long after, Adam had come into the law library and I pointed him out to Bruce, who had been very impressed. In fact, he was so impressed that I had to put my hand over his mouth before he announced it to everyone present. Nobody disputed the fact that Adam was hot.

"What's he doing?" I asked, pretty sure I didn't want to know.

"I don't think you want to know," he answered, confirming my suspicions.

"Wonderful. Just when I thought the night couldn't get any better." I sloshed down some more alcohol. Maybe I would be lucky enough to have a blackout.

"Now that's interesting," Bruce said, apparently analyzing whatever Adam was doing. I wanted to know now. I had to admit Bruce was usually on target with his observations.

"Tell me," I said resignedly. "It's better that I hear it. It'll help me regain my sanity."

"He's chatting up a blonde."

"What's so interesting about that?" I asked, wondering if I had done something awful in a past life to deserve this night. The last thing I needed at this point was to watch the guy who I secretly wanted pick up some other chick.

"He looks bored. Like he's just going through the motions. She, on the other hand, is pouring it on. She just leaned over and practically shoved her tits in his face."

"Classy," I said, feeling my stomach starting to roil. "I want to leave." A month and a half ago he sat in my room when I was scared so I could fall asleep, and for a brief moment it had felt … intimate. "Don't be an ass, Lily," I told myself sternly. "You were female, available and alone in the same bedroom with him but you were both too tired to do anything about it. That's all it was."

"Not yet you don't, sister! He needs a reminder of what a truly sexy woman, who's worth the effort, looks like. He hasn't seen you in a month and I want to see his reaction when he does. Come on."

"Come on where?"

"To the dance floor, of course!"

He yanked me out of my seat and I staggered after him, although I really couldn't tell you why I did. Bruce just had a way of compelling me to do things. The pounding music was starting to give me a pounding headache and I had a feeling that if any more lights flashed in my eyes I might go blind. I really wasn't in the mood to shake my booty but Bruce wasn't going to take no for an answer. We got out onto the dance floor and Bruce starting channeling his inner boy band, busting out all of his fanciest moves.

"What are you auditioning for?" I shouted at him over the music.

"One of us has to catch your boy's attention and you're moving like you're in a body cast," he shouted back, swiveling his hips like Elvis in the early days. "It's too bad Jason was on call tonight. If he were here we could have gotten really raunchy."

"And what happened to showing Adam a woman worth the effort? I don't know that having a threesome under the disco ball would exactly set me apart from his current companion."

"She's not his companion anymore. He ditched her."

"Are you sure that she's not just blowing him under the table?"

"I just love your girlish charm," he yelled back at me.

"I feel the same way about you," I responded. Hearing that Adam had changed his mind about Ms. Titty cheered me up a little and I found myself loosening up a bit. Eventually, I got lost in the music and I let my mind drift.

"I think you have an admirer," Bruce shouted a few minutes later.

"I have many admirers," I joked.

"This one is a tall, dark and handsome prosecutor." Suddenly, he backed up and practically doubled over laughing.

"Are you choking on something? Because I don't remember any of that Heimlich shit from Girl Scouts." He punched me in the shoulder, still laughing his ass off. "Ouch! What the fuck is wrong with you?"

"Come on Lil. Will you try to look like you're having *some* fun for Christ's sake?" he shouted/growled through his self-induced mirth. He grabbed my hand and spun me around twice. Not a great idea after three Martinis. I wound up facing the other way and when the room stopped spinning too I looked up and saw Adam reclining in a chair at a table not far from where we were, with an amused look on his face. He smiled and waved. I furrowed my brows and Bruce yanked me back around.

"Why didn't you wave back?" he demanded with a maniacal smile. He was so intent on looking like he was having a blast that he was now dancing like a muppet.

"Because he's laughing at me!" Bruce looked like he was having a spasm. Someone would probably call the paramedics.

"He's not laughing at you. Well, maybe a little, but not in a mean way. More in a 'she's pretty adorable' way. I'm telling you!"

"I'm not adorable," I said, feeling unreasonably irritated. "Chipmunks are adorable. I'm empowered!"

"Since you're so liberated I guess you don't care that he's seriously checking you out."

"He is? Not that it matters."

"How often am I wrong?" He had me there. "So after this song, we'll walk back to our table past him. Stop and say 'hi' and try not to look like you're having a colonoscopy."

The song ended and Bruce started fanning himself like a Southern Belle and acting more effeminate than I had ever seen him act before. Ever. Good grief! This performance deserved an award. He practically skipped off the dance floor. I sighed, tried not to look nervous and walked in Adam's direction.

"Lily, fancy meeting you here!" Adam shouted with a smile. I tried to figure out if there was an insult in there somewhere. Maybe I hadn't heard him well enough.

"You're not going to call me Lilith?" I asked suspiciously.

"Feeling succubus-like this evening?"

"Perhaps some other time," I yelled back and he actually laughed.

"Hello! I'm Bruce!" Bruce said, holding his hand like he expected Adam to kiss it. He just gave it a quick shake instead. "Lily is keeping me company while my partner, Jason, is on call at the hospital where he works."

"In case you didn't catch that, Bruce was telling you that he's gay and therefore we are not here together in the romantic sense. Why he thinks you would care isn't really clear."

Bruce scowled at me and then rolled his eyes. "Would it kill you to be a *little* nicer, Lil?" he demanded.

"What?" I sputtered, feeling appalled. "If you think that wasn't nice you should hear the things he's said to me!"

"Well, he didn't say any of them tonight. I think you should apologize for being so unfriendly." My mouth literally popped open but Bruce just continued to give me his most reproving look. I sighed.

"I'm sorry I was unfriendly," I shouted. I mentioned how Bruce could compel me to do things, right? Sometimes I wondered if he had mind-control powers.

"I accept your apology," Adam answered, looking like he was trying not to laugh. I wondered if the busses were still running so I could throw myself under one. Bruce took his cell out of his pocket and read a text message.

"Oh shit! Jason got called in and I have his keys. I have to run. Maybe one of the girls can take you home, Lil. Or better yet, let me call you a cab."

"It's okay. I can call one."

"I'll take you home," Adam cut in. I looked at him in shock. Bruce looked at him with glee and beat it out of there so fast he practically left a dust cloud in his path. He was gone before he could say "beep beep." I guess that Adam was taking me home. Oh God.

ACKNOWLEDGMENTS

I would like to thank Karen, Michelle, and Rosette at Literati Author Services for going above and beyond for me in their role as my publicists. I would also like to thank my terrific Street Team, The Jury, for their enthusiastic support and loyalty. It means a great deal to me. Thanks to my friends, Taryn Plendl, Jennifer Stevens, and Joyce Turner-Blanker for being funny and cool authors. Thanks to everyone who took the time to write a nice review for The Law of Attraction. Thanks to all the readers and bloggers who have given me their support over the months and patiently waited while I found the rest of Gabrielle and Braden's story in my head and in my heart. Finally, last but never least, thanks to my wonderful family who I love. I have the most amazing husband and kids!

ABOUT THE AUTHOR

Once upon a time … N.M. Silber was a criminal defense attorney who got up each morning, donned her power suit and sensible pumps, downed a gallon of coffee and set out to "fight the good fight" while trying to not go insane. Having a dark sense of humor and a sarcastic wit helped — a lot. Another thing that helped was reading. As escapism was the goal, she liked to read romance novels, especially really funny ones and really sexy ones. Then one day something beautiful happened — she read one that was both funny and sexy at the same time. She hung up her power suit, put away her sensible pumps and moved her coffee mug to her computer. Now she writes funny and sexy romance novels herself and she lives happily ever after.

In her former career N.M. Silber was a criminal defense attorney working in a major city on the East Coast of the United States. She had several non-fiction articles published and edited a legal journal before turning her attention to writing novels. Using her experiences in the criminal court system as a starting place, she developed the engaging cast of characters and the humorous story lines of her romantic comedies.

www.ingramcontent.com/pod-product-compliance
Lightning Source LLC
Chambersburg PA
CBHW070623130626

46556CB00001B/448